D1333107

NO IDENTIFIABLE REMAINS

No Identifiable Remains

~~~~~~~~~~~~

JOHN TAGHOLM

Quartet Books

First published in 2008 by
Quartet Books Limited
A member of the Namara Group
27 Goodge Street, London W1T 2LD

A catalogue record for this book
is available from the British Library

ISBN   978 0 7043 7131 6

Typeset by Antony Gray
Printed and bound in Great Britain by
T J International Ltd, Padstow, Cornwall

FOR SALLY

CONTENTS

PART ONE

Mis en Place

Chapter 1

Even now, five hours after the accident, his hand was still shaking. He felt as detached from it as he did from his surroundings.

The small hotel room was dominated by an old black and white photograph of a mountain waterfall which had been blown up to cover the whole wall in front of him. To one side were a basin and a small shower with a dirty plastic curtain hanging lopsidedly across its front. There were two windows, one giving on to the main road, the other on to a tiny alley, the view from each half obscured by a tangle of bright red geraniums. It was now dusk and the colour was already draining from the room. His unsteady hand reached out to turn on the television, pausing for an instant before pushing the button.

He knew already the images that would greet him and the flames on the screen reflected across his pale face. His eyes were impassive as he watched the rescue crews working amongst the wreckage. A line of ambulances stood waiting for the dead and injured, blue and red lights joining the pink of the setting sun. From the edge of the cornfield drifted thick black smoke, spoiling the early evening sky and casting a shadow across the chaos.

He looked up at the waterfall tumbling towards him and recalled leaving his house that morning. The tall plane trees in the square opposite seemed to shimmer and rustle, disturbed by a breeze he could not feel. It was the end of a long hot summer and the leaves were dry and tired. He had glanced behind him as the silvery under-leaves waved in the early morning. Did he sense then that something was going wrong, that this parched rustle was a portent of what would happen later? Or was it a reminder of what he was leaving behind? However illogically, the trees came first in his *mis en place* of the day's events. Guilt can take you this way.

*   *   *

The train had been full. It was Friday, and for some a long weekend in Paris was already beginning in north London. As the grey and yellow express pulled slowly out of St Pancras International, the women in a group around the table to his right, were shrieking with excitement as a bottle of champagne was opened with a staccato pop. Their chatter continued as the train sped through the endless suburbs, interrupted only by the various ring tones of their mobile phones. He gathered they were escaping their husbands for a hen weekend in Paris and, without the restraining influence of their partners, their conversation was personal and raunchy.

He was sure they were among the dead.

He watched the North Downs give way to the flat Kentish plain, before the South Downs triggered the announcement that the train would shortly be entering the Channel Tunnel. More excited cries as the express plunged into the black tube. Within moments of emerging into France, as though it had been fired from the barrel of a gun, it was travelling across the open landscape at over 250kph. The buzzing of mobiles, vibrating on the tables in front of them, marked the greetings sent by the French networks to the new arrivals.

The girls grouped together to send picture texts to their loved ones, blowing kisses to their phones. He could see them all now, frozen like the images on their mobiles, the pretty blonde girl with wire-rimmed glasses, her tubby friend with the piercing laugh, the quiet one with the sweet smile and the dark haired, sun-tanned girl who had opened the champagne.

He made his way to the buffet car, four coaches in front of him. He left his laptop on the table and also his mobile phone,

12

which he forgot and which lay hidden under his copy of *The Times*. He was escaping the jollity of the carriage which failed to match his mood.

He swayed gently as the train sped through the low sandy hills to the east of Charles de Gaulle airport. It is around here, in a series of long, banked turns, that the track begins to sweep south westwards towards Paris. Just after Ermenonville, the D549 crosses the line, a minor road over a non-descript bridge on the way to Othis. Some people may have heard of Ermenonville, the birthplace of Rousseau. But no one had heard of Othis. Until this day, that is.

The petrol tanker rumbled through Ermenonville sometime after 11a.m., he learned later, en route, via Othis, to the airport. No one could be certain why the driver, Roland Taricquo, took this route, but afterwards it appeared that he always did. Whatever, he never would again.

Why the accident happened was still a mystery, but approaching the bridge, at about 60kph, Roland Taricquo failed to negotiate the slight bend in the road and ploughed straight on. The crash barrier collapsed under the combined weight of the tanker and its full load of aircraft fuel.

As he sped towards the bridge, the driver of the train could see this happen but, in the split second it took to register the falling debris and the crumpled nose of the tanker erupting through the bridge, he was under and beyond it. Ten seconds earlier, the whole train would have made it. As it was, the falling tanker severed the train in two, exploding on to the eighth carriage, detaching it and those behind, from the first half of the train.

The aviation fuel exploded almost immediately, a giant fireball that seemed to suck in the on-rushing carriages as they spilled crazily off the rails. Still travelling at over 160kph, one of the carriages was flung in the air and was sliced in half by the bridge. A second and third carriage became wedged under the bridge and the rest of the train piled up behind them. Not that this was really visible, since the flames and smoke were so intense that the bridge had entirely disappeared. The carriages towards the back of the train, with nowhere else to go, were forced to either side of the blazing wreck, some shooting upright through the fencing to the west of the track, ploughing into a field where, miraculously, after two hundred metres they ground to a halt. The carriages that sheered off to the east did not fare so well, breaking up as they hit the steep embankment, catapulting over the road spewing bodies and luggage left and right. A giant four wheeled bogey careered through the air before disappearing beyond the burning mass. It was the lethal projectile which, seconds earlier, had killed the four young women with their mobile phones.

At first he hadn't realised his luck. The impact of the tanker falling on to the train, only a few carriages behind him, had flung him across the buffet car, his coffee spilling in an arc against the opposite windows.

It took two kilometres or so for the amputated train to come to a halt. In that time, the two CCTV cameras stationed either side of the bridge had neutrally recorded the disaster to disbelieving monitors in a control room near Paris. Even before the driver of the train gathered his senses to call the same room, the emergency services had been mobilised.

Getting up from the floor of the buffet car, he heard the driver announce that there had been an incident and that passengers were to remain in the train. The next few moments were to begin a chain of events that were to change his life. He made his way back to his carriage, afraid that his computer and phone may have been thrown to the floor and damaged. These worries evaporated as he approached the carriage just before his own. All faces were turned away from him, towards the connecting door. It framed a view he would never forget. In the distance was a scene he could only compare to film images of the Second World War, clouds of black smoke rising from burning carriages.

From the dense cloud emerged figures, some running, some staggering.

Compelled to do something, he and several others climbed down through the gap, onto the track and began to walk towards the appalling scene. The closer he came, the images were augmented by sound. The suck and roar of air into the blazing mass, the crack and snap of bending metal and the awful cries of the injured and shocked.

The true horror of the accident could not be seen from the south side of the bridge, or what was left of the bridge. The black smoke was a protecting veil over the dreadful sights that lay beyond. Some of the passengers who had blindly staggered their way out of the inferno were injured, others merely lost and bewildered. The closer he came he could also see the dead and maimed, flung indiscriminately out of the coaches as they slammed into the bridge.

He was so shocked that at once he became a victim rather than a rescuer. The wind was driving the smoke into his face and with it came a smell he'd rather not consider. He moved to the side of the track, towards the embankment and the high wire fencing that protected the track. Beyond it was a small wooded hill with sandy paths leading inwards. At one point the fence had been neatly breached. Just beyond it, half buried in sand, lay the four-wheeled bogey so lethally expelled from the colliding train.

He scrambled up the bank, hardly daring to turn round, towards the edge of the copse. Hanging from the branch of a tree, like some ghastly totem, was a holdall, ripped along one side, its contents spilling down the tree. And from inside the woods came the incongruous call of a mobile phone, repeating and repeating the main theme of *The Ride of the Valkyries*.

Moving along the edge of the woods, he came to the road along which Roland Taricquo had spent the last few seconds of his life. Crossing to the other side, he could look down on the full scale of the crash. In the distance he could see the long line of track arrowing towards the mayhem. In front of him, like a vast painting, lay the scene of a major battle. In the cornfields between him and the track, eight coaches had zig-zagged off the track, two of them on their backs. People huddled in groups, or knelt by the dead and injured. But most of them stared back at the blazing carriages by the bridge. Even through the smoke, the orange heart of the fire pulsed furiously. At least five coaches were compressed into this hell and as the first fire-engines roared by behind him, it was clear there would be no survivors.

One of those coaches was his own. Somewhere in there were the four girls so recently full of life. It was like watching his own death. He shrank back into the woods, blinking as the ambulances rushed on to the scene. He could not go forward, so he turned back and retraced his steps, keeping in the woods parallel to the railway, the lost mobile still ringing hopelessly.

As he reached the point where the six surviving coaches had come to rest, he stopped and looked down at the passengers who had stayed behind, now hugging themselves with a mix of relief and guilt. As he watched, his body began to shake uncontrollably and sweat sprang from every pore of his skin. He crouched forward and vomited over the ferns and willowherb.

A little further on, out of sight of the train, the woods petered out on the edge of a large field left fallow. Beyond that another bridge led over the line. He felt as though he had been encased in double glazing, the sounds around him muted, his vision slightly distorted. He could think of no logical reason to move forward, but he did, one step in front of the other, staring ahead as if intent on some distant object. He crossed the line on the bridge, not bothering to look to his left towards the bedraggled group of survivors and the horizon beyond, thick with smoke. The village sign said Beaumarchais, but he did not register it as he walked along its tired main street. At what point do instinct and reason join forces? And were the reasons that caused Oliver Dreyfuss to pause in front of Le Cheval Blanc so deeply laid that he could not see them? He stopped and did not care to know why.

His lightweight blue suit was dusty and torn at the knees and elbows. He took off the jacket and put it over his shoulder before walking into the tiny room that served as a reception. His request for a room was met with apparent indifference by an old man whose wife normally did this sort of thing, but who was at the market in Meaux. He opened the door to his room and locked it noisily, shutting out the events of the day. He sat on the bed and the afternoon slowly gave way to dusk. He had yet to see the waterfall tumbling towards him.

The news networks tried to make sense of what had happened to the 9.01 from St Pancras International to Paris Gare du Nord. The first reporters on the site could only describe the scene in front of them, guessing at the numbers of dead and injured, at the chain of events that led to the devastation they were witnessing. As the night drew on, he watched the television reports become increasingly confident, the conjecture give way to facts. The death toll rose by the hour until, by midnight, over two hundred had been confirmed. By now the computer data from the check-in at St Pancras International had related passenger names to seats and coaches and had resulted in sombre forecasts. One hundred and thirty passengers had been travelling in the four coaches at the heart of the fire. Since little or nothing remained of these carriages, the chances of recovering any bodies, or parts of body, were thought highly unlikely.

He took his eyes from the screen and took a ticket out of his wallet. Seat 54, forward facing, carriage 11. The tanker had fallen on carriage 12, obliterating it completely along with the three carriages behind. The remaining six coaches had either crashed into the embankment or jackknifed into the fields. Reports now confidently suggested the death toll at around three hundred and fifty. He was thus witness to reports of his own death. His body was exhausted, on the point of collapse.

He got up and stood in front of the sink and looked at his face in the stained mirror. Oliver Winfield Dreyfuss. Male. Age: 37. Height: 5' 11". Weight: 12st 3lbs. Status: Married.

And dead.

Chapter 2

The plate glass windows on either side of her office narrowed to a wedge beyond which, across the Thames, was the old Billingsgate Market building, topped with its matching dolphin weather vanes. HMS *Belfast*, scourge of the North Atlantic in 1940, was moored just below, her great guns now redundant. Ship and building, their glories in the past, anachronisms against a backcloth of steel and smoked glass. Daily she watched the river rise and fall, nagging at the groynes and crevices, sluicing the City clean. Of everything, she thought, except its sins.

Sonya Dreyfuss's desk was six or so metres in from the converging glass, so that she usually had her back to the grey blue water and the spectacular waterfront. Now, though, she was sitting on the edge of the desk, tapping a heel against one of its chrome legs, as she listened to the caller. After a while she responded.

'I'm sure he thinks we're being entirely unreasonable, but, in my opinion, all we have done is offered him a price which he thinks is too low. We haven't called his mother a *putain*. Let him stew a little and we'll see which way he turns.'

She was talking to one of her assistants and she did so lightly. Nevertheless it was a decision clearly made. 'Call everyone in now for the meeting, could you please?'

Sonya Dreyfuss called her company 3MS and for the few people who didn't know, she was always happy to tell them why. 'Money. Money. And Money. We try to make even more money for high worth individuals. We try to make more money than anyone else by selling the companies that people have bust a gut to build up. And we try to help fast growing companies buy other companies so that, in the end, they can make even more money. Simple.'

Her team, five women and five men, filed into the room and sat around a walnut table the shape of a pear drop. The gentle badinage that played to and fro between them subsided as she sat down and pushed her papers in front of her. She had begun to talk when the door of her office opened and her PA came across to her.

'Excuse me, Sonya,' she said quietly, 'but there are news flashes that one of the St Pancras trains to Paris has crashed.' 3MS Capital did a lot of work with France and most of the people around the table had made the journey many times.

'We have nobody on it today,' the PA said quickly, the immediate answer to the obvious question.

'Thank the lord for that,' said Sonya holding the remote and bringing up Sky News. There was a 'breaking news' strap across the bottom of the screen indicating that a train had been involved in serious crash about 70 kilometres north of Paris. Without further information, Sonya pressed the mute button and got on with the business of the day. An hour later, though, the meeting ground to a halt as the first pictures came in of the stricken train. Although the screen was easy to see from the table, many of the group got up and stood in front of the monitor, shaking their heads. Words were not necessary to debate what they were seeing.

She dissolved the meeting shortly afterwards but out in the office everyone kept watch on the various screens hanging from the ceiling. Sonya, too, could not take her eyes from the unfolding drama and she abandoned her routines to watch the uninterrupted coverage. What misery, she thought, for the thousands of people connected to the dead, injured and missing. What a ghastly emotional and logistical mess. Even though the images she was seeing had been through an editorial filter, many were still harrowing enough for her to take her eyes from the screen and look out towards the river.

It was around 7pm that the call came through. It was her assistant, sounding puzzled and a deal less confident that she had earlier. 'It's St Pancras' Customer Liason on the line. A Mr Harries.'

'Hello,' Sonya Drefuss said, with a query in her voice.

'Mrs Dreyfuss, as you will have been aware, there has been a serious accident with one of our trains. My colleagues and I have the task of confirming who was on the train. Excuse me for coming straight to the point, but our records show that a Mr Oliver Dreyfuss bought a ticket for the 9.01 train and was checked in at 8.25 this morning. We have to ask if this may be your husband?'

There was a pause.

'I think there might have been a mistake.' Sonya Dreyfuss was confident that there had been. 'My husband had business in London today. He was looking at sites for a new restaurant.'

'I sincerely hope you are right, Mrs Dreyfuss, but I have to caution your optimism. There may be a chance that your husband,' here he hesitated just a second, 'might have overlooked to tell you what he was doing. Or he might have bought a ticket and given it to someone else. Unlikely, now that our anti-terrorist precautions are increasingly watertight these days. Names on tickets, passports and addresses are carefully checked to see that they match. I hate to sound pessimistic, but I must ask you to try and get in touch with your husband.'

With this he gave two special direct lines that she could call should she have news. She, in turn, gave him her home and mobile numbers, but even as she did so she felt no real concern. This was one of those simple administrative errors that happen all the time. Nevertheless, the moment she put down the phone, she dialled her husband's mobile.

'The number you are calling may be switched off. Please try later.'

She called Oliver's London office. Another recorded voice told her to leave a message. It was too early for him to visit the restaurant, but she tried it anyway. 'Hello, François, it's me. Has Ollie been in?'

'No, madam. He said that he probably would not come in tonight. We have several covers but no one he knows.'

A life of being absolutely logical, of assuming nothing and taking nothing for granted, enabled Sonya to believe that, lurking somewhere, was an obvious explanation to the problem in front of her. Not even a frisson of fear crept into her. She went to her private bathroom and stood in front of the mirror, her face lit by carefully diffused light. Sonya Dreyfuss. Née Burn. Age: 36. Height: 5' 8". Short blonde hair. Wide eyes. Strong, narrow mouth.

Very much alive.

Before she left her office, Sonya Dreyfuss sat at her desk and sent an email to her husband. 'Ollie. Please contact me as soon as possible. S'

Sonya had met her future husband at his first restaurant, a brasserie in south-west London, not far from the Wimbledon home they now shared. Oliver Dreyfuss was chef/patron, cooking part of the week and playing front of house the rest. Often, as is the nature of running restaurants, he did both, as he was on that first visit. It was a busy night but every so often Oliver's face could be seen in the porthole window in the swing door to the kitchens. Ignoring her companion, she watched him come in and out of vision, his black curly hair falling over the collar of his whites, calling out orders and occasionally catching her eye through the circle. Sonya was not there by accident. She had read about this up and coming restaurant, named after its photogenic owner, in a newspaper and she was aware of its growing reputation. It appealed to Sonya that it was not in the high street on the hill, with its rich shops and estate agents, but lower down the slopes towards the suburban housing and the railway lines. No part of Sonya was ever entirely at rest and it was her natural curiosity, her instinct to acquire, which had made her so successful. She knew he had seen her too and when she had finished her main course of duck with poached pears, she told the waiter that she would like to congratulate the chef. Later, Oliver came over to her, his whites stained with the efforts of cooking for seventy covers, to confirm whether she had liked her meal. A year later they were married. That was five years ago.

From the back garden of their home in Wimbledon, it was possible to see eastwards over what appeared to be the whole of London. It was late when she got home, and the panorama, with The London Eye at its centre, twinkled in the falling light. She sat for some time, sipping at a glass of wine.

She was startled when the doorbell rang and for an instant she believed it was Ollie. But then, just as quickly, she realised he would not ring the bell and by the time she got to the door an unfamiliar apprehension had taken hold. It was immediately confirmed when she saw two police officers standing in front of her.

'Mrs Dreyfuss?' She gave a slight nod.

'May we come in?' She opened the door and then, as she clicked it shut, she had the ominous feeling that nothing would ever be the same again. For a second she rested her forehead against the cool stained-glass of the door.

'Mrs Dreyfuss?'

She took them through to the living room where they sat down. It was the woman who spoke first, introducing herself as Sergeant Maureen McCulloch and her partner as Sergeant Robert Stands. She forgot their names immediately for her mind had raced to the conclusion that the modern police service sends women round to break bad news.

'We understand from the authorities that you don't think your husband was on the train to Paris this morning.' It was a statement, not a question, and her answer carried nothing of the confidence it had earlier.

'Well, yes. He always tells me when he is going to Paris, which he does quite a lot.' She kept her eyes on the female sergeant.

'We know you may find this distressing,' Sergeant McCulloch said softly, 'but we have further reason to believe he might have been.' Sonya Dreyfuss remained composed and the policewoman continued.

'We'd like you to look at this video image.' She held up a mobile phone and turned it towards Mrs Dreyfuss. On one side of the picture was a young woman with her mouth open, as if she was shouting to the person taking the picture. At first she wasn't sure why she was being asked to look at the image, until she saw the face in the background. It was her husband.

Sergeant McCulloch could see the reaction on her face and slowly put the phone on the coffee table between them. 'Mrs Dreyfuss, the photograph was taken in carriage 11 of this morning's train at 11.36 a.m., French time and sent to the young lady's husband. She was with a group of friends travelling to Paris for the weekend. It appears that, by chance, your husband was in a nearby seat. At 11.58 a.m. the accident happened and although nothing is absolutely certain at this stage, it appears that coach 11 was one of four to have borne the brunt of today's casualties. We have reason to believe that your husband may be one of the dead.'

It was as if Sonya Dreyfuss could hear every sound in the world. The tick of clocks, the gurgle of plumbing, the drone of aircraft, the rumble of trucks on West Hill, the whole ambient roar of London, buzzed in her head, the denial forming itself even before she spoke.

'No, it can't be,' she said in a voice that was more matter-of-fact that she had intended or felt. 'Is there a body?'

The sergeants looked at each other. It was the woman who spoke again.

'Mrs Dreyfuss, accident investigators say that the fire which engulfed those carriages was so severe that the chances of finding any bodies, or bodies that can be identified, is extremely unlikely.

I'm sorry. We felt it was important to talk to you as soon as possible. May we ask if there is anyone who could be with you tonight?'

Sonya Dreyfuss nodded. She had plenty of friends, she said, and she would call them once they had left. She wanted them to go so that she could organise the facts for herself, reach her own conclusions. Once again she was given a number to call if she needed help or information.

At the door she realised she had been right. It was a barrier between now and then, an impassable watershed dividing certainty and doubt. She shut her eyes and the picture message of her husband, fuzzy but undoubtedly him, played in front of her eyes. Could she remember the last time she had seen him, or would this image always be the last memory of her husband?

Two instincts fought inside her, grinding together like tectonic plates. The emotional side, which wanted to cry out, and the rational which sought desperately to assemble the clues which would confirm their error and her husband's existence. As a businesswoman, she would not have allowed this to happen. Emotion would play little or no part in her decision making. And confronted as she was in this case with contradictory information, she would have demanded further investigation.

She picked up her wine and looked out over a darkened London. She dimmed the lights in the room so that she could see beyond her own reflection. Her emotions surprised her, a mix of anger and frustration. 'You bastard Ollie,' she said to herself.

It was going to be a long night.

Chapter 3

She walked from her apartment in the Marais, up through the ghastly modern development of Les Halles, wondering, as she always did, why it was allowed to replace the old market, and then past the specialist catering shops that supplied the capital's restaurants, until the hinterland of the Gare du Nord gave way to cheap bars and massage parlours. It was a glorious late summer's day and she smiled as she walked, full of anticipation. Even the pimps and pickpockets lurking at the entrance to the station, watching the tourists and out of towners arrive at the terminus, couldn't dent her feelings. For a split second, as she ran over the wide stretch of cobbles in front of the terminus, she gave a small skip of delight. Robert Doisneau could not have caught this moment better, so quick and unconscious was it, but if it had been frozen on film, it would have shown a woman of uncommon beauty. Her looks were an accident of genes, for her parents were physically unremarkable and her sisters, although attractive, were plain in comparison. Her dark hair was cut short, her eyes were wide and, like her mouth, slightly too large for her face. This conjunction of shapes, however, taken as a whole, was quite arresting and enough to make both men and women pause and look again at this young woman. But her looks were both a blessing and a curse, for they acted as a barrier between what she was and how she was perceived. But for this moment, on a warm September day, with her head thrown back and her feet off the ground, she was entirely herself.

Entering the station concourse, the sounds of the city were replaced by a sharper and more specific collection of noises contained under the arc of the great roof which spanned the platforms. In here was concentrated the excitement and anxiety of travel, the mystery and intrigue of arrival and departure, the beginning and end of other worlds.

Karyn Baird was in the curious cocoon that happiness can bring, a euphoria untested by time or experience. Two months earlier she had met Oliver Dreyfuss at a site meeting at La Mission, a new restaurant being developed out of an old bank near the church of St Sulpice. She was a manager with the group that Oliver's company was in partnership with, overseeing this and several other projects. Site meetings at the best of times could be stressful affairs and this one, she now recalled, was worse than most. Working with builders is like juggling with mercury and progress on key aspects of the reconstruction of the interior was behind schedule. Karyn had spoken to Oliver on several occasions, but this was the first time they were to meet. She was given a hard hat as she entered the site between columns of dull porphyry supporting an elaborate pediment. If the exterior betrayed the building's earlier life, the interior had yet to indicate its future direction. A shaft of sunlight from an oriel window, high on the wall opposite the entrance, was alive with swirls of dust. The demolition work was just about finished and in various parts of the large room builders were at work. At the centre of all this stood a man wearing a three-quarter length leather coat studying a plan. He, too, was wearing a white hel– met so at first she was unable to see his face. He then turned and looked up towards someone standing on a scaffold platform to her right and she saw that he had dark hair, which now fell loose from his helmet across his forehead. She assumed this must be Oliver Dreyfuss, one-time chef, now restaurateur. She intro- duced herself and he then did something which caused her to smile. He put his hand to the brim of his helmet, raised the brim slightly, and said, 'Yes, hello, I'm Oliver Dreyfuss. How very nice to meet.' He looked directly at her and she noted that when he smiled his whole face smiled with him. They shook hands and, as he gestured towards a quiet corner, he took her elbow and began to talk.

'This is a marvellous site and you have done wonders so far, but standing there just now I had a real doubt. I would like to share it with you and see what you think.' It was quite clear to Karyn that he meant it and she was pleasantly surprised. She knew that she was good at what she did, but she was also aware that, particularly in France, she was seen as a woman first and only then as a professional. Men paid lip service to her, their eyes betraying their obvious purpose, flirtation.

'We have the bar running parallel with a straight line from the entrance with tables on the left. Standing there just then, I think it's going to feel too cold, too angular. I think the punters will feel exposed, like dining on the flight deck of an aircraft carrier.'

'*Un porte-avions,*' she said.

'Yes, absolutely,' he agreed.

'You've read my note, then?'

'I don't think so. Was I meant to?'

She was staring at him now, knowing he was telling the truth. She fished about in her narrow briefcase and brought out a piece of paper which she handed to him. He turned slightly away from her to read it.

'*Un cuirassé.*'

'Yes, but I think aircraft carrier conveys better what I felt than battleship.' They were both smiling.

'So what would you do?' he asked as they walked back to the middle of floor. Here she peeled away from him.

'Imagine I'm the bar,' she said.

'Difficult,' he replied.

She shuffled in a narrow arc, placing small bits of brick and wood behind her to outline the shape she was describing with her feet. The debris had brought the bar round at a right angle. She moved towards the door.

'This way,' she explained using her arms, 'the bar encloses the diners. It also allows a much better station for the *maître d'* and a passage way here through to cloaks.'

'I don't disagree,' he commented, wanting to hear more.

'But there is something else,' she said.

'You surprise me.'

'I don't think it should look modern, as it does in the designer's sketch. I would much rather have an old fashioned *zinc*. I think the exterior dictates that we should be more traditional.'

Now it was his turn to walk the space, which he did by marching out of the site onto the boulevard before retracing his steps through the marble columns. When he reached her line of runes, he turned left and followed them until they petered out. He walked on a further ten feet or so, before putting his hands in his pockets and looking back towards her.

'I agree. Let's do it. Coffee?'

There was not one element of flirtation during the hour that followed, although she felt increasingly drawn to this English-man with a French name. His grandmother had married someone vaguely related to the French soldier famously, but wrongly, accused of being a traitor. Later she had left her husband to settle in England and, along the way, gained an extra 's' in her surname. Co-incidentally, her background was a mirror opposite, her mother having married her French step-father who brought the family to Paris. Although they talked most of the time about the progress of La Mission, the trig points for a deepening relationship had been laid.

Since then they had met twice and each time her interest in Oliver had moved to another level. He had spoken affectionately about his wife and had described a little of their life together. They emailed each other more often now, lacing their business with personal touches. They continued to match French words which they wouldn't normally use in conversation, but at no point could these exchanges be regarded as inappropriate.

But her mood this morning told Karyn Baird that she was

happy in a way that she could not previously recall. She felt relaxed in the company of this man, at ease with herself. She did not have to over-promote her talents, or exploit her looks. Their professional relationship had flourished and their joint steward-ship had put the progress of La Mission back on course and given it a new dynamic.

Just as a blindfolded man will, when told he is about to drink a glass of orange, for a few seconds at least, believe he can taste orange even though he has been handed a glass of milk, so Karyn Baird remained in her sunny state as she entered the Gare du Nord, even though the signs that would destroy it were all around.

'All services are suspended,' warned the arrivals and departures board. A tannoy message advised passengers that due to a serious incident there would be no further trains today. Karyn failed to register either of these warnings and it was only when she saw the crush of people at the foot of the escalators leading to the departure lounge that she realised something had happened.

French trains may be the envy of the world, but they were constantly prone to industrial action, so at first Karyn felt nothing but irritation at the prospect of Oliver's delayed arrival. But snatches of overheard conversation dissolved her bonhomie. True fear, real distress, spreads like electricity. A woman next to her, holding a mobile phone to her ear, turned and pleaded with her.

'He won't answer. Why won't he answer?'

Another woman collapsed against her partner who helped her to a seat. Now everyone seemed to be using their mobiles, their faces betraying extreme anxiety. Karyn fished out her mobile and tried Oliver's number. It rang, and she held her breath. The ring tone kept beat with her heart, which would have stopped if she had been able to see where the phone was ringing. The steel bogey which had ripped through Oliver's carriage and killed the group of women had, together with the force of the crash, expelled any loose objects in a wide arc around the track. Some, like Oliver's laptop, ricocheted around the carriage before being engulfed in flames. The phone was catapulted out through a hole in the roof and landed, thirty metres away in soft earth. Its ring tone was now lost amongst the sirens and shouted instructions which filled the scene. Not long afterwards, it stopped and it was later picked up by a *pompier* who put it amongst the growing collection of property which would later be returned to their owners or their families. And to help identify the dead.

An area of the Gare du Nord was now being cordoned off and a *gendarme* with a loudhailer asked all those waiting for the 9.01 service from St Pancras International to gather behind the taped area. Climbing on a trailer normally used for luggage, and accompanied by a man in a smart blue suit, the policeman addressed the crowd of some two hundred people.

'Ladies and gentlemen, it is now confirmed that the 9.01 from London St Pancras International was involved in crash at approximately 11.30. I am sad to tell you that there are reports of many casualties, many deaths.' At this point, a collective groan rose from the huddled group. 'This is Philippe Gendebien from the company who will tell you about procedures from now on.'

Desperation prevents you listening properly, ruins your concentration and the information that was now being given was hard for Karyn to take in. She did hear that the accident had taken place near Ermenonville, not far from Charles de Gaulle airport. She looked around at the weeping faces, some hopeful, some hopeless and knew she had to leave. It was not a logical decision, but she had to get to the scene of the accident, she had to be there, to know what had happened, to find Oliver.

She hurried down to the RER and caught a train to the airport. Her resolve kept her panic in check. She knew she would have been unable to stay at the Gare du Nord, a helpless victim passively waiting for further news. Half an hour later, she picked up a taxi at the airport, and one hour after leaving the train terminal, guided by the thick smoke that rose from the crash site, the taxi dropped her at Beaumarchais. She walked along the road to the bridge where, two hours earlier, Oliver had crossed in the opposite direction. She took the path by the perimeter fence, following the line, until she could see six coaches alone and incongruous, with several policemen standing guard around them. She could see the smoke now and with panic rising in her, quickly realised that the six coaches had somehow miraculously escaped the accident. Six coaches out of, say, eighteen, she calculated, lessened the odds but at least there was some hope. Moments later, though, as she came out of the woods, her hands rose involuntarily to her face. Ten ambulances, their back doors open, were receiving injured passengers, some on foot, others on stretchers. But what made Karyn shrink back, was the row of bodies lining the side of the road, each face covered with a blanket or bloodied sheet. Here and there, arms and hands, some badly distorted, poked out from the shrouds. The dead had been left so that the injured could have priority, an awful indignity but clearly the right decision. The police, who had established road blocks to all but emergency vehicles, had not had time to seal off all access to the scene, so Karyn was able to move through the rescue vehicles towards what was left of the bridge.

If the south side of the bridge had given her some hope, the north side almost completely destroyed her. She wept as she looked down on the appalling scene and had to support herself against a road sign. 'Can I help you, ma'am?' She felt an arm go round her and a blanket was draped over her shoulders. 'Those without serious injuries are being grouped over there. Do you need help?' She turned and saw a *pompier*, his hands hidden by black gauntlets, his helmeted face protected by a plastic shield.

'Thank you,' she said. 'I'll be fine.' She looked across to see where the *pompier* had pointed, and saw a small group of people. She walked closer and scanned the faces. Oliver was not amongst them. She stood and waited, the blanket still keeping her warm and, as the sun disappeared from the sky, watched as each new survivor arrived. By dusk, she knew he was either dead or badly injured.

She lied when she phoned the hospitals later and said that she was his wife. By midnight, neither his life, nor his death, had been confirmed. She returned home and although she didn't want to, she turned on the television. By two in the morning, the death toll had reached almost four hundred and the search for victims was still going on. She eventually fell asleep in front of the television, her short black hair sticking up in tiny eruptions, the lids of her eyes grey with exhaustion, her mouth turned down in sadness. Her crumpled face was reflected in an old silvered mirror.

Karyn Baird. Aged 26. More dead than alive.

Chapter 4

Oliver was not aware of having slept, but the warm sun on his face and the low grumble of the television must have raised him from a fitful rest. It was 6 a.m. and the live relay from the crash site showed the same sun glinting on the tangled wreckage of the train. The scene was less frenetic now, slower and more deliberate, as the final sweep for survivors was drawing to a close and the forensic experts, in white protective suits, moved amongst the burnt out carriages like ghosts. A reporter, her face orange against the rising sun, referred to a sheet of paper in her hand as she announced the grim toll of dead, injured and missing. The number of confirmed dead had not risen substantially overnight and hovered just below four hundred, but the figure did not include the twenty-seven passengers so far totally unaccounted for. Relatives of the missing were being contacted now and the reporter confirmed that a list of their names would be broadcast later.

Oliver rubbed his eyes, trying to push back the tiredness he felt. He stripped off his clothes and walked into the shower and allowed the cold water to bring him into the morning. He pressed against the dirty white tiles as the water rolled down his neck and back. So he was not quite officially dead. How curious to be a spectator of your own demise. He looked at his suit and shirt lying on the floor of the bedroom and wondered what he was doing. Perhaps the shock of the accident had so deranged him that he was having a sort of breakdown. He consciously pushed back images that he had seen the day before, bodies torn and destroyed by the force of the crash, a hand caught in a chunk of wreckage, a detached leg lying by the track. Was it these horrors that had caused him to walk away from the accident? Was the trauma too big for him to cope with, so that he had instinctively drawn a veil over it and pushed it to one side as though it had never happened?

He walked up and down the room drying himself with a thin white towel trying to make sense of his actions since the crash. Perhaps he knew, as he looked down into the inferno that had been his carriage, that he was being offered an opportunity to escape. Sometimes the body takes over from the mind, leaving logic behind, so that reason can only be deduced later. Yesterday, he didn't choose not to be a survivor, he simply gave up thinking and his body had gone its own way. Now, this early morning, he did have a choice. He could go back and become a survivor, his actions explained as the result of shock. Sitting naked on the edge of the bed, it dawned on him that yesterday he had fled more than the horrors of death. He had instinctively fled his own life.

He dressed and went downstairs where *Madame* was at the bar. She looked at him and said '*C'est terrible, n'est-ce pas?*' At first he did not know how to respond. 'Yes,' he agreed and then added 'Horrible.' He asked for the bill. 'You have no baggage, *monsieur*?' He was about to say 'no', when he realised that an explanation was necessary.

'I had an argument with my wife and I had to leave the house in a hurry, you understand.' This seemed entirely reasonable to the stern-faced woman, who offered the wisdom that everything is different in the morning. 'I couldn't agree more, *Madame*.'

And then, realising what she had said, the woman put her hand to her chest. 'Except for the poor people on that train.'

He stepped out into the soft morning air, walking away from the little hotel, away from the accident, away from the mill of reporters and emergency workers, his mind working on only what was directly in front of him. He wanted to get away, to change his clothes, to look anonymous to disappear into the landscape. He didn't want to ask himself why. Unhappiness is hard to admit to. Men, more than women, feel the need to carry with them an aura of invincibility, and Oliver was no different. He projected confidence, a confidence he did not always feel. Perhaps, as he looked down at the blazing wreckage, he had a surge of fear that his life had not been what he had wanted, and he had been given the opportunity to see it end. It was this he couldn't cope with. He had escaped with his life but suddenly that life had been presented to him for what it was.

Fear motivates strange actions. The rustle of the trees as he left home just twenty-four hours ago was seen by Oliver as a reflection of his guilt at not telling his wife he was going to Paris. By now she should know that he had been on the train, but he did not want to call her. Karyn, who was the reason for his journey to Paris, would also be desperate for news, and yet he could not bring himself to contact her, either. For the moment he didn't want to question why. He was caught in limbo and he abdicated responsibility to anyone but himself. What was making him flee he could not articulate but somewhere in him he carried the reasons like a dead weight.

In the inside pocket of his blue suit, his wallet contained 1,000 euros, drawn from his company account the day before yesterday to pay for some elaborate setting plates that Oliver had commissioned in Paris. They were the only immediate comfort he had, the means to continue his anonymity until he had focused more clearly on his predicament.

Right now, he wanted to be swallowed up by his surroundings. Above and ahead of him, there were a steady stream of planes landing at and leaving Charles de Gaulle airport. He began to walk towards them, knowing that he would be inconspicuous at an international airport. The road soon became a track, but the planes became bigger and those coming into land crabbed across the sky above him. The track took him to the tiny village of Moussy-le-Neuf and then on to a main road. In the distance he saw a signpost with the symbol of an aircraft and turned to follow it until he came to the outer fence of the airport. By nine o'clock he was just one of a thousand or so travellers in the futuristic departure lounge.

In the surreal world of an international airport, artificial light means that day and night barely exist. The clothes shop he entered was open eighteen hours a day and here morning looked just the same as evening. Oliver bought a pair of jeans, two T-shirts, a crew-neck sweater and a lightweight waterproof top. He peeled off the necessary euro notes, thankful for the cash. He changed in a cubicle in the toilets and it was only when he sat down with a cappuccino at one of the cafés, that the full realisation of what he was doing, and could do, came to him. It is easy to feel that you don't exist in an airport. Everyone is so intent on the business of travel that they see only themselves. He watched now as a woman, pushing a luggage trolley piled with suitcases, collided with a small child and barely acknowledged his cries as she continued steadfastly on her way.

His eyes followed a policeman, a sub-machine gun held across his chest, as he slowly patrolled the concourse. Spooning the foamy milk from his cup, Oliver was aware that CCTV cameras were indiscriminately recording every movement in the concrete and marble hall. But for now, these electronic eyes could look but they couldn't see, for there was no reason why they should pick out the solitary figure at the corner of coffee house. Even so, Oliver got up and wandered over to a Timberland shop where he picked up a baseball cap, a pair of tough boots and a small rucksack. Pulling the brim of the cap low over his eyes, he then went into a bookshop where he bought several maps. As he wandered out of the airport, his blue suit was crushed in the rucksack on his back and when, shortly afterwards, he dumped the clothes in a rubbish bin, he felt that he was discarding one part of his life. What he was replacing it with, he had no idea.

As he walked out of the departure lounge, he felt suddenly

very vulnerable, as though all eyes were on him. Perhaps he had been foolish to come to the airport where his instincts had told him he could merge into the crowds. In fact, here everyone's moments were accounted for and hidden eyes were constantly scanning monitors for any unexplained behaviour. Perhaps he had been seen entering the toilets in one set of clothing and leaving in another. But then lots of travellers did this. Still, he would feel better to be somewhere else.

Oliver was ready to disappear into France, to remain anonymous until he heard the confirmation of his own death. What he would do then, he could not say, but that was his short-term goal. The first bus announced its destination as Melun, a reasonable sized town that he had seen on the map. Here he would look for another hotel that would not demand his passport for identification.

Melun is built on a sweeping bend in the Seine, the river alive with barges. Oliver watched them from the bridge, which was festooned with baskets of geraniums. The barges were enormous, travelling slowly but pushing powerfully through the water. The one passing underneath him now had a line of washing strung across the deck, where a dog lay asleep. A woman with a patterned skirt and colourful shirt, was washing down the small area behind the cabin, her large arms brown and freckled. Supported by a crane at the very back of the boat, hung a Renault 5. This was a self-contained world, a floating mobile home where work and life was lived to an ever changing landscape. Oliver spent some time on the bridge, watching a succession of barges and imagining the lives of the families on board. There were several hotels along the quay and he picked the one whose green shutters were dirty and unpainted. It was tall and narrow and seemed to lean to one side. A small man in a large knit cardigan gave him a key and indicated that the room was on the top floor. There was no lift and he was breathing heavily by the time he reached the top. The climb was worth it, for although the room was tired and smelled fusty, the two shuttered windows looked down on the river. Oliver sat and continued his observation of the lives floating by in front of him.

Hungry and in need of a drink, he ventured out in the early evening and found a bar with a television. Wall-to-wall coverage of the crash had now stopped, and it was half an hour before the national news programme began. Other people in the bar were paying little or no attention to the screen. Outside, people strolled along the pavement and the cars rumbled over the cobbled street. The outside world, though, ceased to exist for Oliver when he saw his name on the screen, one of nineteen passengers confirmed missing and presumed dead. Of those nineteen, six had been French. An English forensic expert, his words translated beneath his face, explained that further tests were being carried out. Oliver expected the other drinkers in the bar would be looking at him, but he was just another figure enjoying *un verre* after work.

He ordered another kir and enjoyed its sweetness. On the wall above him a photograph showed a young couple kissing on a boulevard in Paris, a moment of pleasure caught in the middle of a busy scene. He stared at the picture wondering if it would ever be possible to experience the freedom and comfort the couple projected, their lives apparently without cares, their focus entirely on one another. A barge hooted on the Seine and he left the bar into the shadow of the street.

Chapter 5

It was a gift to the media, whose sensibilities did not run too deep. The forensic scientist stepped carefully across the charred ground. He was framed by the arms of two cranes which were in the process of clearing the wreckage of the coaches not directly involved in the fire. In his hands, held out in front of him like an offering, he carried a white plastic container. He was wearing an all-in-one white protective suit and against the blackened background, he and his cargo took on an ethereal quality. 'All that is left of Coaches 10 and 11,' were the headlines in one paper. 'Ashes to Ashes,' said another. 'The identities of nineteen people,' the voice-over on Channel 4 News reported, as the camera followed the progress of the scientist over the twisted tracks, 'are contained in this capsule no bigger than an average thermos flask.'

Sonya then watched the scientist, the same man that Oliver had seen half an hour earlier on a different channel in another country, explaining that whilst it was possible that DNA traces might be found of passengers so far unaccounted for, there was a chance that there would be 'no identifiable remains'. The phrase echoed around her head like a loose cannon, disturbing her reason, destroying her perspective, ruining her plans. 'It's not possible,' she muttered to herself. And then slowly repeated the words 'no identifiable remains'.

She stood and paced up and down, unable to concentrate. 'How could he do it?' Sonya Dreyfuss was not used to being thwarted but now, on two fronts, she was left frustrated and impotent. She had so much to say to Oliver, so much to ask. And now he was no one, nowhere. She couldn't even talk to a body.

'How could this happen?' she repeated to herself, half in anger, half in astonishment.

She watched as jagged pieces of carriage were lifted on to low-loaders to be taken away, the sparks and white light of oxyacetylene cutters biting into and separating the compressed metal.

The phone rang and she looked hard at the receiver, deciding whether she should answer it. She did and immediately regretted it. It was the policewoman, Maureen McCulloch.

'Yes, I'm holding up fine thank you. It's been a shock of course, and these news reports just seem to make things worse. Yes, I'll be in about six. Yes, see you then.'

What fresh hell is this, she thought as she sat overlooking the garden. For a moment, she almost decided to start smoking again. Events were to get no better later.

Maureen McCulloch was everything you could hope for in a police officer. She was kind without overdoing it, she was busi- nesslike without being brusque and she was bright, a combination of qualities that Sonya liked in the men and women she em- ployed. And she was straightforward enough to ask difficult questions without embarrassment.

'At the moment we have to assume that your husband is dead. And, since we have heard nothing to the contrary from you, that he was, indeed, on the train.' Here she looked straight at Sonya, who met her gaze in the same unblinking way.

'And now we have this.'

'You keep handing me mobile phones,' said Sonya. 'Just how many people did take photographs of him?'

'No, Mrs Dreyfuss, this is your husband's phone. It was picked up by a fireman at the site. Debris from many of the carriages was flung far and wide. I am sorry to have to give you such a tangible reminder of your husband, but we felt it was important to return it to you as soon as possible.'

'But does this mean,' Sonya picked up the phone before

finishing her sentence, 'that Oliver may have survived the crash and dropped the phone afterwards?'

'It is unlikely, Mrs Dreyfuss, very unlikely. Several possessions from people in carriages eleven to eight were found afterwards. But there were, as you know, barely any remains from those coaches. I would not build up your hopes.'

'But there is a chance?'

'Until we get the results of the DNA we won't know.'

'But what about no identifiable remains? I heard the phrase just now.'

'Quite true. The train was hit by a lorry carrying aircraft fuel. The heat of the fire was such that it is expected that there will be no identifiable remains of some passengers.'

'So there is a chance that there might never be any real closure on this?'

'Mrs Dreyfuss. There were sixty-four people in that carriage. Only two have been identified and they were towards the back. The impact was at the other end, where the lorry dropped. The chances of his survival, and those around him, are virtually nil. I'm sorry to have to be so blunt.'

'So, he doesn't exist.' For a moment neither spoke.

'And, cruelly Mrs Dreyfuss, I must now ask you for a possession of your husband's from which we can take a DNA sample. A comb, perhaps, or a toothbrush. It will help, to use your word, in the process of closure.'

Sonya looked down at the mobile and the policewoman followed her gaze. 'We've checked the phone and there's nothing there.'

Sonya got up and went upstairs to the bathroom where she picked up Oliver's hair brush. As she handed it to Sergeant McCulloch, she said,

'I could be giving you the only trace of my husband left to me.' The policewoman carefully put the hairbrush in a plastic bag.

'As you know, Mrs Dreyfuss, we can offer counselling, but I'm sure that you're aware of that.'

Sonya was impatient with this 'softly, softly' approach, being treated as though she was bone china and might shatter at any minute, so she acknowledged what the policewoman had said with a quick nod of her head. When she had gone, she felt angry and at odds with the world, her world. She picked up Oliver's mobile from the table in front of her and held it in the palm of her hand. Forty-eight hours ago, Oliver would have cupped the phone in the same way. Phoning who, she wondered, squeezing it in her fist. She got up and went to her study where she attached a charger to the phone and, sitting at her desk, watched the information come to life on its little screen. She was nervous, a feeling she was unaccustomed to, and when the screen told her that there were two missed calls, her apprehension increased. She hesitated before scrolling to Call Register and then again before discovering who had called Oliver after the crash. To find that the first call was from herself almost made things worse, for she could imagine it ringing alone amidst the horror of the accident. She stared at the name of the second missed caller.

Karyn.

Karyn Baird. She knew who she was, of course. Oliver had spoken of her on several occasions but not in a way that would make her, Sonya, believe that there was anything between them. But now she wondered and the more she turned it over the angrier she became. If only she could confront him and demand an explanation. She turned back to the phone and quickly ran through the list of Oliver's last calls. Karyn's name was there only once. She recognised all of the others, the restaurant, his accountant, a chef who he was trying to persuade to work for him, his bank manager. A perfectly innocent list for a man running a business in this country and about to start another in France. Even the missed call from Karyn had a simple explanation; he was working with her and she needed to check something, or confirm the time of his arrival.

But why didn't he tell her he was going to France? Perhaps,

now, nothing was innocent. The night closed in around her as she sat turning over in her mind the events of the past two days. The television was a dark and threatening presence in the corner. Had she but known it, her husband's name and that of the other missing passengers, was at that exact moment being broadcast on the early evening news. When the phone rang she again hesitated before picking it up.

It was François, the *maître d'* at the restaurant. 'Sonya. How are you? We've just heard. I'm coming over. Poor you.' His words were spilling over in his nervousness. 'He must have arranged to go to Paris at the last minute. We had no idea. Oh god . . . '

'François. I know, it's terrible. But I'm OK. It's not one hundred per cent confirmed that he's dead, but they've told me not to hold out any hope.' Even as she spoke to him she realised that, although she had known about the possible death of her husband for at least a day, no one else could have been aware that he was on the train. As soon as she had said goodbye to François, she picked up the receiver again.

'Gordon. Have you been watching the news?' She did not need to announce herself.

'Yes, it's terrible. Awful.'

'Well, it's even more complicated than that. Oliver was on the train and he's amongst those posted as missing, presumed dead.'

She could hear his mouth drop open, the correct response caught somewhere in his throat.

'But did you know he was going?'

'No I bloody didn't,' she said bitterly.

'I'll come over immediately,' he said eventually.

'No, you can't,' she said. 'It would be entirely inappropriate. Yes, I do wish you were here, but you can't. He's fucked it all up for the moment and we'll have to go to ground for a while. I'm going to have to phone around now and break the news before they see his name on the box.'

For the next hour, Sonya called her friends and family,

explaining her delay in letting them know on the initial uncertainty about what had happened to Oliver. Everyone assumed that it was just another routine journey that Oliver had been making to France so she did not have to tell them the truth, not that she ever intended to do so. When she had finished, she unplugged the phone and lay down on the sofa. It was dark in the room now and although her shoulders ached from the tension of being on the phone, her eyes were wide open and her fingers were slowly scratching the cushion that lay on her stomach. She was focusing hard and her eyes had narrowed in concentration. She was unable to let go and allow emotion and fatigue take over.

Abruptly she stood up and walked surely through the darkness to the corridor and then to Oliver's study. The switch by the door turned on the side lights and she went over and sat at his desk. This was familiar territory for her. When they first lived together they had agreed, like cats or robins, to keep away from and respect each other's studies. But it wasn't long before she abandoned her side of the bargain. She looked around now at the accumulation of papers and postcards, the books jumbled along the shelves, the random scatter of objects on the desk each, presumably, carrying some message or memory for Oliver. Right in front of her, propped on the keyboard of Oliver's computer, was a postcard of an aircraft carrier. Curious, she picked it up, and turned it over. *Did you have something like this in mind?* read the message. *So cosy. Look forward to seeing you Monday. K.* It had been sent to the restaurant and he must have brought it home. So he wasn't too concerned about her seeing it, she thought. But, then again, there appeared nothing for her to be worried about.

She turned on the computer. She had no qualms about what she was about to do. If Oliver could deceive, she could invade his privacy. Sonya was a lot more adept at computers than her husband and was quickly able to review his recent work and emails. She had been here before. Nothing is sacred with a computer, she thought. Somewhere in this neat and precise box of high technology could be found everything that Oliver had done on it. Even what he had deleted she could find. Old fashioned love letters you could hide, but the electronic trail was indelible. She looked first at his emails from Karyn, leaning forward at the screen to read each new message. It was all reasonably mundane stuff until she came to the final email, which was headed *interpretation please.*

> I am standing on the lid of a saucepan. The edge is just like the blade of an ice-skate and I am sliding along the pavement with perfect ease. And then I am in the country, and the pavement stretches out in front of me and I am going faster and faster. The feeling is glorious and even in the dream I cannot believe how all this is possible on the edge of a saucepan lid. And then, somewhere in the distance, a voice that I recognise as that of an older friend of mine, Miriam, starts to criticise me. I can't remember what about, but she has never spoken to me like this before, and it takes away some of the exhilaration I felt from my slalom on the lid.
>
> Isn't it funny how the mind takes us? No doubt you will have a perfectly rational explanation.
>
> K.

Sonya read the email again and thought that it was an odd message to exchange with a working companion, but it was still within the bounds of what Jane Austen might have called 'propriety'.

Sonya was now drawn to a series of red exclamation marks alongside several emails from Jane Masterton, Oliver's acountant. A number of these had spreadsheet attachments and for the next hour Sonya carefully examined a topography only too familiar to her, a matrix of figures, forward calculations and summaries. Even as she read, one part of her became the women in the glass and steel office overlooking the Thames, a surgeon dispassionately examining a body. She knew exactly what these figures were saying since she had determined their course some months earlier. Sonya followed the trail into the folder containing all previous messages from the accountant and made several notes on a scrap of paper on Oliver's desk. It was only after doing this that she ventured to open the one folder that might have attracted her first: *personal.*

Sonya was surprised to find just two documents, which she opened without the same sense of confidence she had with the spreadsheets. The first was marked *poem 1:*

> The names of those who in their lives fought for life
> Who wore at their hearts the fire's centre
> Born of the sun they travelled a short while towards the sun
> And left the vivid air signed with their honour

Sonya then opened the second, marked *poem 2:*

> The sense of danger must not disappear:
> The way is certainly both short and steep,
> However gradual it looks from here;
> Look if you like, but you will have to leap

Sonya was aware of a motor-scooter screaming noisily up the hill towards Wimbledon village and a dog barking in a nearby garden. The fragments of poetry and the array of financial figures, ostensibly so different, carried the same message for Sonya. Each upset Sonya's carefully prepared and regularly used route map to Oliver's character. For Sonya, it was like waking up in the morning and finding that someone had completely changed the layout of her desktop, or the dials in her car.

Sonya Dreyfuss bent her head down, so that her chin was almost touching her chest. Her eyes were closed, but there were no tears. How was it, she thought bitterly, that at one and the same time there is no Oliver and yet more of him than she knew before? How could he do this to her? How could he betray her so?

Chapter 6

Even as she entered the *place* at St Sulpice, she had not decided whether to go into the church there or continue onwards, across Saint Germain, to Notre Dame. Autumn had now arrived in Paris and a brisk wind was whipping the browning leaves off the trees and spinning them along the pavements. The walk through the Luxembourg Gardens had not lifted her spirits and the beautiful little clothes shops which dotted the area she passed without a glance. Paris was in full flow and cars jostled for space in the narrow streets around the square towers of St Sulpice. Karyn decided to continue on towards the Seine, figuring that she would be less conspicuous amongst the crowds in Notre Dame than in the more intimate interior of St Sulpice.

She cut down the rue de Buci and then along the narrow rue St André des Arts towards the Pont Neuf. It was cold out of the sun and she turned up the collar of her coat. The wind whistled along the Seine, which had taken on the same colour as the grey sky, and the lights on the *bateaux mouches* stood out in the narrow stretch of the Seine between the Left Bank and the Île de La Cité. The swifts and swallows that screamed and swooped around the gargoyles and giant buttresses had long since departed for the south, leaving the great cathedral to the pigeons and the crows.

She entered through the west door into the vast interior where groups of tourists looked upwards to the stained glass windows and, who knows, to whatever was beyond. Various tour guides were explaining the glories of the cathedral in German, Japanese, English and Dutch so that, threading her way through them, Karyn heard a *mélange* of tongues, almost a mad new language.

She was heading for a small side chapel in a dark corner of the nave. In the days that followed the accident, she had found concentration difficult and this journey to the church was an attempt to regain some sort of focus. She now knew that Oliver's was one of the missing bodies and that the chances of finding any remains were virtually zero. She dropped the euros into the box and the metallic clunk of the coins cut across the taped organ music which murmured around her. She picked out a narrow, tapered candle and regarded it for a second before lighting it on the flame of another. She slotted it into a holder on the metal stands amongst the other burning candles. And now, her face lit dull yellow in the flickering light, she wondered what to think, what to say. On one level, she had no problem with the idea of Oliver having no body. Standing there, in the heart of the great church, it was easy to feel the spirit of Oliver Dreyfuss and to imagine that it was possible to talk directly to him. She formed the sentences in her mind, oddly intimate amongst the tourists and tour guides.

– Oliver, it is odd to say I miss you for we have so little history to miss. But wherever you are, I miss you. Perhaps you are 'travelling towards the sun' like that poem you sent me. It's hard to put into words but I think I connected with some history in you, a history that maybe not even you knew about. You must know that you are very much alive to me. I only regret that I never had the chance to say I love you.

Karyn spoke the last words out loud and, self-conscious, she looked behind her to see if anyone had heard, but the church carried on without her.

She spent the rest of the day at La Mission, which was now nearing completion. Not surprisingly, some of the joy had now gone out of the project and she went through the motions of her job with little enthusiasm. Oliver's visits to the site had always enlivened proceedings and he was missed by the whole team, and not just Karyn. The *zinc* had now been installed and it curved round in front of the entrance just as they had discussed a few months ago. She leaned against it, looking at designs for the menu covers and matchboxes. It was wrong to think of these tasks as trivial because, had Oliver been with her, the process would have seemed important and fun.

She looked around the restaurant, the high ceilings, the tall windows, the sense of space and yet the feeling of intimacy. She could not help compare it to Notre Dame. Both were arenas where people came to seek satisfaction and, some would say, both were spiritual.

Her mobile chirruped on the bar top, interrupting her thoughts. It was her boss, Patrick.

'We have a little bit of a problem, Karyn.' Karyn listened. 'With the death of Oliver there will be a delay in the funds due for completion. We are currently talking to his accountants but I suppose they are not sure of their ground since Oliver has not officially been declared dead.'

Karyn hated the way he was talking, the cold acceptance of fact, and it troubled her enough for her to respond sharply.

'He was a friend you know.'

'Yes, I know, but life must go on and we are 700,000 euros short of what we need and friend or no friend we have to take action. We need a contingency plan and I want you to work on it. And see what more you can find from Oliver's end of things.'

Karyn flipped shut her phone. Sentiment and money don't mix. Life must go on. She turned the phrase over in her mind and wondered what was the point of death. Was Oliver's death to be filed along with all the other documents that accumulated during the term of their co-production? She was being unreasonable, she knew, and she could not expect Patrick to share her sense of loss but she condemned his lack of intuition.

Cars rumbled noisily over the cobbled street. The flower shop on the rue de Buci was, as usual, alive with colour and next door at the butchers, a line of customers examined the meat behind the glass displays as if their lives depended on it. The cafés were full, people bustled by with shopping bags, intent on this and that. Life did go on.

And it was cruel.

If she had carried her religious thoughts through to the evening, she might have reasoned that, just as the Lord taketh away, so the Lord giveth. It was true that part of Karyn refused to believe that Oliver was dead and yet it was equally true that she was well equipped to deal with his passing away. She felt that she had a spiritual connection to the man who had so recently come into her life, which would exist regardless of his physical presence. So, in a sense, Oliver *was* alive to her and her senses were open to all that he might show her now.

When Karyn returned home that night, to her small apartment just off the boulevard Raspail, she had begun to wonder how to tackle the *pepin* that her boss had given her. Was there merely a temporary problem with the cash flow, or was it more serious? Could she put on hold her feelings for Oliver? She looked out above the jumble of roofs over which it was just possible to see the tops of the taller trees in the Luxembourg Gardens. She decided that she had been lucky. Instead of having to put Oliver behind her and 'get on with life' as Patrick had instructed, she had his permission to continue being involved with Oliver, however painful that might be.

She turned on the television and sat through the end of a game show and felt a drowsiness begin to take her over. She was quickly brought back to her senses when black and white images of the crash flashed on the screen in front of her. It was a promotion for a documentary later that evening which promised 'previously unseen footage' of the recent disaster. Could she sit through that? She got up to start supper, chopping garlic and onions as she debated not just whether she had the courage to sit through the programme, but the morality of watching an event which had just three days ago claimed so many lives. How quickly disaster can be turned into a form of entertainment.

Television is the least brave of mediums needing, for most of its output, to please the greatest number of people, and offend the least. It cannot campaign like a newspaper and often it is forbidden from taking sides. And, in the one arena where it should excel – pictures – it often censures itself to the point of blandness. In the case of the crash, however, the authorities, both rail and television, were faced with a genuine dilemma. The CCTV cameras sited all along the railway track allow each and every kilometre of track to be monitored all the time. So the 9.01 from St Pancras International that fateful morning was recorded for most of its journey. And the dreadful moment when the petrol tanker plunged through the bridge onto the express was recorded in graphic detail by two cameras near the bridge and a third further down the track. The security staff who watched the footage as it happened were stunned by the images of the catastrophic accident. These terrible pictures were made available to the investigation team and, by one means and another, they also found their way to a television current affairs' producer. It was immediately clear that the accident footage was much too strong to show, but it was decided that the recording made by the camera further down the track, by the second bridge, was just about acceptable. Other footage from the crash site, recorded by several different crews, also demanded careful editing. At no time of the day or night could television show pictures of severed heads and abandoned limbs.

And so it was, later that night, that Karyn Baird settled down with a glass of red wine, to watch what the producers called 'Anatomy of a Disaster'. Although she was unaware of it, Karyn began watching the programme with her wine glass in front of her face, so that her eyes were only just above the rim. She began to cry, quietly, as the grainy CCTV pictures showed the train slowly pulling out of St Pancras International. All so normal, she thought. Turn back now, she wanted to say. There was commentary on the high level of security and safety along the track. But the CCTV footage was inter-cut with close-ups of a petrol tanker, obviously reconstructed, and the narrator pointed out that not even the best laid plans could cope with what happened next. The pictures that followed appeared misleading. They showed an empty stretch of track with, in the far distance, a bridge. There was no commentary, no music and no sound. Suddenly, at the top of the screen, it was possible to see a train emerge from the bridge. But immediately Karyn's eyes were drawn to what was happening behind, as an explosion of what appeared to be white light was followed by the shocking sight of a coach rearing up at frightening speed to one side of the bridge. A second coach seemed to break in half as it collided with the bridge. The flash of white light had now been replaced by dark smoke, although, disturbingly, it was possible to make out the shape of succeeding coaches rearing up as they collided with those in front. Karyn now held her clenched hands in front of her face as the pictures were played again in slow motion.

It was not until this second showing, that the narrator mentioned the miraculous escape of the engine and first six coaches, for now this part of the train had come to rest at the bottom of frame, not far from the camera that recorded the ghastly scene. The commentary spoke of the fortunate passengers, about two hundred, who had been in this part of the train. The petrol tanker, the voice explained, had severed the express two coaches after the buffet car, and the force of the falling tanker had been so great that the two parts of the train had been pulled apart like a cracker.

This single, unmoving, camera shot was compelling. In the distance the smoke increasingly shrouded the vague details of the mayhem. In the foreground, bewildered passengers began to emerge from the train, each and everyone turning to look back along the tracks. Now the programme showed carefully selected footage taken by the first camera crews on the scene, flaming carriages, huddled survivors and stretchers bearing the injured to ambulances. Because Karyn had seen some of these pictures before, they did not carry the same impact as the CCTV recordings. The programme returned to these and the commentary spoke of how some of the surviving passengers walked back along the track to bravely try and help. Here Karyn could see half a dozen figures, walking separately, making their way towards the conflagration. None of them moved with any real purpose, knowing what would confront them in a few moments, nor did they look at each other. These black and white figures on a railway track reminded Karyn of survivors from a concentration camp, isolated by their ordeal, unwilling or unable to connect with their surroundings.

And now, towards the top of the screen, the leading figure turned abruptly to one side to head for the embankment. In that moment, in that split second before the passenger left the screen, he was turned sideways to the camera. He was nothing more than an accumulation of dots, of pixels and, as such, completely unrecognisable. But there was something, a way of moving, a disposition of body, that caused Karyn to shoot forward in her seat. And then the figure was gone and Karyn, irrationally, picked up the remote and attempted to reverse the pictures.

She stood up and stared at the screen. She could barely move. Although the programme credits were now playing, all she could see, frozen in a black and white blur, was the outline of a man who she was convinced was Oliver. Fool, she said to herself, you are seeing things. It's what you want, so you are trying to make it happen. You're fantasising.

But yet the image remained, indelible, and she sat down and wept.

Chapter 7

The barges began to move at first light, grumbling under the bridge below his window as a brisk wind tugged at the metal shutters. Oliver had slept badly, waking with a start on several occasions with vivid images of the accident. The awful smell that came from the burning wreckage he could still taste in his mouth. As he listened to the town coming to life, his drab room slowly taking colour, he thought again about how close he had been to death. His face was damp with sweat. The shock was still fresh with him and he doubted he would ever shake it off completely. But on this windy morning on the banks of the Seine, thousands of other unknown lives below in the strange town, he began to see a little more clearly. His reactions since the crash were far from the irrational acts he had first thought. Yes, on one level the shock caused him to flee the horrors of the accident, but on another he had used it as an excuse to blank off difficulties in the rest of his life. He had been like the captain of a one-man submarine, closing the hatch and sealing himself off from the world. Sitting at the window looking down on the barges he afforded himself a rueful smile and at once recognised it as a small token of normality.

Oliver was used to taking decisions himself. It was a simple case of sink or swim. When his father had died of cancer Oliver was nine years old, an only child. His mother had taken the death very badly and so, in the space of a few days, Oliver learned to cope with the radically altered landscape of his life. His mother never remarried, so he remained head of the household until he left to do his first *stage* in France when he was seventeen. She died whilst he was away. By this time, his self-reliance was ingrained and it helped him professionally and, for a while at least, in his private life. Women found his singular resolve very attractive and many wanted to conquer and disarm him. But Oliver's emotions were quite tightly sealed and his relationships were always short term. What made Sonya so attractive to him was that she never tried to get through to him like that. The notion of 'fortress Dreyfuss', as she called it, suited her because it mirrored her own character. They were two highly successful young people, running their lives in parallel, making no great claims on one another, but comortable with the privacy that each afforded the other. Or so it had seemed.

So it was no real surprise to Oliver that, in the grey light of this September morning, he did not want to phone Sonya and that he had little guilt at what she might be feeling at the news of his 'death'. She was so remarkably self-controlled that it was impossible for him to imagine her even grieving his loss. The very thought of this made Oliver angry, not because he had any illusions about the importance he played in Sonya's life, but because, even with an event as important as death, Sonya's emotional defences would be tightly in place. In this sense, they deserved each other.

But there was more, a succession of events with Sonya, some so small that they barely registered in his conscious memory, that had steadily accumulated in him like a great wall of water behind a high dam. Even now, as he tried to establish what had brought him to be sitting here in a strange room in the middle of France, he could recall nothing in particular, aware only of this enormous pressure inside him which blotted out detail and from which he was desperately trying to escape. And then, for the briefest of seconds, like a subliminal frame in a film, he saw Sonya's face and he knew the image was taken from the events of a Sunday morning in early June a couple of years before. Her face, sharply defined by the morning sun, was leaning towards his and her eyes, green and steady, were looking into his own. But, as quickly as the image came to him, it was gone, shut down by an emotional circuit breaker over which he appeared to have no control. Oliver was left with the familiar uneasiness which he had become to regard as normal and which he had learned to live with and deny, like a steadily growing cancer.

It was Karyn he wanted to call, to apologise and to ask for help. But he was frightened. He had told her that his visit to Paris was professional, but the truth was that he wanted to see her. Although he felt a great comfort in her presence, he could not gauge her feelings for him and now that he had let her believe that he had been killed in the crash, he was totally unsure what her reactions would be if he called. But there was something else. Having, by chance, found himself in this cocoon of anonymity, he did not want to abandon it just yet. And it would have been unfair to give her the responsibility of knowing he was alive. This woman, though, had an intuitive wisdom which he needed desperately. But he couldn't move forwards or backwards. He was between two worlds, both of which he didn't yet understand. He knew he would have to, but for now, like an animal hibernating for winter, he wanted to seek the shadows and go to ground.

There was another problem, though, which he could barely acknowledge. Would their fledgling relationship survive him telling her that his company could not afford the final payment on the Paris restaurant? He did not want to present her with failure, particularly a failure he could not comprehend, another factor in the labyrinth which he was unable to unpick. It was partly shame that caused Oliver, successful restaurateur, married to the strikingly attractive and extremely wealthy Sonya, to freeze now. Such malfunctions are not permitted to those who are so clearly blessed. It was not possible to talk about failure with Sonya. It was an unacceptable word in her lexicon of life and went hand in hand with never apologising and never explaining.

If you are certain, you never entertain doubt in yourself or in others. When had he first felt like fleeing from this overwhelming certainty? Was there even a moment, a nano-second, in that first meeting in the restaurant, the tiniest blip on his radar, that warned of what lay ahead? No, he had been enveloped in her sureness. If he had shown his capacity for self doubt to Sonya then, what would have happened? He shut his eyes but he simply could not imagine the scene, however much he now wished it had happened. And then, apparently unbidden, another memory floated to the surface.

It was a Monday morning in the early days of their marriage. The success of his restaurant had meant that he could now employ a chef and this particular Monday, with the restaurant shut, he was running through some options for the new menu which he would later suggest. Sonya was at work and he was alone all day. Like most chefs, Oliver was a pickpocket of other people's recipes, lifting a process here, an ingredient there to produce something of his own. Some he would simply reorganise or bring up to date, others, which he felt had slipped into the public domain, he merely tested and made only minor adjustments to the presentation. As the day wore on, the kitchen contained a mix of intense smells, garlic, saffron, coriander and spun sugar. The hours compressed and he barely realised the afternoon had disappeared when Sonya came into the kitchen. She kissed him and then went over and flicked on the extractor.

'Do you want to hear my news?' Before he could reply she had sat at the kitchen table and kicked off her heels. She then proceeded to tell him about an unwelcome takeover bid she was involved in, describing in cruel detail and not a little humour, the various players and their foibles. 'And you know what,' she finished, 'no matter what happens we'll make well over a £100,000. Don't you think I'm clever?'

The question was rhetorical but he agreed anyway.

'And so, where are you taking me to celebrate?'

He looked down at the array of dishes in front of him, some neatly arranged and others partly eaten, as if a successful dinner party had suddenly been interrupted. Even now, lying on his bed 500 kilometres from home, he remembered clearly what he had cooked: fillets of John Dory with saffron ratatouille sauce, *artichauts à la barigoule*, a mussel soup with coriander, duck coated in lavender and honey and a panacotta topped with a spun sugar dome. By now the saffron sauce had developed a dry crust and the oil had seeped from the ratatouille in a brown stain.

He paused, but only briefly.

'The Connaught?'

She clapped her hands together as she jumped to her feet, all in one movement. 'I'll change.' And she disappeared. It was what she wanted.

And, now, in Melun, in a room that had probably seen a thousand disappointments, he raised his fingers to his nose half expecting to smell the garlic and see the faint yellow blush of saffron.

He got off the bed and returned to the window where the floating odours of cooking had perhaps prompted his thoughts. 'And what had I been doing all day, Sonya?' he asked quietly.

A young boy sitting on the roof of a barge, his arm around a black and white collie, waved up at him and Oliver raised his arm in response. The boy could no more have heard him than Sonya did.

He checked out of the hotel, handing over a few more precious notes from his dwindling supply and asking for directions to the station. It was only when he watched the double decker train pulling into the station, the Paris commuters waiting patiently on the platform, that he realised he could not climb on board. The noise of the wheels on the track and the sheer bulk of the train, made him draw back and he felt pin pricks of sweat all over his body. How foolish of him to think, so soon after his trauma, that he could put it behind him and resume life as before.

He contemplated walking the eighty or so kilometres to Paris, following the Seine until he arrived at the centre, but that would have taken him at least four days and the idea did not appeal to him. So he caught a bus, which carried him through the southern sprawl of Paris, via Orly airport and the crowded autoroutes, to the Port d'Orléans. Arriving in Paris this way, he thought, you could never guess what pleasures lay beyond this ugly hinterland, the jumble of dual carriageways, high voltage pylons and graffiti clad walls.

The bus dropped Oliver at Montparnasse. Suddenly here, in this familiar city, Oliver felt exposed again, just as he had at the airport. He had Karyn's address, hardly any distance away, but he guessed she would be at her office, or on site. He couldn't just turn up, like a ghost. He stopped at a café on the boulevard Raspail and pretended to read *Le Figaro*, just another Parisien.

*   *   *

Even as Oliver took his first sip of *café crème*, barely half a kilometre away, Karyn left her flat, a black cap covering her short hair. Karyn had been taught by her father that women, particularly attractive women, had an advantage over men when it came to finding information. With men, he said, it might take three phone-calls, maybe five, to get what you wanted. Women, he explained to his daughter, could achieve it in three or less. Karyn invariably found this was true and after the shock of seeing the programme the previous evening, she had made a call to a girlfriend whose boyfriend worked for TF1, the channel which had shown it. Karyn didn't explain why she wanted a recording of the documentary and the boyfriend didn't ask.

She cut down the rue du Bac, before turning onto the boulevard St Germain towards place de la Concorde. The boyfriend had arranged for her to watch a VHS recording in one of the viewing rooms at the channel's headquarters, just off the Champs Elysées. Jean-Paul met her at reception and as he handed the tape to her his eyes appraised her and the slight smile on his face indicated that his helpfulness was not without a price. She took the tape from him and, looking at him directly, said that she needed to be left alone if he didn't mind, which she was sure he didn't.

Once he had gone, she dimmed the lights in the room and then spooled the tape forward to the end of the programme. Her heart beat faster now as the images rushed toward the point she was looking for. She pressed the half speed button, and the passengers leaving the train slowed down. It was the lead figure she was interested in and she watched his progress up the tracks, an unrecognisable figure in a dark suit. She waited until he turned to his left and then froze the image. It was nothing more than a blur in different shades of grey. She moved towards the television on her hands and knees, so that her nose was almost touching the screen. The outline of the figure was worse here, but she felt that by being so close and staring so hard, that she might give sense to the surreal pattern of dots. She was startled when the pictures automatically animated and the figure began to walk to the edge of the screen. She pressed the freeze button, but the man in the dark suit was no clearer than he had been before. She sat back in her chair, rewound the sequence, and watched it again in normal speed. It was only now that she recognised what had caught her attention the previous evening. It was a certain way of walking, a slightly limping gait that was somehow familiar. But the figure was the size of a little finger on the screen and no matter how many times she watched the sequence she could not be sure that she was not fantasizing, willing the grey bundle to reveal more, to be Oliver.

She took a pen out of her bag and scribbled a note on a piece of paper and left it on the television. 'Jean-Paul. I did not want to disturb you. I have taken the tape home to look at it more carefully. I will give it to Sylvie tomorrow.' With that she put the tape in her bag, left the building and returned to her apartment, where she played the section of the tape into her computer. In

Photoshop, she enlarged the images, frame by frame, but still the blurred images refused to reveal the identity of the person they made up. It was only when she watched the tape at normal speed, that she felt the faint skip of recognition. But it was not enough for her to make her feelings known. However, it was a slender thread to hang on to and as she lay down on her bed she acknowledged the debt to the candle she had lit the day before.

*　　*　　*

Sonya Dreyfuss lay in the arms of Gordon Turner. He was an exceptionally good-looking man, with wavy ginger blond hair flecked with grey and lazy eyes. Their affair was almost a year old and she felt this room was nearly as familiar as her own bedroom. She looked at Gordon by her side, his face relaxed and easy, the slow rise and fall of his chest. His demeanor reflected his character, accepting and uncomplicated and Sonya adored his lack of doubt, his apparent contentment with himself. She probably loved him, she thought, and she certainly loved having sex with him. His apartment was in a comfortable mansion block between Victoria station and Westminster Abbey. From the window in his bedroom, they could just make out the tower of its religious rival, Westminster Cathedral, its ugly red brick tower made ruddy in the afternoon's sun.

'I didn't mean to do that,' Sonya said quietly.

'I'm glad you did.'

Sonya had arrived a couple of hours earlier having realised, in a sort of delayed reaction, that she didn't have to fabricate a story for Oliver in order to be with Gordon. Nevertheless, she was tense and uncharacteristically uncertain about what to think since Oliver's death. Gordon listened sympathetically to Sonya as she described the agitation she felt and her anger at Oliver for going to France without telling her. Perhaps it was the release of her anger, or perhaps the anger itself, that made Sonya feel incredibly sexual. When Gordon put his arms around her, she kissed him violently on the lips, her teeth clashing with his. She lay on the bed, her skirt riding up her bare legs as she raised her knees, and pulled Gordon down on her. She unzipped his flies and, pushing her knickers to one side, guided him into her. She felt an enormous relief as he filled her up and she grabbed the back of his trousers to pull him further in, so that her instincts obliterated any other thoughts. Gordon, excited by this fierce abandon, became even more aroused and he roughly undid her shirt and pushed up her bra to kiss her nipples. She felt his hands slide under her ass and she raised herself so that he could reach her vagina. She came shortly afterwards, grunting noisily and she felt him follow shortly afterwards, thrusting himself right into her, his milky sperm filling what felt like every corner of her body.

For a moment neither of them moved. And then he carefully got off her and lay down beside her. Sonya's skirt was crushed up around her waist and one breast was bare beneath the bra which was skewed across her chest. He lay his hand on her vagina and felt his own semen warm his fingertips.

'I didn't mean to do it because I didn't think I could,' she said as a means of explanation. 'I always felt I could control Oliver and now that he's not here I was suddenly at a loss. It's been really bothering me. Why did he lie to me? Why did he go to Paris? Why didn't he tell me about his financial problems?'

'If you go on any more like this, I'll be thinking that you cared for him more than I thought,' Gordon said, casually zipping up his fly. He turned and propped himself on his elbow. 'I expect you could easily find out, anyway,' he said. 'If you really wanted to.'

She looked back at him.

'If it's going to bug you it's going to bug me. Find out from this woman, whatshername?'

'. . . Karyn Baird.'

'. . . from Karyn Baird what was going on. It's tough having no body, but at least you could find the truth of what he was up to and bury that instead. And I don't mean to be flippant.'

Sonya lay looking at the ceiling. She felt his fingers move against her, slippery and warm. But now her mind was back in charge and she considered what he had said.

'Will you come to France with me?' she asked.

'Mmm,' he said. 'As long as we fly.'

She looked at Gordon and laughed briefly and wearily. Not far away Big Ben boomed out the time and down below in the street the wail of a siren disappeared into the distance.

Chapter 8

It was a blow so unexpected that it left him breathless.

Oliver had walked along the narrow street where he knew Karyn lived. He had felt reasonably safe here and had paused not far from the green double doors, into which had been cut a smaller door that led, he assumed, to a communal courtyard and then on to her flat. One part of him hoped that he would see her coming through the doors, another dreaded the moment. For the first time since the accident, he now felt there was some proper purpose to his actions, although he had not begun to formulate the words that he would say when they did eventually meet. He had observed the doors for half an hour or so and then, despite the risk, he had continued on down towards La Mission, keeping in the shadows as much as he could. He could not wait in the nearest café to the site since it was used regularly by the teams working on the restoration. Instead, Oliver had found a seat in the shade of a plane tree from where he could watch the comings and goings from the restaurant. If she had been there, she would undoubtedly have come out for lunch, but by 2.30pm there was no sign of her so he had given up and for the next two hours he had walked around the Luxembourg Gardens. He had observed the women with their children, some running free, others being pushed in elaborate buggies and, as he had with the families on the barges, he wondered at their normality, at the distance he felt from them.

But then he had been drawn back to watching the double green doors. He had entered the cobbled street only half expecting to see Karyn when he had been stopped in his tracks as he saw her coming the other way. She was hurrying along, her head lowered, as though rushing to a meeting for which she was late. She quickly opened the doors and the clatter of them closing had rolled along the street with a certain finality. He hadn't moved and neither had she looked towards him. He leaned back against the wall to his left and had closed his eyes. He had waited for a few seconds before resolving to ring on her bell and announce himself. He pushed himself away from the wall and as he did this he collided with someone rushing along the pavement. For a second he had stared at the man, who, expecting an apology, had stared back at him. Failing to get one, he shrugged and took the few further steps to Karyn's door. Oliver heard the man press a buzzer and announce himself. 'Hi, Karyn, it's me Jean-Paul. You naughty girl. I've come about the tape.' As he said this he looked back at Oliver who was still standing there motionless. There was a moment's pause before the door clicked open to let the man in, a moment in which Oliver's mind seem to go into reverse. As the door clattered shut once again, Oliver was stunned and strangely breathless as though he had taken a heavy fall playing rugby. He looked back at the door as if somehow willing the previous scene not to have happened. But it had, and the rush of thoughts were more than he could process and he froze. Then his responses became confused and his next actions were as illogical as those of a computer infected by an unknown virus.

He began running down the street, turning instinctively along a narrow alley which funnelled him down to the boulevard Raspail where he dashed across the road up towards the rue du Cherche-Midi. He passed the *boulangerie* where his mother had taken him on one of his early visits to Paris. As he continued along the street, no wider than a car, he stumbled on a curb in front of the shoe shop he had been told about by Karyn during one of their innocent lunches. In the window was just one shoe suspended in a diamond of mirror glass reflecting it from every angle. He connected to none of this as he ran on down towards

St Germain, passing close to the restaurant at St Sulpice without giving it a thought. As he reached the boulevard St Germain his stamina gave out and gasping for breath he hailed a cab. When the driver asked him where he was going, Oliver looked at him blankly and then said the first thing that came into his mind. They crossed Pigalle, by the sex shops and the prostitutes that had so fascinated him as a young man in the capital, and began to climb towards Montmartre. The driver stopped in the small square close to the Sacré Coeur, hard by a café where he had once worked as a *sous chef* although he neither saw it nor registered its new name and exterior. Oliver's only aim was flight and he was unaware that he had chosen a route that linked his past. Our instinctive moments are perhaps our most predictable.

He now stood looking over Paris but as a madman would, seeing nothing and yet staring hard at some distant object. He slumped onto a bench in the gardens in front of the church and began to cry, quietly and unremarkably as the whole of Paris beneath him went about its business.

And now huge feelings of guilt began to overwhelm him. At the very point when he had come close to touching normality again, he had fled at the prospect that Karyn might be conducting a life without him. The sheer absurdity of his reaction brought him face to face with his selfishness. How dare he react this way when the people on the train had been killed, torn to pieces, burnt to nothing? He had survived and he had left them, dead and screaming in the wreckage. He didn't have any rights now, he couldn't ask for anything, hope for more than what he had, he simply didn't deserve it, his display of jealousy an outrageous indulgence. This purgatory into which he had stumbled was just reward for a guilty man.

But, suddenly, he was somewhere else, as if this shock had dislodged part of the emotional log jam which lay at the heart of what had brought him on this strange journey. Perhaps the very darkness of this Paris night had made him remember its very opposite, a day of luminous clarity in the first months of his relationship with Sonya. It was a glorious April afternoon in Newmarket and he recalled the sun shining on the flanks of the thoroughbreds as they loped around the paddock. He had no interest in racing but he was happy to go along with Sonya, this new force in his life. She was part of a syndicate which owned one of the runners and he stood with her, the trainer in his brown trilby and the tiny, wiry jockey.

The spring air was so clear that everything seemed sharp and in focus. Even the smell of the animals was clean and precise and the horses' hooves sprang from turf electric green in its early season freshness. She gripped his hand with excitement and he watched the fierceness of her gaze as the thoroughbreds sped towards them in a blur of browns and coloured silks. It was the intensity of that gaze that sprang to his mind now, the absolute concentration and the total exclusion that came with it. Had he been entranced at the time? Or, in that moment, did he detect a different Sonya, a glimpse of another woman that came and went in a second just as the horses flashed by the winning post.

They stayed that night in a country house hotel in amongst the stud farms and training establishments which surrounded Newmarket. As soon as they got into their room she kissed him and thrust him back on the bed. She sat on him, somewhat bigger than her jockey that had come in triumphant a few hours before.

'Did you see it? Wasn't it magnificent? What power.' With each statement, she pushed down on him with excitement. 'Did you see how he changed pace two furlongs out, opening up his body and stretching away? Magic.' But this was not a preamble to sex. He looked up at her face and he knew that, for that moment at least, he didn't exist, that Sonya was locked entirely in her own imagination.

Two more nudges with her knees and she climbed off him and went into the bathroom. 'We're up in the morning to see him go out first string. I'll get a 5.30 call.'

Oliver swung himself to the side of the bed and adjusted his clothing. He looked at his watch and wondered whether François would have arrived at the restaurant. He was such a careful, precise man that Oliver could see him walking through the front door now, adjusting the lace curtain which half covered the front door even though it had not been disturbed. He would walk over to the ansaphone and check on the bookings before calling back to confirm the reservations. This was why Oliver tried his mobile.

'Hello, Oliver. We have eleven bookings for this evening, you will be pleased to know.' Oliver smiled at the comfortable predictability of his *maître d*'s response.

'Just looking ahead to tomorrow, is there anyway you could reschedule the chap from Layton's, or deal with him yourself?' François was the epitome of politeness but even so Oliver could just detect the slightest hesitation before he replied. 'Of course. I'll let you know what we come up with.'

Sonya was still in the bathroom and Oliver slipped out of the bedroom and left the hotel. A brisk easterly was chasing away the remnants of the day, but Oliver reckoned it would be light for another hour. It wasn't a very important meeting, was it? He wanted the answer to be no but he knew the truth to be different. It mattered to François because choosing new wines for the restaurant was one of his great delights and he wanted Oliver to be there to share his pleasure and to confirm his skills. Oliver had not put on an overcoat and the wind caused him to pull up the collar of his jacket. The old railway line which ran in to Newmarket had once crossed the road here and he could see the raised embankment which defined its route running away to his right. The tiny station was now no more than a platform, a faint reminder of the days when even the smallest community was served by rail. He sat on the edge of the platform. At the hotel, they had told him that during the Great War, when the Derby had been run at Newmarket, some of the runners had arrived here by train. He imagined them coming on to the platform, frisky and nervous, ears pricked at the steaming train, wondering what they were doing here. He had a similar feeling now.

By the time he returned to the hotel, Sonya had changed. She was wearing a long black skirt with a wide leather belt and a small black jacket, like a matador's. The raised waistline accentuated her slender figure, as did the black ankle boots. She wore the black pearl nestling just above her breasts. She looked stunning.

'I'm so looking forward to tomorrow morning', she said, taking both his hands and in that moment his decision to return to London evaporated.

He could not tell himself, on this dark night in Paris, that he had not enjoyed seeing the horses on the gallops early next morning, or that the sight of sixty or more horses coming up the long slope towards him had not been thrilling, or that being at the centre of the yard as the horses were led back hadn't fascinated him. It was just that he knew he shouldn't have been there any more than he should be here, on a bench at midnight, looking southwards across Paris.

But, high on the hill of Montmartre, Oliver was beyond making sense of his feelings. He had become his emotions. What he did next was driven by some force deep in his system, beyond his brain and his conscious mind.

* * *

On certain days, flights coming into Charles de Gaulle from London take a low, lazy turn over Paris and those sitting on the right side of the aircraft as it begins to bank are given a breathtaking view over the city where at night the white tower of the Sacré Coeur is lit up like an Apollo rocket. And so it was that Sonya looked down on the marble church where her husband sat alone and invisible three thousand metres beneath her. Gordon had his hand on her knee which, in a perverse way, she found both a comfort and an irritant. They had discussed a plan of action for Paris or, more accurately, Sonya had outlined what she was going to do. Paris may be the city of many people's dreams, but not Sonya's. The hotel rooms were too small, the inhabitants too rude and there was something about the faux romanticism of the place which set her teeth on edge. She wished she was flying with Gordon to New York or Vienna, more pragmatic cities in which to conduct an affair.

Sonya had booked the Hotel Montalembert, smart and chic but where the rooms, if you can get one, are still on the smallish side. The hotel was not far from the site of La Mission and Karyn's apartment, the address of which she had found in Oliver's computer. During the flight she had become increasingly convinced that her husband had been having an affair with her and the anger she would have expressed to him was now stored up for Karyn. And it was clear that however much she wanted Gordon's support, he would have to remain in the background. She looked across at him now, sitting impassively by her side, his eyes closed, his face relaxed, his longish ginger blond hair perfectly sweeping by his ear. His face showed no signs of tension, as if the problems of life had somehow not marked him and she admired his calm assurance. She turned back to the window and heard the low rumble beneath her as the undercarriage came down.

So not more than a few hours since Oliver had stood on almost the same spot, by the side of a tall plane tree in front of the church of St Sulpice, Sonya watched the door of the restaurant that would soon become La Mission. One part of her was detached, wondering about the business, running through in her mind the figures she had seen on Oliver's computer, confirming what her own projections had been and smiling at her own wisdom. How little Oliver knew. But the smile faded. What did that matter if Oliver was dead?

It was night-time and the building was dark and sombre,

hinting more at its former life than its future one. Sonya thrust her hands deep into the pockets of her overcoat and turned back towards the hotel knowing that tomorrow she would meet the woman who caused her husband to die.

*   *   *

Karyn had watched the tape again and it was making her ill. She was helpless and no matter how often she looked at the footage she could no longer convince herself any more that the series of black and white dots sparkling in front of her were someone she knew. She sank back and aimed the remote at the television and watched it turn to black. Even the buzz on the door was slow to divert her attention.

The handsome young producer should have been warned by the look on her face. He had come to reclaim his tape and perhaps pursue Karyn in other ways. He was shocked at the vehemence of her reaction when he suggested they had a drink in return for his favour.

'You bloody fool, you cretin, you are just like all the others. Have you no other idea in your head? Are you led entirely by that thing between your legs?' At this point she threw the nearest object to hand in the direction of his groin. It was the TV remote and it pinged off his hip and smashed against the wall. 'And if you call me naughty in that tone of voice again I will personally slice off your testicles and drop them in the Seine.' She glared at him and the very coldness of her look told him not to respond. He nodded and turned to leave but just as he was closing the door his male pride made him turn back to shout a clever rejoinder at her but even as he did the tape he had come to collect was flying through the air towards him so that it was all he could do to catch it and scuttle off down the stairs.

Karyn slumped onto the sofa, angry with herself, angry with the world. How ridiculous to feel like this, she thought, caught between a relationship that was never consummated and one that never would be. Her pulse was racing, but as she looked at herself reflected in the blank television screen it began to slow, her shoulders began to drop and the anger began to seep away. She wandered over to the window and looked out into the Paris night. The street was lit by a series of small lamps which cast regular pools of light along the cobbles across which the strong wind was blowing leaves in erratic patterns. A dog trotted into view and cocked his leg against one of the lamps. In her bones she felt that winter was not far away.

An hour or so later, perhaps still guided by the candle she had lit in Notre Dame, she picked up the phone to speak to the producer she had so recently abused. She agreed to meet him for a drink in a bar on the rue de Buci, a noisy narrow place the very opposite of the intimate restaurant he had suggested. In amongst a throng of people she apologised for her behaviour but before he had time to follow up his advantage, she told him the story of Oliver, omitting her hopes that he was still alive. He had to lean forward to hear her, for she spoke in a low flat voice that was barely audible in the crowded bar. In the end, it was he who apologised to her and, although he could not take his eyes from her sad and beautiful face he could do no more than kiss her hand when she had finished. 'I'm sorry,' he said, 'I wish I could have helped more.'

She walked home slowly, meandering through the streets not wanting to go back to her apartment. She felt defeated, exhausted and as she passed in front of the Palais de Justice one of the *gendarmes* standing on duty, perhaps catching a hint of her sadness, was minded to say '*bon soir Madame*' a gesture which caused her to turn and give him a small smile.

It was gone eleven when she pushed open the door of her apartment to the sound of the phone ringing. She was so tired she picked it up instinctively and even before she spoke a woman's voiced asked in English, 'Is that Karyn Baird?'

'It is,' she replied. 'Who is this?'

'This is the widow of Oliver Dreyfuss. I think we should meet, don't you? I will be in the library of the Hotel Montalembert tomorrow morning at eleven. I think you will be there.'

The line went dead and Karyn stood for some time holding the phone between her thumb and her forefinger before dropping it into its cradle.

Chapter 9

The library of the Hotel Montalembert is variously described as cool, intimate and comfortable. Only one of those adjectives was appropriate as Karyn entered the carefully lit room, which took its name from the two black lacquer bookcases flanking the modern fireplace in which the eternal flames of a gas-effect fire burned in minimal chic. The neutral tones of the room were contrasted by the large red cushions on the sofas. But it was in one of the grey leather faux 30s armchairs that Karyn saw a woman whom she assumed was Sonya Dreyfuss. Karyn had no instinct to dislike this woman. Oliver had never spoken critically of her and, despite the abruptness of her tone on the phone the night before, Karyn had been given no cause for antipathy. Indeed, as she walked to the hotel that morning, she felt a large degree of sympathy, even companionship, for the woman who had so recently lost her husband. And yet, as she paused by the door leading into the library and she saw Sonya sitting there something shifted inside her. Sonya was wearing an elegant black suit which would have been masculine had not the slim jacket been cut almost to her knees. Under the jacket she had a white shirt with a beautiful silk tie in a mix of mauve or orange silk depending on which way it caught the light. She wore black shoes with high heels made of transparent plastic at the centre of which ran narrow steel supports. This was not the outfit of a woman in distress. As Karyn moved towards her, she stood up. They needed no introduction..

'Mrs Dreyfuss, can I say how sorry I am about your husband. He is a huge loss.' Sonya's response was the slight movement of her head, as if she were avoiding a small fly. Karyn continued. 'It was a horrible shock for us all but for you it must have been terrible.' Karyn was aware of the eyes coolly appraising her.

'And, but for *you*, he would be still here.' Sonya said quite evenly.

'But for his *job*, he would still be here,' Karyn responded in the same tone.

'Don't,' she said sharply, so much so that a passing waiter turned and looked towards her. 'Don't pretend any sort of innocence with me Karyn Baird. He was coming to Paris to see you.' She emphasised the word 'you' as if she was spitting it out towards the other woman, not in anger but in controlled venom.

For now, Karyn did not want to enter battle with this woman. 'Of course he was coming to see me, Mrs Dreyfuss. We have a business relationship.'

'You have a relationship,' Sonya fired back. 'I suppose it will give you pleasure to know that I had no idea that Oliver was coming to Paris. So his,' and here she hesitated, 'his death was all the more shocking. You understand what I am saying?'

Karyn measured her words carefully. 'I had a relationship with Oliver, but not a *relationship*,' and here she pronounced the word in the same pejorative way that Sonya Dreyfuss did.

'Are you asking me to believe that you didn't sleep with my husband?' Sonya responded coldly, not really making it a question. The same waiter glided by, but this time did not turn towards the two women.

'I'm not asking you anything,' replied Karyn, 'I'm telling you.'

'But I don't believe you. I have seen some of the correspondence between you both and it is not, shall we say, entirely innocent.' She gave Karyn the sort of look a school teacher does to a pupil who has made a feeble excuse about homework.

'But not entirely compromising,' replied Karyn firmly. 'Look, you'll have to believe me because I'm now the only one who can tell you the truth.'

'Exactly,' said Sonya. 'You would say that. But I don't believe you. Why should I? He would have told me if he had been coming here on business but he didn't because he was coming here to *fuck* you.' She said the word deliberately, with extra diction.

Karyn was not going to rise to the bait. She knew she was in the right, but only partly so. She would gladly have slept with Oliver and from the background she came from the thought was almost as bad as the deed. Maybe this showed in her face and she looked into the eyes of the woman standing opposite her, a woman who had shared the bed and body of Oliver Dreyfuss.

'Can we stop this?' she asked Sonya, who then gave a sort of grunt, half-way between a laugh and an exclamation.

'But why? My husband sneaks off to Paris to be with another woman and gets killed on the way and we have to change the subject. Come off it Karyn Baird.'

'I'm here in a professional capacity as well,' Karyn replied trying to parry the invective.

'Well, I'm not,' said Sonya. 'I'm here in a purely personal capacity as the wife of a husband who is now a pile of dust. Thanks to you.'

Karyn was standing opposite Sonya, but now she felt all the strength leave her legs and she suddenly sat on the edge of the sofa.

'Is it getting to you now?' Sonya looked down at her as she spoke, the dominant animal in the fight. 'Well it should. He would be here now but for you. You should feel wretched.'

'And do you feel wretched, Sonya?' Karyn asked, looking up at the woman who had now become her opponent. 'How bad do you feel? Or do you just feel thwarted because you didn't know what Oliver was doing?' As soon as she said this, she wished she hadn't. She wanted to snatch the sentence back. No amount of anger or hatred would change the truth that lay between them. The man they both loved had ceased to exist.

'I am sorry, Mrs Dreyfuss. I should not have said that. You

77

may rest assured that I never had sex with your husband. I would like you to believe me.' But she knew from the cold eyes that were now looking through her, that Sonya Dreyfuss was not prepared to accept this. What came next, though, took Karyn completely by surprise.

'I don't think you came here to sympathise with me,' Sonya said with a cool finality. 'You came here to ask for money. I know that your project is in trouble and that Oliver owes, or should I say, owed quite a lot of money. Almost 600,000 euros, isn't it? Not a lot really, but I expect the lack of it could scupper you. Am I right?'

Karyn continued to stare at Sonya.

'Well, the further bad news is that Oliver's business partners haven't got a brass farthing between them. I think he always assumed that he could fall back on me and, once upon a time, he might have been right. But now . . . '

Oliver had never spoken to Karyn about his financial position but he had told her enough, or she had deduced enough by reading between the lines, that there was a no-man's land between his business affairs and those of his wife. She therefore chose to disbelieve part of what Sonya had just told her and the very comfort of this knowledge helped balance the bad news that she had just heard.

'You do me an injustice, Mrs Dreyfuss. Even though there is an outstanding business issue with Oliver it was to express a sense of loss that I came here today. I'm sorry for us both.' With that, Karyn turned and walked out of the library, through the small, beautifully decorated lobby and out into the bustle of Paris. She felt as empty as the city was full.

* * *

Sonya Dreyfuss rarely showed anger. She merely internalised it and used it later as a weapon. Even as she watched Karyn leave the library her feelings for the woman were hardening into a strong pellet of dislike. How dare she lie to her? Of course she had slept with Oliver but she had the cheek to stand there and deny it. And although it was hard to admit, her anger was fuelled by the way Karyn had looked and conducted herself. This was a beautiful woman and the very thought that this combination had been irresistible to Oliver made it certain that Sonya would not let the matter rest. This was unfinished business. Her contempt for Karyn was so complete that she had longed to tell her, to flaunt the fact even, that La Mission could never succeed because she had made sure it couldn't. But she was too wise, too cunning, to score a cheap point like that. She kept this information for another time.

She took the small bird-cage lift which rattled upwards to the sixth floor and returned to her suite where Gordon was lying on the navy-blue and white bedspread reading a book. He half lowered it as she came into the bedroom. He had known her long enough to recognise the look on her face and to know that he shouldn't say anything. She went over and sat at a small table by a dormer window with views over the nearby rooftops. He watched her turning over the problem in her mind, not registering the classic and familiar view of Paris. He had seen her like this once or twice before, fiercely concentrating on a problem and working it over until she found an answer.

'There's more to this than she's admitting to,' Sonya said without turning. 'All this has been going on without me knowing. I can't believe it.'

A bit like you and me, Gordon mused, but kept the thought to himself. He waited for her to continue.

'She's very beautiful, but not in a conventional way. And she just stood in front of me denying she'd had a relationship with Oliver. Very cool indeed. I know one thing.' Here she turned and faced Gordon. 'I need to find out more about Miss Karyn Baird.'

Gordon hesitated before speaking. 'Whatever you say. But

does it really matter that much? I mean, Oliver is dead and whether he slept with this woman or not is purely academic.' He got off the bed and walked over and put his hands on her shoulders. They both looked out of the window. 'And it has given us a clear path to be together.'

She continued to gaze over the jumble of Paris roofs. 'Sure, but you need to understand something. I thought that I knew my husband, could second guess him always. I can't just let this lie. I need to file it away and the only way I can do that is to find out what he saw in this bloody woman and why.'

'But . . . '

'But nothing Gordon. It's like I've lost Oliver twice and I don't like it. On the one hand it is all so final. On the other, totally incomplete. I've got to know more.'

Sonya stood up and pushed Gordon towards the bed. He fell back and put his hands behind his head as she knelt on the end of the bed, facing him. She took off her jacket and it fell to the floor. She undid the buttons of her shirt with one hand, pulling off the tie with the other. She unclipped her black bra and her breasts fell forward. Gordon's hands were still behind his head as she now undid his fly to release his cock. She lent down and kissed it whilst holding its stem as you would a microphone. She then rubbed its blunt tip against her nipples, first one side and then the other. Standing on the bed she undid her trousers and flicked them onto the floor. Keeping on her knickers, she pulled them to one side so that when she straddled Gordon she was able to guide him into her. Gordon was barely moving as Sonya rose up and down on him and it was only as she bent forward towards him that he took a nipple into his mouth. Moments later he had his hands on her ass as he pushed up into her.

'Go on,' she said. 'Push it into me.' And he did, until their movements became more urgent and she began to breathe in the short gasps that told him she was about to come which she did with a series of deep grunts. Seconds later he followed and he was aware of her watching him as he did.

'I love to see you come,' she said breathlessly.

For his part, Gordon thought that Sonya's sexuality worked in direct proportion to her anger so that as she rolled off him and into his arms he concluded that her discontent was an unexpected bonus. There was a predatory quality about Sonya, taking him from above as she often liked to do. He could see their bodies reflected in an antique mirror on the wall opposite, Sonya turned on her side so that her body resembled a Henry Moore sculpture, a series of round almost abstract shapes. He put his hand on her and felt the slow rise and fall of her breathing as she slipped into sleep.

PART TWO

Plat Principal

Chapter 10

He cut up the chicken with six deft slices of the big cleaver and put them in the hot casserole to brown, flicking them over from time to time with a small wooden spoon before lifting them out and tossing in chopped onions, bacon and garlic. He looked out of the window and over the sizzle of the cooking he could just hear the mewing of the two buzzards that regularly circled the valley, their big wings spread wide to catch the thermals rising from the hills below. He returned the browned chicken pieces to the casserole, tipped in a slug of brandy, lit a match and watched the low blue flame spread over the mixture. When it had died down, he poured in a bottle of red wine and added a couple of bay leaves. He brought the dirty red liquid to the boil and then turned down the flame and left the dish to simmer.

Walking across the small kitchen he now turned his attention to three large sea bass which lay gleaming on the stainless steel surface. Cutting off their heads and tails he carefully filleted the fish before scraping the bones, head and tail into a large pan ready to make a fish stock. And so the hours went by as Oliver did the tasks in front of him. He had grown a beard now and in his whites he was barely recognisable as the man who had stumbled off the wrecked train only one month before. He wiped his hands, removed his apron and left the kitchen. It was four o'clock and he had a couple of hours before he needed to prepare for the busy Friday night service. He followed a grassy track which led out of the town and up a steepish climb between fields of stubble. The blue sky was filled with billowing cumuli and their shadows chased across the open landscape. The higher he went so the wind picked up, blowing his long hair and tugging at his shirt. He was making for a point about two kilometres further on at the junction of the ridge path and the one he was on now. It was here that a small copse of tall beech trees stood in lonely glory overlooking the landscape. A fallen and rotting log was the seat that Oliver regularly came to in order to sit and take in the view.

In the distance directly below him the small town was dominated by a magnificent abbey which, lit by the afternoon sun, stood out like a giant white liner against green trees which rose up beyond it. High above him, so high they were invisible, the skylarks sang their endless songs interrupted only by the continued mewings of the two buzzards. Up here Oliver felt the timelessness of the place, the clay and flint path underfoot that had carried travellers to this spot for eight hundred years to be rewarded with the exact same view that was in front of him now. It was an appropriate place for a man who had ceased to exist, for here he felt part of a tunnel in time, existing neither in the past nor the future and strangely distant from the present.

He looked down on the town where, once upon a time in another life he had spent a short holiday. Even as a teenager he had wanted to be a cook and he had read about this small town which had somehow managed to find itself with two Michelin starred restaurants along its winding main street. And now, nearly twenty years on, he had come back. Oliver had spent one more night in Paris before fleeing here. He had slept on the bench in front of the Sacré Coeur and sometime in the early hours of the morning he had walked down the long stairs from the church to the bus station at the Gare du Nord and by seven o'clock he was in the outer suburbs heading towards the rising sun.

Oliver had realised that to live his new life he would need a job but it was not to the smart restaurants that he applied. Oliver needed to remain as anonymous as he could, so it was to one of the lesser restaurants that he went in search of work. The world of the kitchen is a law unto itself defined by a complete disregard for the sort of rules that govern most working lives. French employment law is such that it is very difficult to fire someone if you employ them officially. And so when Oliver offered his services as a chef on a cash basis, no questions asked, no papers shown, he was welcomed without hesitation. He had, though, already shown his prowess by preparing a range of dishes in the sort of time demanded by a busy kitchen. The man who opened his arms to him, Bernard Chichilian, had been a Michelin starred chef until brandy and claret had begun to undermine his skills. Reformed now, he had been running Au Fil du Temps for almost three years and knew not to look a gift horse in the mouth. This Englishman who went by the name of Oliver Cobden, could cook and speak French so the less questions he asked about his past the better.

The wind had picked up and the sun, lower in the sky, had turned the side of the abbey pink. Oliver lived in a small flat almost within the shadows of its great walls, a comfortable living room with windows on three sides and wide floorboards covered with threadbare rugs. All his transactions were in cash. He had no bank account and to all intents and purposes he did not exist. He invented a background for himself but was cautious not to give too many details in case he forgot them himself. In many ways, he thought, the French loved to get one over on the state and he felt safe in this community. He had been accepted in the town for he was friendly and both understood and respected the way the French did things.

But he was not part of the hills around him, nor of the kitchen which now contained him. He did not deserve the beauty of his surroundings nor the routines of his job. The money he was given at the end of each month, paid in cash by Bernard, he felt guilty in receiving, unable as he was to put any value to his life. He was merely surviving, moving from moment to moment to join up the minutes, hardly daring to question his existence.

He wandered slowly back down the hill and re-entered the kitchen, his own for the evening since Bernard was taking the night off. He felt safe in this cocoon, particularly during service when he was so busy his mind had no room to think about anything else but the preparation of the food. He did not question how long he could go on like this. For now, he was happy not to exist.

Sometimes, in the swirl and clamour of the cooking, Sonya would appear to him, as if the steam and sizzle acted as a camouflage behind which Oliver could view his thoughts in comparative safety. He had been cooking like this when he had first seen her through the porthole of his kitchen. Confidence radiated from her and he wasn't the only one to turn and look at her as she spoke and laughed with her companion, about whom he had no recollection. It was she who asked to see him at the end of service and he felt the rip tide of her vivacity draw him effortlessly towards her. A splash of water scalded his hand now, the hands that he remembered wiping self-consciously in front of her as, to his surprise, she told him about himself. She had quoted a headline from the previous Saturday's *Financial Times*: 'The Irresistible Rise of Oliver Dreyfuss'. He was flattered and the memory made him grimace and he banged the large ladle he was holding noisily against the stainless steel work surface. He felt his squad look over to him in surprise for he was not given to such gestures. It was Sonya who had appeared irresistible, vivacious, direct. He could see her now wearing a grey silk shirt with the single black pearl of her necklace resting on her brown skin just above the divide of her breasts. Wouldn't any man have been attracted? He placed the lid on top of the tureen, cutting off the memory and allowed the routines of the kitchen to take over.

There were over sixty covers and the four hours between seven and eleven were compressed into what felt like thirty minutes. One hundred and eighty dishes to be cooked and approved, the clatter of the kitchen and the increasingly noisy restaurant forming a bath of sound in which he worked. He had come to treasure this time, the flames leaping from the copper pans, the shouted orders, the film of sweat on his forearms. Later, after the kitchen had been cleaned and the staff departed and a strange silence had descended on the place, he would sit and finish the remains of any bottles left by customers. Sometimes he would fall into a troubled sleep, waking suddenly to attempt to remember the pattern of his dreams. Tonight it was the image of Karyn standing in the middle of an enormous space surrounded by people walking in front of her so that his vision of her was sometimes blocked. Finally, his view was obscured completely but when the people cleared she was not there. He woke abruptly and could only wonder at the sheer logic of the unfettered mind. He wandered home, bone weary and fell asleep fully clothed on his bed where his troubled dreams continued until the early hours of the morning.

*   *   *

She looked carefully at the photograph. To the uninitiated eye it was simply a mountain landscape, with a mass of great misshapen rocks rising above a tree line of dense conifers. In the distance, a series of grey jagged peaks, mottled here and there with snow, stood guard over the scene. But Karyn was looking for something in particular. In the centre of the photograph, which she had taken with a telephoto lens just after dawn, almost indistinguishable from the barren landscape around it, was the distinct shape of a cat. It sat in a small pool of sunlight, its pointed ears back-lit so even at a distance of almost a kilometre there was no mistaking the outline of a lynx.

Karyn had first heard the stories of these beautiful animals when she had visited the Pyrénées with her father. They had stayed in a mountain hotel not far from Bagnères-de-Luchon and on the walls of the bar was an old black and white photograph of a Eurasian lynx. The owner had told her stories of how his grandfather would sometimes see these cats in the forests to the south of the hotel and, with the help of the local newspaper, had taken the picture she so admired. When Karyn's father had left her mother, the holidays ended as well and it was several years before she felt able to come down again to these mountains. Her fascination with the lynx remained throughout, perhaps as a symbol of happier times, although she doubted she would ever see one in the wild. She was told by some locals that the creature was extinct, by others that perhaps a handful still roamed the densely wooded hills beneath the peaks. For years she had walked the paths up to the high pastures but had never seen or heard trace of the fabled animal. It remained a figment of her past, like the marriage of her parents.

It was perhaps not surprising that Karyn should have chosen to come to the Pyrénées after the death of Oliver. She felt exhausted and since work on La Mission had ground to a halt, she took the opportunity to flee the city for the solitude of the mountains. On the day she took the photograph she had risen before dawn and following a path she knew well, had climbed through the woods until the first light touched the tips of the highest peaks. At around fifteen hundred metres she emerged from the tree line. She wanted to record the sharp contrast of sun and shade which made this time of day so special. Ahead of her was a steep valley beyond which the trees rose to the same height she was standing at now. After that the mountains began in earnest.

She set up her tripod, attaching the long lens to the camera before slotting it in place. She worked fast because the light would be gone as quickly as the mountain weather. It was only by chance that she saw the movement. She was adjusting the focus and checking the exposure when it caught her eye. At first she had thought the shape was a rock and she was startled when it moved. She instinctively looked up from the camera but the object was too far away to see with the naked eye. She returned to the viewfinder just as a corner of the sun blinked over the top of a distant ridge. Perhaps the lynx knew of this spot for in an instant the animal was at the centre of a rectangular shaft of light. Karyn could hardly believe her eyes and she was suddenly fearful that she would lose the moment. She took one picture, the click of the shutter sounding like the crash of a falling tree and then another. Adjusting the aperture by half a stop she tightened the zoom and pressed the shutter again. At this moment the cat turned its head towards the camera as if it had heard a sound on the other side of the valley and gently walked into the woods.

Alone on the side of a mountain, chilled by the early morning wind, Karyn wanted to tell someone of her extraordinary good fortune. 'Oh, Oliver,' she said, 'how I wish you were here now.' She wrapped her arms round herself. The lone tear that ran down her cheek might have been caused by the cold but high up here she needed no excuse to cry. And she wept for a loss which seemed to become more acute as the weeks went by. Not a day passed without her thinking of Oliver and now, alone in the empty mountains, she found herself talking to him as if he was by her side. She put the camera on automatic, adjusted the lens and poured herself a cup of tea from a Thermos. Pressing the shutter, she stepped in front of the camera and raised the drink in a toast, looking directly into the lens at wherever Oliver might be and waited for the camera to click.

Now, in the living room of her Paris apartment, she recalled that moment as she looked at the photograph of herself. It was even more important to her than the picture of the lynx, although the one complemented the other. She carefully placed the pictures in the frames she had bought and propped them against the mirror above the fireplace, at the very heart of her room.

*   *   *

Sonya popped the cork and watched the champagne bubble to the mouth of the bottle. She heard Gordon laugh in the bathroom. They were in another hotel room in another country and the reason lay on top of the carefully folded clothes on her bed. It was a picture of Karyn Baird in a transparent folder. Sonya had downloaded it from Oliver's website which was still proudly proclaiming the forthcoming glories of La Mission and the Anglo-French co-operation which was producing this 'destination restaurant'. Karyn's hair was short, her big eyes were wide and welcoming as was her smile. Sonya hated it and took it with her wherever she went to constantly rekindle her anger at what the woman had done to her life.

At first Gordon had not noticed it but one day, about a week earlier, he had caught her staring at the picture. She knew what he was going to say and she cut him off before he started. 'I rather enjoy it,' she said. 'Do you remember how you used to pick at scabs when you were young? It's that mix of pain and pleasure.' But Gordon did remonstrate with her, saying that she had become obsessed with the woman and that they should get away.

Sonya admitted to herself that the more obsessed she became with the life of Karyn Baird and her affair with Oliver, the more intense her feelings for Gordon had become, almost frighteningly so. These were not feelings of dependency, but of sexual need and they reflected that mix of pain and pleasure. So when he suggested that they have a break, away from France and London she said yes with rising excitement.

On a good day, the Cotswolds are no more than two hours from London but the view from their room of the sheep-covered hills was of another world. Not that Sonya wanted to do more than gaze on it from the comfort of her room. It had the proportions she liked, with a large four-poster bed, comfortable sofas and a round table in the window where she could receive a succession of meals without having to see anyone else.

Gordon came out of the bathroom wearing an immaculate

blue suit. He walked over to her and poured himself a glass of champagne, downing it in one gulp. He picked up the white napkin from the tray which held the ice bucket and, as instructed, looked at her without smiling. 'I will be up shortly.' As soon as he had left she experienced a huge rush of desire. She picked up the picture of Karyn and placed it on the table in the window. She slipped off the heavy hotel dressing gown she had been wearing and picked up a skirt from the bed. It was leather and black and it barely covered her. The black shirt she put on next was a size too small for her and her breasts pushed against the buttons and her nipples were sharply outlined against the silky material. And then she stepped into the high heeled shoes, the ones she had been wearing in Paris to meet Karyn. She stood in front of the full length mirror on the door of the armoire and enjoyed running her hands down her body, pausing at the hem of her skirt so that her fingers could touch her vagina.

She then filled her glass of champagne and took it and the bottle over to the sofa where she arranged herself so she could see her reflection in the mirror. She took a sip of champagne and waited. The knock on the door was followed by 'room service'. Sonya watched as Gordon entered the room, the white napkin over his arm.

'You called madam?' he asked.

'Yes,' she said dismissively. 'Could you clear all those things away.' As he filled the tray with the remains of the morning papers, she crossed her legs so that the leather skirt rode even further up her thighs. That she could see herself in the mirror made it all the more exciting and she saw Gordon's eyes turn to her legs.

'Will there be anything else madam?' Sonya uncrossed her legs, licked her finger and cleaned an imaginary mark from her shoe. She knew he could see all of her now.

'I'm having trouble with the plug by the sofa. Could you see about fixing it?'

'I'm not quite sure where you mean, madam,' he said. Sonya got up from the sofa, feeling his eyes follow her. 'It's down here,' she said, getting on all fours and pointing under the cabinet which held the television. She looked back at him and watched him unzip his trousers and release his erection. He bent down behind her and entered her. 'I think you've found the problem,' she grunted, thrusting herself back against him. Even though she was in this position, she enjoyed the feeling of being in charge, the sensation of having her skirt pushed up to her navel, the heels of her shoes digging into the backs of her calves. Keeping him in her, she manoeuvred around so that she could once again watch what was happening in the mirror as Gordon slipped in and out of her. She didn't want to come just yet so she pulled away from him and crawled on to the sofa where she sat with her knees tucked under her chin. Gordon moved towards her on all fours and, pushing her legs apart with his face, placed his mouth on her wet vagina. She enjoyed feeling his tongue search around the wet flesh and she moved her body against him. She wanted him inside her, so once again she moved away from him but this time he grabbed her and trapped her against the wall. She put her legs around him and his cock felt as if it was going right through her. His hands were supporting her by the cheeks of her ass and as she widened her legs his movements became more urgent. They were banging against the wall now and a print of Bath was moving in unison. Seconds later Sonya began to come which she did, noisily and happily, a fierce grin across her flushed and sweaty face.

'You can go, now,' she said as she fell on the bed and felt him ooze out of her. The picture of Karyn had fallen from the table and now lay face down on the floor.

Chapter 11

Karyn Baird woke with a start and for a moment could not think why. And then she registered the ringing of her phone and glancing at the clock by her bedside, wondered who would be calling her at this time on a Saturday morning. It was the last person she expected. Her boss Patrick. He was not apologetic and he came straight to the point.

'It's going down the pan, Karyn. Unless we can raise getting on for a half million we'll have to pull out and, as a distressed seller, you know what that will mean. I had no idea that Oliver's company was in such a mess.'

She carried the phone into the living room and stood by the fireplace. Karyn had reported to Patrick about Sonya Dreyfuss's steadfast refusal to bail out her husband's company, although she had not gone into the details of why Sonya was so unco-operative. If she had, she may not have received the following instruction.

'I want you to go to London to see Mrs Dreyfuss and try and broker a deal.'

Karyn's response was instinctive. 'I don't think that will be possible, I'm sorry. She was adamant that she wouldn't help.'

'I still want you to go,' was the immediate reply. 'I want you to propose a business deal. We'll have to pay more, of course, but with the way things are no one else is interested.'

Karyn was looking at the picture of herself offering a lonely salutation to the camera. 'But what makes you think she will change her mind?'

'Well, consider this Karyn. If it was to be known that the boss of one of London's leading venture capital houses was not prepared to do a deal to help her recently deceased husband's business find its feet, thus putting at risk scores of jobs, how do you think that would sound?'

'But that's blackmail.'

'No, Karyn, that's business.'

To have refused to go would have meant explaining her position so, against her better judgement and with a feeling of dread, Karyn flew to London and found herself walking along the Thames, past the ominous bulk of HMS *Belfast* towards the offices of 3MS. The river was high and from it rose its own particular smell, neither foul nor sweet. From a passing pleasure cruiser came the distorted commentary of a guide telling the story of Traitors' Gate, a low archway in the wall of the Tower of London on the opposite bank, where enemies of the state made their final journey. How appropriate, she thought, as she swung through the glass doors of 3MS' gleaming home.

Karyn imagined that Sonya had agreed to see her in the same way that a cat loves to play with a mouse. There was no warmth in their meeting and no preliminary small talk. Although she couldn't see it, Karyn's picture was tucked into Sonya's business diary.

'You know what we say here,' began Sonya looking out across the river. 'We say that restaurants are the barometers of the economy, the seaweed of boom or bust. Last year they were opening at the rate of one a week, now maybe one in the last three months. And bookings are down across the board. And you know what that means, don't you?' She didn't wait for a reply. 'It means people are expecting the worst and looking after their pennies, just as they say rabbits burrow deeper before hard winters. So, quite apart from anything else, why would a sensible company like mine put money into a dodgy restaurant business in Paris?'

Karyn stared at the woman. 'Because Oliver was your husband,' she said simply.

'Oh please don't get me started. Here I have to separate my head from my heart and my head tells me two things. La Mission is a bad bet and you were the woman who slept with my husband.'

'If I had, would I be here now?' Karyn replied calmly.

'Well, I'm not going through that debate again. Where there is smoke there is fire, so the answer is going to be no.'

'My boss, Patrick, is a hard man and has asked me to say this to you.' Karyn replied. Even though she disliked the woman she wanted to distance herself from what she was about to say. 'He thinks you would not like the press to know that you refused to help your late husband's company get back on its feet. You are, after all, famously rich.' Karyn said this without the conviction it needed to strike home.

'I see,' said Sonya, walking towards her. 'First adultery and now blackmail. Not a pretty pair. Let me toss something back at you. How would this hard-man boss of yours like to know of your affair with my husband? Perhaps he may see this as the reason I won't fund your little project. I imagine he wouldn't like that.'

Karyn had expected this response. 'But it would not be true.'

'Truth,' the other woman said slowly, 'is a somewhat elastic commodity where I come from and I think you are guilty as charged.'

Karyn stood up to leave, but paused and looked back at Sonya. 'For a woman who has recently lost her husband you show neither sadness nor understanding. I cannot think what Oliver saw in you.'

'Ditto,' said Sonya, turning back to the river.

*   *   *

From above, Sonya watched Karyn walk along the Thames towards Tower Bridge. It was a month since their first meeting in Paris and in that time, with Gordon's help, she had compiled quite a dossier on 'the woman who killed my husband' as she frequently described Karyn. She knew about her father, who had left her mother and now lived in Geneva. Karyn had been thirteen at the time and she pictured the young teenager's confusion at the splitting up of her parents. She knew her mother had remarried a Frenchman and they now lived out by the Bois de Boulogne. She knew of Karyn's success as a designer and her growing reputation for creating unusual and exciting interiors for shops and restaurants. But she could find no blemishes in the background of this woman who, she acknowledged only to herself and with some bitterness, was undoubtedly beautiful. In fact, it was this very beauty that confirmed the hatred she had for her.

There was no satisfaction in being able to condemn Oliver's business to bankruptcy, not even the obvious discomfort of Karyn Baird as she came cap in hand to her. Sonya had encouraged Oliver to embark on the project in Paris in the first place. It was shortly after she had met Gordon, at the time when Oliver's success was beginning to irritate her. The old bank in Paris was a valuable piece of real estate and, unusually, the freehold was for sale. It was far too expensive for Oliver's company to buy, so she had put together the finance to buy it, but had deliberately underestimated the renovation costs. She wanted the project to fail, to halt Oliver's inexorable rise, to have him completely dependent on her once more. She would still have a share of the valuable freehold, so there was no risk for her. This deliberate genetic flaw in the financial plan for La Mission would only have its required impact if Oliver was there to suffer. And he wasn't and that was the fault of Karyn Baird.

She still felt incomplete, as though there should be another conclusion to the events that had so recently overtaken her. Not even telling Gordon over lunch of Karyn's discomfort would dispel her feeling of being thwarted.

* * *

Karyn sat at a café and watched a tug pulling six barges of waste paper pass effortlessly under Tower Bridge on the fast ebbing tide. A large gull eyed her coldly from the embankment wall. She pondered the French word for the way she felt. '*Nul*,' void, empty. She sat alone for over an hour, drinking her cappuccino as the river fell imperceptibly and the buses crawled over the ludicrously ornate bridge. A week ago she had climbed high into the Pyrénées to spend the day in the empty mountains but here, surrounded by people, she felt much more alone.

She was protected from the cool wind which accompanied the departing river by a hedge of bay trees which marked the boundary of the café. It meant that she didn't see Sonya until she had virtually walked past her. She was wearing a long stone coloured mac with the belt tied at the back. Suddenly a man sitting at a table on the terrace of a restaurant further along from where Karyn was sitting, got up and walked towards Sonya. He kissed her on both cheeks and taking her hand, guided her to his table. At first, Karyn assumed this was a business meeting, but when Sonya leaned forward and kissed the man's cheek again, and put her hand on his, she wasn't so sure. There was a familiarity between them, a physical ease. Karyn was craning forward now, curious to know more, but afraid she might be spotted. The man, tall, handsome with blondish hair, now put his hand on Sonya's shoulder, laughing at something she said. The tables of the restaurants along the terrace were now filling with people and Karyn's view became obscured. She paid for her coffee and retraced her steps to find a place closer to the bridge where she could watch the couple without being observed herself. There were several other people gazing at the river so she became just another tourist. It was from here that she watched them finish their meal and kiss. As they did so, the tall, handsome man placed a hand lightly on Sonya's bottom in a gesture that spoke of only one thing.

Karyn watched the scene without pleasure. With a curious leap of logic, she felt instinctively protective of Oliver as though he was still alive and in the process of being betrayed. And then the indignation rose in her as she recalled Sonya's moral superiority in accusing her, Karyn, of having an affair with Oliver. She watched the man take Sonya's arm and stroll in her direction. She turned to the river and waited for them to pass and as she did she wondered how long it had been going on. One month on from Oliver's death it might have been acceptable for Sonya to have found comfort with another partner but she doubted that they had just met. They were beyond her now and Karyn watched them as they turned from the river to enter a narrow alleyway where they paused and kissed again. No, this had been going on some time.

Karyn returned to the café and flipped open her phone. 'I want a number for the Hotel Montalembert in Paris please.' Moments later she was talking to reservations.

'My name is Sonya Dreyfuss,' she said. 'I stayed at your hotel exactly a month ago and I may have left a book in my room. Would you mind checking if anything has been handed in? I'm afraid I can't remember what number room we had.'

There was a pause during which she heard the tapping of keys on a computer. 'Ah yes, Mrs Dreyfuss. You and your husband stayed in Room 40 on the sixth floor. But sadly we have no record of any book being left behind. I'm sorry.'

So within days of Oliver's death, Sonya had brought her lover to Paris. Karyn stood up and walked towards the river recalling her first meeting with Sonya. Karyn had felt guilty because in her heart she believed that she had committed adultery with Oliver. Sonya had sensed this and had played on it but shaking her head and with a rising sense of indignation, Karyn wondered how Sonya could stand there and lecture her on adultery when she was having an affair herself. She looked back along the river towards the green and grey 3MS' building, now obscured by the granite buttress of Tower Bridge. She accessed Sonya's number and when her PA said she was busy simply told her 'She will want to hear the news I have.'

'You're becoming a pest,' were Sonya's first words, before Karyn had even spoken.

'Who did you go to Paris with, Mrs Dreyfuss?' Karyn had expected the question would knock Sonya off her stride but there was barely a pause before she replied.

'Since you ask, I went with an old friend.' She didn't elaborate.

'A man.'

'A man,' Sonya confirmed.

'Such a close friend that you shared a room,' Karyn continued. 'And a bed.'

Sonya's response was not what Karyn had expected. 'I was married to Oliver, the man you were having an affair with, for five years. He is then killed, obliterated, in an appalling accident and a few days later I come to Paris to confront you. Yes, I needed some support.'

'You don't need support, Mrs Dreyfuss. You don't need anyone. You came to Paris with your lover and then had the gall to accuse me of sleeping with Oliver.'

'You know, you're not very good at this,' Sonya said mockingly. 'In a moment you'll be threatening to expose my affair, as you call it, unless I cough up some money for your restaurant. Now, why don't you go back home to France and leave me to run my business. You've caused enough trouble.'

'Did you enjoy your lunch? You seemed to be receiving a good deal of support throughout it. And some of it was of a frankly sexual nature, wouldn't you agree?'

'So we've turned detective now, have we? Spying on me over lunch. How undignified and how completely pointless. It is over a month since Oliver's death and there is absolutely nothing wrong with me having lunch with a male friend. So I would suggest that this concludes our business.'

With that, Karyn heard the line go dead.

*　　*　　*

Sonya Dreyfuss had conducted many tense negotiations on the phone and over the years she had developed for her voice the equivalent of a poker face. She would not betray her feelings to Karyn, but during the course of their conversation she flicked open the pages of her diary and pulled out the picture of Karyn. Picking up a pencil from her desk she began to lightly tap the face, as if she was pricking the pastry base of a flan tin. When she eventually put down the phone, the point of the pencil was placed at the centre of Karyn's forehead and held in place by the end of her index finger. She did feel anger at her own carelessness in having had lunch so publicly with Gordon, but she quickly converted this into a further and ever deepening hatred for Karyn Baird. The pencil had now pierced the plastic folder which contained the photograph and had left a light but unmistakable mark between the eyes of Karyn Baird.

Chapter 12

The media is at a loss with the everyday, the ordinary. It preys on disaster, feeds on misery and deformity. It has an insatiable appetite for what is wrong, unusual, abnormal. So when Jean-Paul, the producer of the documentary about the train crash, learned that forensic pathologists, who had worked on the aftermath of the Twin Towers attacks in New York, were coming to help with the final stages of the French investigation, he proposed a follow-up film. He discovered that, even a year after the death of nearly three thousand people in the World Trade Centre buildings, there were no tangible remains of over half of them. Sophisticated DNA matching had been set up so that even the tiniest fragments might help reveal an identity. In comparison, the 901 disaster, as it had become to be known, was a relatively simple affair. But nineteen people were still entirely unaccounted for and the insurance companies, ever slow to settle, wanted the best teams brought in to help confirm the deaths. So the ill-fated 9.01 from St Pancras International spawned a second film for Jean-Paul and more pain for all those connected with the tragedy.

He began filming at the crash site, as the final touches were being made to the bridge which replaced the one destroyed in the accident. 'Barely fifty days after the worst rail crash in French history,' his guide voice-over began, 'and there is hardly a trace of the accident which claimed over four hundred lives. But to this day, there is no trace at all of nineteen human beings who were travelling on the fateful train. This is the very spot where many passengers were reduced to ashes. Identifying them has been a painstaking process. But those nineteen were obliterated

beyond ashes. Vapourised. Now a crack team of forensic pathologists has been flown in from New York to help bring their
experience of working on the aftermath of the World Trade
Centre attacks. What will they find?'

The leader of the team, the head of the Department of
Forensic Biology at the New York Coroner's Office, was inter-
viewed at the Paris morgue where the body parts and ashes had
been stored. In a room lit by bleak overhead lights, he outlined
the problem: 'In so many ways, this is the Twin Towers in
miniature. The combined forces of the train and the aircraft fuel
were similar to some extent to the conditions we were faced with
at Ground Zero. And you know,' here he paused as if to take
stock of what he was going to say next, 'of the 2752 people
killed, over 1200 have yet to be identified. The probability is,
most of those never will be. Can we help find the nineteen
unaccounted for on the train? We'll try, but . . . ' His words
trailed off and Jean-Paul knew that when he came to edit this
sequence, he would leave this pause in place.

A model train expert had been commissioned to create a
working scale model of the train, which was now being
assembled in the studio on a length of track which curved
around towards a bridge in an exact replica of the opening
scenes of the film. Four of the coaches had no roofs so that the
small figures representing the nineteen passengers could be
seen sitting in position. Jean-Paul recorded several takes with
the model train travelling up and past the camera before a
series of shots with the camera tracking along the stationary
train finishing on the four key carriages which were at the heart
of the accident. Then he placed the coaches in the positions
they had finished after the crash and, using a small hand-held
camera set on a slow shutter speed, he recorded a sequence of
semi-blurred images which he would cut together with the
CCTV footage he had used in the first documentary.

Jean-Paul asked his researcher to pull in images of the unaccounted for passengers and on the desk in front of him now lay pictures of the nineteen people who ceased to exist that morning in France. He intended to cut these stills into close-up shots of the wreckage and, as with the sequences of the train, he wanted to merge a mix of classic portraits shot on a rostrum camera with more jagged images recorded hand-held. But first he spread all the photographs on the floor of the studio and panned over the images from above, repeating the sequence several times from different angles so that in editing he could mix the takes together. The shots of the nineteen, for whom there were no identifiable remains to date, would form the backbone of the film, to be inter-cut with the work of the American forensic pathology team and interviews with the friends and relatives of the missing.

He worked his way through the pictures of the nineteen victims. Some of the photographs they had received from the police, others from telephoning the families of the missing. Sonya had emailed two pictures of Oliver and that morning Jean-Paul had persuaded Karyn to lend him some of the photographs taken of Oliver on site at La Mission, one of which had been used in the web-site. Jean-Paul had felt no embarrassment in talking to either of the women about such a sensitive request. Sonya was pragmatic and agreed almost immediately. Karyn was reluctant at first, but Jean-Paul had not become a leading documentary maker without considerable powers of persuasion.

The recording of all these images was tedious work so that after a while all the images seemed to blend into one. Each photograph he shot in several different ways but with one standard technique running through them all, a shot of the full-face defocusing into a ghostly blur.

Jean-Paul came to the images of Oliver late in the day. They showed Oliver wearing a short leather coat in the unfinished interior of La Mission. Two of the shots were in profile, in a third he was turning to the camera. All three pictures had been taken full length, so in order to get the close-up he needed, Jean-Paul had to zoom right into the face. As he did so, the quality of the image deteriorated and it was this that occupied Jean-Paul's attention at first. He called his graphic designer down to the studio to ask if the image could be improved electronically and although the answer was yes, he was told the difference would be marginal. So Jean-Paul played around with different shot sizes until he decided to take a break. He brought a plastic tumbler of wine and some cheese from the canteen and sat in the darkened studio with his team. At various points in the room, monitors held the still image of Oliver Dreyfuss staring into the gloom. Removed from the responsibility of directing sequences, Jean-Paul was now looking at a monitor away to his right whilst sipping his wine. Something about the face looking impassively at him was beginning to disturb him. At first he thought it was because he was imagining the strangeness of this man not existing at all, in any shape or form, except in this one dimensional image. He got up and walked over to the monitor. Although he had been working with the picture for an hour or more, he was now seeing it for the first time. He was certain he recognised this man from somewhere, but he couldn't place where. He roamed his memory, recalling where he had been in recent weeks, but he couldn't find a match for the face in front of him. It's not important, he thought, and carried on late into the night recording the faces of the luckless passengers.

*   *   *

For Karyn, it was displacement therapy. She was putting the finishing touches to an article she had written to accompany the photograph of the lynx. She had not fully realised how important the picture was until one of her colleagues at La Mission, whom she was commiserating with on being laid off, commented on the excellence of the still.

'But I thought they were extinct in France,' she said when

told it had been taken in the Pyrénées. 'This is an important story. You must talk to someone in the press.' So now Karyn was concluding the story of herself and the lynx which she was about to send to the features editor of *Le Figaro* magazine, with whom she had spoken earlier. It was odd, though, for as she sealed the envelope, a sadness came over her. The picture represented a very private moment, both in the sighting of the animal and the strange moment of rapport it produced with Oliver. And now this was about to become public. In sharing the experience, she would lose a part of herself in the same way that some African tribes believed that having their photographs taken somehow reduced them. She shrugged, accepting that she had sealed the fate of the picture with the licking down of the envelope.

It was almost midnight when she left the apartment and the air carried the unmistakable smell of autumn, of leaves turning brittle and brown by a cold and drying wind. She delivered the package by hand at the offices of *Le Figaro* and returned slowly along the Left Bank, towards the Île de la Cité. She crossed Pont Neuf and made her way to the western edge of the island where it narrows to a point, splitting the Seine left and right. She often came to the bench by the willow tree that spilled over the river and now she sat alone and listened to the river and the ambient rumble of the city beyond.

When she returned home, she was surprised to see the red light flashing on her phone indicating a message was waiting for her. She looked at her watch. It was gone one and she wondered whether she would listen to the message now, or leave it until the morning. She pressed the button.

'Karyn. It's me, Jean-Paul. Listen to me, I know it is very late but would you call me. It's very important.' What could be so important at this time of night, wondered Karyn, but before she could think any more uncharitable thoughts, he continued. 'I think you might be able to help me. Please call.'

Karyn looked at herself in the mirror above the fire, an ornate eighteenth century antique that had been a twenty-first birthday present from her father. The mirror glass itself was slightly faded at some points so that her face was partly obscured by a dark patch. Her eyes were tired and she stared at herself for several seconds before picking up the phone.

'Jean-Paul, it's me. You called.'

It was clear that he had been expecting her. 'Look, I don't know how to put this and I don't want to upset you, but ... ' At this point Karyn was regretting calling, but what he said next woke her abruptly. 'You know when I came to see you and you threw that thing at me.' He waited for Karyn to say something, but she remained quiet. 'Well, just before I came up some bloke who was hanging around your door, collided with me. He looked slightly mad and even though it was his fault, he didn't apologise.' Karyn wondered where this was leading.

'Anyway,' she felt him hesitate again. 'Anyway, I was filming the pictures you gave me today and it suddenly hit me that I had seen him. Oliver. I'm sure he was the guy in the street.'

Karyn had two instinctive responses, each contradicting the other, so they collided in her mind and rendered her speechless. 'But that's impossible, he's dead,' one part of her said. And in another, she felt the rekindling of the fire of hope that had been fading inside her.

'Karyn. Are you OK? Please say something.'

'How sure are you?' Karyn asked the question softly but clearly.

'I'm not, but I thought I should share this with you.'

But why was he telling me this, Karyn wondered and although even the slightest chance that Oliver was alive began to fill her with joy, her response was cautious. She had not told Jean-Paul the full story of her feelings for Oliver, only that he had been a close working companion.

'You must be wrong,' she said. 'He would have contacted his

wife immediately if he had survived the crash. And me, for that matter. Of course he would.'

Karyn could hear the doubt in Jean-Paul's voice. 'Look, I'm really sorry but if it's not him it's someone very similar. But you're right, he would have been in touch with his wife before now. I'm sorry if this has disturbed you. I'm probably wrong. If you want to call me, I'm on the mobile tomorrow.'

She walked over to the window and the familiar view of the cobbled street. Her heart was racing as if she half expected to see Oliver looking up to her from under one of the lamps. But the street was empty. A collision of emotions was still taking place within her, a sweeping joy that Oliver might just be alive and a corrosive doubt that she was once again deluded. And now a vague unease that, if he had somehow survived the accident, why had he not contacted her? Could she have been that mistaken about him? Surely she had correctly identified that her feelings for him were reciprocal? But amidst this swirl of doubt and hope she was experiencing a rising excitement which was filtering through her body and which would keep her awake for most of the night.

Chapter 13

This was a land travelled through and fought over, unloved by the rest of the country, the runt of the *départements* that make up France. Seven hundred years ago, the Crusaders rode over it at the beginning of their journey southwards towards their distant enemy. For more recent soldiers, this became the greatest battleground of all where today, a hundred years on, the dead are still being uncovered and the old bombs continue to claim their victims. Once upon a time tanks scuttled over this open landscape dashing to, or retreating from, the coast, planting their tracks in the broad fields. The old farms, villages and towns have been destroyed and rebuilt by different generations resigned to being pawns in a larger game. Today the hoards that invade it to head south wear a different uniform and pay as little heed to their surroundings as did their predecessors. These are holidaymakers drawn towards the sun and the apparently grey, flat northern plains of northern France are there to be hurried through on the way to Provence, Tuscany and beyond.

This is a land of survivors, thought Oliver. Each weather beaten farmer that ploughed the land had a depository of stories of survival and struggle handed down from father to son. Off the main roads, in the valleys hidden in the folds of the hills, like seagulls bobbing in the swells of a big sea, small villages lay hidden along meandering rivers. This land of strange and open beauty was Oliver's new home, his horizons bounded by the hills of Picardie and the valleys of the Somme and Authie. This dramatic landscape contained him, just as his work did, protected him with new boundaries. The local people, each with their own histories of displacement and loss, were warm and hospitable and recognised Oliver as one of their own.

It was his day off and he was walking close by the river Somme eastwards towards Amiens. The route followed a contour some fifty metres above the river, an effortless path worn by the passage of time which afforded views on all sides. This was not the part of the river that saw the fighting of the Great War, but a fuller more tranquil river which flowed to a wide, sandy estuary. Oliver worked at the restaurant as often as he could, for it was easier on those days to think of nothing else but the routines of cooking. He was forced to take the occasional day off by Bernard who did not want his star chef falling ill. It was these times he found more difficult and so he filled them with specific tasks in order that he was never really alone with himself. Today he was walking to the cathedral at Amiens which, he recalled from his stay as a teenager when these things didn't really matter, was one of the grandest in Picardie.

He entered the town along the river, but seeing the imposing cathedral dominating the town on the opposite bank, he crossed over on a small bridge and made his way up to the flamboyant building which had stood there for over eight hundred years. This part was easy, for now he could become a tourist and absorb himself in the glories of his surroundings. The exterior of the church he regarded as unsuccessful, the solid mass of the church too big for the slender spire with the two towers on either side unbalanced and unimpressive. But walking into the church through the huge west door, he was amazed at the scale of the interior into which he stepped. A long line of slender columns supported a magnificent vaulted ceiling of enormous height. Somewhere, an organ was gently filling the space with sound and in the side chapels candles cast flickering shadows on the ancient walls. Oliver was almost alone and he stood in the centre of the cathedral looking up at the grey ceiling which seem to explode like a firework from the tops of the tapering columns. He sat at the end of a long line of wooden chairs and for the first time in weeks just stopped, closing his eyes and allowing the music to take the place of his thoughts.

How long he remained like this, he couldn't be sure but when he opened his eyes it was because he was aware that someone had sat near him and was muttering a prayer. He looked across the aisle to the parallel row of seats where an old woman in a long black coat was leaning forward and resting on the back of the seats in front of her in prayer. Although lined, she had a handsome face which appeared completely calm and at ease with itself as she spoke to the gilded figure in the far distance of the church. Although not a churchgoer, Oliver nevertheless felt ashamed that he had not even thought of saying a prayer for or to anyone. What children, grandchildren, friends and loved ones was this woman now uniting in her prayers? He felt his exclusion from the world creep over him like the beginning of a fever. What was this life he was now leading? How could he sit here without reference to anyone? And then the suppressed images began to rise in him, pictures that he had condemned to a hidden dungeon in his body. The four women on the train, their faces frozen forever in his mind, inextricably linked with the severed limbs and broken bodies strewn around the bridge, the ghastly debris hanging from the trees, the roar of the wind, the cracking of the metal, the sheer horror of it all too great to comprehend. He looked up at the great stained glass window and watched the colours blur and bleed. Did he not have a duty to acknowledge them now, to include them in this strange existence he was now calling life? He could not say the words but to the dead he left behind he paid homage and offered a silent apology.

The woman now stood up and as she entered the aisle Oliver saw her pause and looking towards the altar, give the slightest bow before turning to leave the cathedral. As she arrived at the huge door, the light flooded in and she became a silhouette against the bright light of the exterior before disappearing.

He could not bow to the altar as she had done, for the gesture would have been too artificial and nor did he feel the release that he presumed she felt after her visit to the church. But he did sense a shift inside him, as though one part of his life was closing and another opening. He looked back down the long nave and its solid lines of marching columns. The very permanence of the cathedral appeared to mock the artificiality of his life, a life, as he acknowledged with a shrug, that didn't really exist anyway.

He wandered around the great stone interior. A series of wide stone steps led him from the chancel to the nave. As the stairs rose they curved and narrowed, drawing the eye upwards and beyond. Passage up or down the stairs was pre-ordained by this line of sight so that the steps on which his feet were now treading were worn into graceful shallow dips. His feet had contributed imperceptibly to the gradual erosion of the tough stone, an infinitesable wearing down. For a brief moment he saw his own life with Sonya in the same way, a series of events, like the tread of a thousand anonymous feet, that had gradually worn down the original Oliver Dreyfuss.

But at least he could see it now, admit that it had happened.

Just outside the cathedral, he stopped at the statue of Pierre of Amiens, otherwise known, according to the inscription underneath, as Pierre the Hermit. Yes, he was a hermit, a hermit from his own life, leading a routine existence devoid of complication. He had simplified it, demanding little from anyone and having very few demands made of him. And he felt wretched, unconnected and sad.

Oliver knew there was a train which would take him back to Abbeville, where he could pick up a cab to take him back home, but after his thoughts in the cathedral, he still could not trust himself with trains. So he decided to wait for one of the infrequent rural buses. He had an hour and a half before the next one left, so he went into a bar overlooking the Somme and ordered a beer. The smell of black tobacco and *crèpes* being prepared behind the bar accompanied the bitter taste of the drink. He picked up the local paper, but soon tired of parochial stories of local councillors and gruesome car crashes. Later the bus rattled along the pretty south bank of the Somme, through Picquigny and Longpré-les-Corps-Saints and then to Abbeville where he took a taxi for the last leg of his journey.

It was too early to go to his apartment, so he dropped into the restaurant where the last diners were finishing their meals. He was given a *pichet* of red wine and some bread and cheese. He was joined by Stephanie, one of the waitresses who, as the last customers departed, kicked off her shoes and plonked her feet on the chair next to Oliver. She was an attractive woman with long black hair tied back behind her head in a loose ball. She came from the south of France and spoke with a distinct accent which occasionally Oliver had difficulty understanding.

'So, *Monsieur* Cobden, how are we?' she asked mockingly. 'You can't stay away even on your days off, can you? What a strange one you are.'

'You're right,' Oliver replied, raising his glass of wine with one hand and pouring her one with the other. She had just worked for four hours and there was a flush to her cheeks which, in the candlelight, made her look like a model from a painting by Caravaggio.

'So when are you going to take me to dinner somewhere else?' she teased, a big smile across her face.

'Where do you suggest?' Oliver smiled back.

'Well,' said Stephanie holding up her hand to count her fingers, 'there's Michel Bras at Laguiole, Pierre Gagnaire in Paris, Georges Blanc at Vonnas.' She listed three of the best restaurants in France. 'But then there's this little *bastide* not far from where I was brought up. A simple farmhouse, but in the hands of *Monsieur* Ducasse, something different altogether.'

Oliver knew she was talking about La Bastide de Moustiers, a sumptiously comfortable hotel with brilliant food deep in the rugged hills of Provence close to the Gorge de Verdon. And, looking at her across the table, he knew she was serious and that, if he chose to lean forward and look her in the eyes and say 'yes, why not', he could take her away for a weekend and more. But, for the second time that day, he was brought face to face with himself and he felt a distinct uneasiness. His inability to commit to his past life disqualified him from doing so in this.

'I seem to have lost you,' Stephanie said, breaking into his thoughts.

'There's nothing I would like better than to spend a few days with you at La Bastide,' he lied. 'But, you see, I'm sort of spoken for.' This was the first time he had acknowledged to anyone the existence of that past life and the woman in it. It was almost a shock to hear himself tell her this.

Stephanie gave a mock pout. 'So who is this mysterious woman then? She must be very patient because your nights off come along once in a blue moon.'

She was surprised at the seriousness of his response. 'I'm not sure she is patient,' he said simply. 'I don't seem to be very good at telling her how I feel. And she has her life to lead.'

'Ah, she's married?' He shook his head. 'But you talk as though she was on the moon. What a strange man you are. In fact, since it's late and we've got a drink in front of us, why not fess up and tell me just a bit about yourself. You don't get to your age without a little bit of baggage, after all.'

As much as he felt trapped, Oliver also realised that this was the first intimate conversation he had had in many weeks. The old woman in the cathedral made him aware of the lonely and selfish existence he was now leading and now this attractive younger woman was helping him define what was missing in his life.

'It's very hard for me to talk about,' Oliver said.

'That can mean only one thing,' she replied straightaway. 'That you're married or that you've got a problem with the law.'

He looked directly at her and wondered, just for a second, if he would tell her the story, but then the moment was gone. He placed his hand on hers.

'Thank you,' he said. 'You have made me feel different tonight. You're right on both counts, but I can't say more. Maybe one day.' He got up and kissed her on the cheek and moved towards the door.'

'Just one thing,' she said and he looked back towards her.

'Do something about that beard.' She heard his brief laugh as the bell above the door signalled his departure.

Later, lying on his bead scratching the untidy stubble, he thought about the first time he had met Karyn. Although she made an enormous impression on him, only now could he understand what it was that had subsequently made her so important to him. It was the very absence of conflict, an overwhelming ease that seemed to flow through him when he was with her. What a fool he had been not to tell her this then. Instead, here he was alone on a narrow bed, in the shadows of an ancient abbey, in a strange town leading a life that wasn't his own. The room was plunged into darkness as the big lights, illuminating the ancient monument, automatically clicked off at the first chimes of midnight. He turned over to sleep, but his eyes were wide awake and he listened to the distant barking of foxes haunting the moonless night.

Chapter 14

The rain fell incessantly, as if it knew it was a weekend. Karyn watched it lash against her windows, hurled there by the fierce winds which were shaking the trees of the very last of their leaves. She pulled the cord of her dressing gown even tighter and sat on her sofa, tucking her legs under her. On her feet she wore thick socks. It was eleven o'clock in the morning, but the side lights in her room were lit against the steel grey skies outside. Earlier that morning, two copies of *Le Figaro* were delivered by courier and she had put them to one side until now.

She slid the sections of the paper apart and the colour supplement slipped to the floor. She bent forward to pick it up and there on the cover was her picture, at first just a view of mountains and clouds but there, at its centre, the fabulous lynx. The headline declared: *The Lynx Lives in France. The extraordinary story of one woman's quest for the animal thought to be extinct in France.* Inside there were photographs of her as a child and a picture of the hotel in the Pyrénées. Her story took up six pages of the magazine and she read it fearfully, expecting errors to leap out and shame her. On the front-cover was the photo she had taken on automatic as she raised her mug to an imaginary Oliver. To every other reader, however, she was merely toasting the success of her discovery.

The wind rattled the windows and the rain drummed on the lead roof above her, but Karyn's mood was in contrast to the weather. Jean-Paul's call had set up a chain reaction which would ricochet throughout the weekend, rain or not. She had resolved the doubts of the night before and was now delighted that the article had appeared in the magazine. She was not traducing that special moment high on the mountain, she was sending it out with the hope that the one person she wanted to share it with, would read it. She was now convinced that Oliver was alive and that, whatever his reasons for not getting in touch with her, she should respect and understand them. She looked up at the rain splattered windows and imagined Oliver out there, somewhere.

During the stormy night, she had tried to picture what Oliver had felt after the accident. Shock, certainly, but what would that have led him to do? She reasoned that he could not have planned his disappearance but that the accident had triggered a series of responses within him which, out of the blue, offered him the opportunity to walk away from the life he had been leading. Did she include herself in that life? Probably not. She reasoned that she was part of the process of change in Oliver's life and that he was on the point of realising this when the crash so violently interrupted his metamorphosis. So, on this dark and dismal day in early autumn, with the threat of winter not long away, Oliver was alive. Somewhere.

Karyn's 'study' was one corner of her living room, a glass topped table in a stainless steel frame, which she had designed herself. An elaborate lamp, in the shape of a metal giraffe, stood on the desk and lit the screen of a slender laptop. The shelves above were also metal and were lined with an array of books and papers, not neatly stacked but somehow appealing to the eye. Propped here and there were mementoes of her life, stones picked from beaches, old postcards, portraits of her parents and, attached by sellotape to the front edge of the lower shelf, the two poems Oliver had sent her with, between them, the photograph of him wearing the leather coat. As the screen came to life, Karyn wondered how, in this age of instant communication, computer records, CCTV, twenty-four hour monitoring and satellite tracking, it was possible for someone to disappear. She concluded it wasn't and, patting the keys in front of her, began to make a list. An hour later she decided that, of the eleven ways she might begin to trace Oliver, the most obvious weren't going to be available to her. She wouldn't be able to see his bank statements to check where he made cash withdrawals, nor overlook his mobile phone bill or examine his sent email box. But then, she thought, if he didn't want to be discovered then he would be careful in these areas. What would the police do if they believed there was a possibility that Oliver was still alive? Simple. They would get the TV networks to put out a picture of Oliver under the title 'Have you seen this man?'. They would begin to talk to friends and family, to ask if they had any idea where he might go. And, of course, they would examine the scene of the accident for evidence of his leaving it.

She had been this way before in the summer sunshine, not that she had registered the weather that horrible day. She picked up the autoroute at Porte de la Chapelle, passing under the rue Périphérique where she noted the traffic was at a standstill, as it so often was. Her own car was being buffeted by the wind and the giant trucks smothered the small Twingo in clouds of spray. She continued beyond the huge Citroën factory, where the autoroute quadrupled in size to form a twelve lane artery in and out of the city. She passed under the runways of Charles de Gaulle airport and then the railway line itself. She looked up at the streamlined bridge, where high speed services had been resumed, and felt the first hint of apprehension. On the autoroute, it was impossible to tell whether it was still raining or not, but turning off at the next junction on to a minor road, she was relieved to find that it had and that there was not a lorry in sight.

Just as Jean-Paul had discovered a few days earlier, it was as if the accident had never happened. She parked the car, and even before she arrived at the bridge, she heard the roar of an express passing, perhaps not as quickly as it would have done before, but still at high speed. The wind was blowing hard from the east and her coat was moulded to her back as she was pushed towards the bridge. The first thing she saw were the flowers, lines of them, put there since the bridge had been reopened. Most were wrapped in transparent cellophane which shivered in the wind and set up a strange, irregular crackle. She almost dared not look down onto the tracks for fear of what she might see and when another train came rushing through, she put her hands to her ears.

She left and walked towards the woods on the other side. Slithering down the slope, she continued alongside the protective fencing towards the next bridge and clambered up. Here was the view that she recognised from the CCTV footage, colourless and empty. She closed her eyes and imagined the six stranded coaches in front of her and the mayhem beyond it. It was here that the bundle of snowy black and white dots that she thought might be Oliver had left the train and walked back towards the billowing smoke and stricken carriages. He had then veered off to the left, where the guard fence must have been destroyed by the crashing carriages or debris. It was not difficult to guess that he would have fled the horrific scenes and there was really only one way he could have gone, back towards where she was now standing. On one side of the bridge, the road rose between trees and disappeared into the forest. On the other side there were signs for the village of Beaumarchais, where she now turned.

Once upon a time Beaumarchais had been a true village, a community of farm workers living off the fertile land all around. And then the slow spread of Paris and the decision to build Charles de Gaulle changed it forever, the roar of the high-speed trains and low-flying jets a constant reminder of what it had lost. Karyn stopped at a bar and ordered a coffee. Overhead she heard the thunderous whine of a plane approaching the airport. An old man at the bar, wearing blue overalls and taking an early *rouge*, nodded to her and without removing the yellowing cigarette from his mouth, said 'Crazy, eh? The best farm land in France and they put an airport on it.' She nodded in agreement and sipped her coffee.

The man continued. 'Are you one of the relatives?'

The question took her by surprise. 'Sort of. My boyfriend was on the train.'

'They all come in here,' he said, with his smoker's growl, looking at his reflection in the long mirror behind the bar, a curl of blue smoke rising from his cigarette. 'I suppose they always will.' And then, looking towards her, added 'But life goes on, doesn't it? Life goes on.' He downed the last of the wine and, with a nod in her direction, left the bar. Seconds later, Karyn followed and caught up with the man as he walked slowly down Beaumarchais' main street.

'Excuse me, *monsieur*,' she said, fishing a photograph out of her wallet. 'My boyfriend was one of the passengers but his body has never been found. I still can't accept that he is dead. Would you look at this picture.' She offered him the snapshot of Oliver. He examined it and then handed it back.

'I'm sorry for you, but I can't help.' He gestured with his head. 'You could ask Madame Guiot at the auberge. She knows most of what goes on around here.' He smiled at her and touched her forearm with his freckled hand. '*Bon courage*.'

Madame Guiot came down the wooden stairs to greet her, wiping her hands on her pinafore. She was immediately suspicious when Karyn asked her if she could help with some information about the train crash.

'You're not from the media, are you?' she demanded, straightening the front of the pinny. 'I am fed up with them, lurking around and talking to everyone. What a way to spend your life, poking your nose into other people's misery.'

Karyn shook her head and told her story. She was about to hand the woman Oliver's picture, when she said. 'I wasn't here that morning. I was in Meaux, at the market. When I got back it was like the war. You've never seen such chaos. We were full for the next two weeks, mostly with journalists who drank too much and then were up and gone, like locusts.' Karyn heard all this with a sinking heart. Madame Guiot considered the photograph and scratched her chin.

'Maybe, maybe. Bruno,' she shouted, and then again, 'Bruno.'

Bruno shuffled in, wearing carpet slippers and regarded her mournfully. 'You were here the morning of the crash. Do you recognise him?' He held the picture away from him and then fumbled in his pockets and brought out his spectacles. He studied the photograph for a little longer and then looked over his glasses at Karyn.

'Yes. My wife doesn't allow me to take charge very often, so I remember him. He had no luggage. I thought he might have a rendezvous, if you know what I mean, so I didn't think anything more about it.'

Karyn steadied herself against the counter. 'But do you know where he went?' At this point, Madame Guiot snatched back the picture and looked at it more carefully.

'He might have been the one who said that he'd had a row with his wife, I don't know,' she shrugged.

'But did he say where he was going?' Karyn persisted, but Madame Guiot had reached the limit of her memory. 'They all go to Paris from here. Why should he be any different?'

As Karyn left the hotel, she realised that she was shaking. Oliver had survived the crash and her instincts had been right all along. And, looking to her right, she knew without doubt that this was the direction he had taken the following morning, further distancing himself from the site of the accident. But, as she peered along the street, she felt the vastness of France open up to her, just as it must have to Oliver.

She returned to the café and ordered a cognac and felt it warm her. As her breathing became normal, she unfolded the list that she had prepared earlier. Why didn't she just go to the police, she wondered? She had proof that Oliver was still alive and they would surely find him more quickly than she could. Did she have a responsibility to tell Sonya? Would Jean-Paul help her? No, she wanted to keep this to herself, to find Oliver before anyone else did. It was her crusade to get to him before they did. Or, perhaps, he would come to her. She heard another train rush by as she drained the last of the brandy from the small glass.

Chapter 15

It was as if Oliver's death had not so much freed Sonya as released her into a sort of free-fall. Oliver and she had existed in parallel, maintaining a respectful distance between themselves but nevertheless, like the twin hulls of a catamaran, where one turned the other had to as well. Sonya liked to think of herself as the leader and Oliver the passive follower, but now she was beginning to see that her husband's autonomy helped her to define herself and that his death had brought unforeseen changes. This angered her and she blamed Oliver for it. She was working less hard, she realised, and it was Gordon who suggested, in his laconic way, that she had always wanted to show off to Oliver, to confirm how capable she was. With Gordon it was different, for he was wealthy in his own right and had no need to work. Like Oliver, he made few demands on her, but it was different. She revelled in the freedom she felt with Gordon, but she was aware that she was in a vacuum and that the touchstones of normal existence were absent. Why couldn't she just enjoy this accidental happiness?

As she struggled to define what it was that she had needed from Oliver, she watched a pair of ocean-going tugs manoeuvre an elegant cruiser alongside the great bulk of HMS *Belfast*. On the deck of the modern ship were lined the ship's crew, perfectly turned out in their uniforms, saluting to the motley jumble of tourists and Londoners going about their business below.

The letter which had prompted her thoughts was open on her desk. She picked it up and read it again. In three precise paragraphs of cold, official language, it confirmed Oliver's death. His life insurance company had received notification that the death certificate had been issued by the French coroner. Although there was no definitive DNA matching, the coroner believed there was sufficient evidence to prove that Oliver had perished in carriage 11 of the 9.01 to Paris and that his body had been 'beyond any possible identification'. In the distance the sun was just catching the golden globe at the top of the Monument and it shone for in instant above the cascade of buildings around.

'Bugger you, Oliver,' she said to the empty office. Not only had she been unaware of his journey to Paris, she had been impotent in the face of the legal procedures that had followed the accident. It was this inability to control what was happening which most angered Sonya. And now the final insult. The letter informed her that her husband's life had been insured for £300,000, payable to his estate. Her laugh was bitter, as she tossed the letter on to the desk. Enough to save his French restaurant, but only if she chose to release it since, according to his will, she was the sole beneficiary. And there was no chance she would do that. But what was the point in having manoeuvred this position of financial power over Oliver? Now it just seemed like a futile *coup de grâce* and she felt the frustration settle on her stomach and turn into bile.

She stood at the window and looked down on the Thames. Later there would be a full moon, and the extremely low tide had reduced the river to a narrow stream no more than ten metres wide. On the foreshore in front of her, the retreating river had revealed the uneven line of dock moorings, rotting and blackened stumps of wood, reminders of the days when the Pool of London was a rougher and dirtier place. Sonya smoothed the sleeves of her black jacket and picked up the phone.

'Can you collect me early?' she said to Gordon, before he had time to say anything. 'I need to be taken out of myself.'

She returned to the window. It was the late afternoon of an autumn day and the embankment path had suddenly filled with workers, whose day regularly finished at five, hurrying towards London Bridge station, their coat collars turned up against the chill wind which more often than not blew eastwards down the Thames. Enclosed in their worlds, they looked neither to the left nor right, and certainly not upwards to Sonya standing against the green tinted glass. She despised their petty lives, their limited horizons, their very ordinariness. Her disdain was complete and un-negotiable. She saw herself in a class of her own not driven like the huddle of commuters moving in what looked like a single stream towards the bridge. She imagined for a moment that she held in her hand a remote control which could speed them up or slow them down or, as she now wanted, to turn them over the embankment and into the cold and dangerous waters of the Thames.

The view westwards from Sonya's office had changed radically over the years and only the Custom House remained of the old riverfront. To one side of its elegant façade stood a monstrous building of black glass which was flanked by its exact opposite, a shapeless white block which, as far as she could see, was windowless, a fact she had always found quite extraordinary given the views that the river offered. When she sat on the edge of her desk and looked east towards the darker skies, her window was filled with a panorama barely touched by time for almost a thousand years. The Tower remained solid and unmoved by time and tide, a reminder of the fickleness of passing fashion. It mocked the chrome and glass it now faced just as Sonya dismissed the commuters beneath her.

Sonya looked down at the letter in her hand. So Oliver was dead, but he was not beyond vengeance. His life insurance money would only augment her fortune. La Mission and Karyn Baird could rot in hell. The light outside had now fallen enough for her to be half reflected in the window, her face set and unyielding, her narrow lips closed and her eyes cool with no hint of warmth. At first she hardly heard the phone ringing and then, assuming it was Gordon, she picked it up and waited for him to speak. She was puzzled when the voice spoke in heavily accented English.

'Mrs Dreyfuss? Mrs Dreyfuss, this is Jean-Paul Patrese.' She recognised the voice but said nothing. 'I need to speak to you about your husband.'

'Well there's a surprise,' she said without emotion.

'Sure,' he said, hesitating just slightly. 'As you know, I am a television producer but,' and here he began to speak up, 'before you put the phone down I have some very important information about your husband.'

Sonya's instinct was indeed to put down the phone. 'My husband is dead,' she said flatly.

He quickly continued. 'I have reason to believe he may not be.'

Sonya waited before answering. 'I have a letter in my hand which tells me he is. It confirms the findings of the French coroner.' She could sense him absorbing this information, like a scavenger picking at the remains of a blackened animal.

'I am sorry to confront you like this Mrs Dreyfuss, but I think I may have seen your husband in Paris.'

'Have you ever met my husband, Mr Patrese?'

'Call me Jean-Paul. No, but I feel as though I have. I am working on a second documentary about the accident and I have seen many images of your husband – some of which you sent me. And he was working with a friend of mine, Karyn Baird.'

At the mention of Karyn's name, Sonya pushed herself away from the desk and turned away from her reflection in the window. She was not going to betray her position. 'Yes, I know her. So?'

'Well, I think I may have seen him outside her apartment just a few days ago.'

Sonya cut the connection and held the phone away from her, looking at the finger which continued to press into the red button on the receiver. She could not allow this confusion into her life. It had to be cut off, cauterised, exorcised. This was some sort of trick played by a cold-hearted journalist to get her involved in his film. She had in her other hand the truth about Oliver. He didn't exist, he was nothing, not even the tiniest fragment of anything, he was beyond even dust, consigned to some sort of infinity.

But the other hand, so firmly clasping the phone, told her something else. A seed had been planted which now, only seconds later, was beginning to spread doubt through her body. 'Damn you Oliver. May you rot in which ever hell you're in.'

Sonya's office had been fitted with a light thermostat which, when activated, automatically adjusted the lighting inside to correspond with the level of light outside. It could work in both directions, making the office lighter as night came on or, as now, it could dim the lights so that, as darkness fell, the inside lights became more subtle and could enable her to sit at her desk and look out at the panorama of the Thames. The flashing lights of a small jet blinked across the horizon as it banked into its approach to City Airport.

Sonya still held the phone in one hand and the letter in the other but in the few minutes since the call from France she knew which one she could not ignore. She scrolled through her phone for 'call register'.

'Mr Patrese.' It wasn't a question. 'I will help you.' That she was lying mattered not at all to Sonya. It came as naturally as smoothing her short hair, which she now did with the sweep of the hand which still held the letter from Oliver's insurance company.

'But first I need you to tell me exactly what you know about my husband and I want the details of this so-called sighting of him.' In the space of a few minutes Sonya had changed direction, picking up the scent of a distant prey, suddenly alert and focused.

She could hear the excitement in his voice as he replied. 'I'm grateful, Mrs Dreyfuss. Your husband was working on a major new restaurant in Paris, as I know you are aware. I gather he was coming to Paris for a meeting with Karyn Baird when the accident happened.' There was no suggestion in his voice that the meeting would have been anything other than a routine one about business.

'Of this much I am aware, Mr Patrese, but, apart from the ghost of my husband you saw outside that woman's apartment, what makes you think he could have survived the accident?'

'Well, he looked very real to me Mrs Dreyfuss. I cannot swear that it was him, but I do know this . . . ' He paused and she waited. ' . . . there is one way he might have escaped. There is just a chance that he might have walked through to the buffet car, one of the six coaches that survived, before the impact. It is possible, don't you think?'

Sonya stood up. She had been led so firmly to believe that Oliver could only have perished in the accident that she had not even begun to think of any way he might have survived.

'This is a dangerous game you are playing, leading me to believe that my husband might still be alive – all for the sake of your so called documentary. It would make a good story, wouldn't it? Perhaps at my expense?'

'I assure you, Mrs Dreyfuss, that . . . '

'Oh, don't give me all that,' she interrupted. 'You're in this for yourself and you couldn't give a toss what it might do to me.' Out on the river, a police patrol boat cruised slowly up the middle of the river now alive with the reflections from the buildings on either bank. It was swallowed into the shadows of London Bridge before Sonya spoke again. For now, Jean-Paul Patrese had served his purpose but, she acknowledged to herself, he might be useful in the future.

'I assume you want to interview me?'

It was the last thing Jean-Paul expected to hear but he was quick to agree.

'I am coming to Paris next Tuesday for a few days. Where shall we meet?'

He gave her an address and a time which she wrote down on a pad. She had no intention of seeing him. After she had finished speaking to the Frenchman she called Gordon and cancelled their evening. She had other plans.

Chapter 16

The rich and particular smell of Gauloises usually betrayed the whereabouts of Bernard Chichilian, sometimes preceding him and always lingering long after he had departed. As Oliver arrived in the restaurant early that Saturday morning, he knew that Bernard was already there. The knowledge made him feel comfortable for there was in the old restaurateur a genial, unquestioning warmth. This morning, though, he noticed an added sparkle to the older man's rheumy eyes.

'Good morning, Oliver. *Ça va?* A glass of champagne, I think.'

'Bernard, it's only eight-thirty. I have at least a hundred and thirty covers this weekend. I'll never last the course.' Oliver said this lightly, with mock severity.

'I shall have to drink to your, to our, success alone, then.' And with that, Bernard turned the cork of the champagne bottle so that it gave a gentle 'pop'. The pale liquid fizzed up the side of one of the two flutes on the table in front of him.

Oliver sat down and cocked his head, waiting for an explanation. Bernard filled the second glass and pushed it towards his chef.

'Now, my mysterious friend, do you remember that rather insignificant chap that ate in the corner of the restaurant one rainy Tuesday evening a few weeks ago?'

'The one that had two starters and two puddings as well as the main course,' Oliver answered.

'Just so,' said Bernard, raising his glass towards Oliver. 'He was the man from Michelin, as I suppose we might have guessed, and he wants to give us a star.'

Even as he heard the words, Oliver felt his chest come alive and the familiar uneasiness run through him. He could see Bernard looking quizzically at him and he recovered enough to pick up his flute and clink it against his boss's.

'Bravo to you,' said Bernard. 'But you don't seem as pleased as I thought you might.'

Oliver looked over the top of his glass to meet the stare of the older man. It was Bernard who spoke first.

'No, don't say anything. I respect your secrets. And, anyway, at this time in my life I have learned to count my blessings. So, *santé*, and thank you.'

Oliver took a sip of his champagne and got up. He placed a hand on the other man's shoulder and gave it a small squeeze. 'You deserve it,' he said quietly and went on into the kitchen.

All was ready for the lunchtime service, the stations meticulously clean. Oliver saw a blurred reflection of himself in the scrubbed steel splash-back above the stoves. He breathed in deeply and as he did so he heard the applause fill the empty kitchen. He felt hot and his skin was covered with a light film of sweat, as it had been that evening. The presenter called his name and as he got up from the table to go and collect his award, he looked across at his wife. Her hands were clapping in front of her face but through the blur he could see her eyes. Although the smile was wide, the eyes were cold and still. He carried the award, an inscribed plate, back to the table and at the party afterwards he noticed that people wanted to touch him, as if some of his success would rub off on them. By this stage, Sonya had left, not that this surprised him.

By the time he had arrived home after the party and the television interviews, Sonya was already in bed and appeared to be asleep. It was a hot night and the bed clothes were thrown back. She was wearing a pair of black silk shorts with the faintest pink stripe and a matching top. He stood and looked at her elegant form curved unconsciously across the bed, lit by a pale light from the curtains. She seemed almost translucent, a delicate glass figure by Lalique. He was surprised to see what she was wearing for, once upon a time, the flimsy outfit used to indicate that she wanted to make love to him. This had not happened for some time and his slight puzzlement was accompanied by sexual arousal, a cocktail which sat uneasily in him.

And then he was aware that she was awake, propped on her elbows looking at him, the whites of her eyes clearer than ever.

'So, the man of the moment returns. I thought I would leave you to your adoring fans and come back early. I hope you didn't mind?' As she said this, she adjusted the thin shoulder strap of her halter top so that, momentarily, her breast appeared from behind the thin silk. 'You really are the talk of the town, *le tout Londres*. And all those girls wanting to meet you. My.' She turned on her side, the rise of her hip pushing the tiny shorts up towards her waist, the curve of her bottom smooth in the half light.

Oliver began to take off his clothes, his eyes on the shape in front of him. He watched as she brought her knees towards her in a foetal position which exposed even more of her rear.

Oliver was naked now, his erection complete.

'Good night, Ollie', she said, drawing the sheet over her. 'I hope you sleep well. After all that excitement.'

The memory of that moment stayed with him, a tiny private incident but one which embarrassed him even now so that he glanced around the kitchen to make sure he was still alone. But what he remembered more was the next day, which was worse. He awoke to a deceptively beautiful June morning.

Sonya was already up when he came down, padding around the kitchen still wearing the black silk pyjamas. She made coffee and warmed some croissants and slid them in front of Oliver. She then pulled up a chair opposite, climbed on to it and sat on its back with her feet on the seat. It was a something he had seen his wife do from time to time, particularly when she wanted to talk to him seriously. As she did it, Oliver's eyes were drawn to that most private part of her body, now slightly revealed by his wife's position on the chair.

'I have been thinking, Oliver,' she began, making her position on the back slightly more comfortable. 'You should open a restaurant in France. In Paris.' She leaned forward to emphasise her point. Oliver looked away to the picture on the wall above the work surface. It was a photograph of a grape harvest in Bordeaux, a picture he had taken as a teenager. A man carrying a container of grapes on his back was in the process of tipping them into the back of a trailer. The man and the tumbling grapes were in dark profile against a blue grey sky. It was a small moment in yet another *vendange*, but caught forever.

It was this conjunction of rememberings that gripped Oliver now. The moment rose in him fully formed, as if it had been waiting to make this appearance. He could recite the words that came next and he did now, this Saturday morning.

'Oliver, you are a star.' Even then the words didn't appear quite right and they sounded strange as he repeated them now. 'It would be a shame to waste your success,' she continued. 'You should use it. Exploit it.'

Her elbows, he remembered all too clearly, were now resting on her knees and her face was cupped in her hands. Her legs were slightly parted and curls of pubic hair sprung from the sides of her shorts like unruly undergrowth.

'I have a business friend who looks after property in Paris. A number of banks are relocating out of the centre. He has to find new uses for them.' She jumped off the chair and left the kitchen only to re-enter moments later with a card which she put on his plate next to the half-finished croissant. She was standing very close to him, he remembered, along with the fact that he had said nothing. The next moment they were making love on the table, a brief staccato affair which was over even before the warmth had left his unfinished croissant.

What stayed with him now, across the distance of time, but as though he was watching a re-enactment of the actual events in front of him, were, once again, her eyes as they made love. So clear. So steady. And so open. By the time she left the room, he still hadn't spoken and he was left with his boxer shorts around his ankles. On the table in front of him lay the business card.

He felt as bad now as he did then. But now the events carried a different meaning and he could only shake his head at the memory. How do we section the past, he wondered, dissect what happened so that the post-mortem will clearly reveal cause and effect? Where first to lay the scalpel along the time line? Make an incision here, too early, and the traces of future malfunction are too faint to perceive. Make the cut too late and there is evidence in abundance, the poison clear for all to see. But there is a moment, somewhere along the line, when an examination can reveal the exact point where an accumulation of events is about to turn septic and demands action.

Oliver knew that this had been that moment in time. And he had done nothing. The sheen of sweat on his face was caused by a mix of shame and embarrassment and, somewhere much deeper, anger. She had taken over his life. No, he had allowed his life to be taken over, acquiesced and facilitated its gradual demise. Success and money often walk hand in hand and when they do they have the power to soften and sometimes disguise reality. Sonya had hated his growing reputation, but he could not see it, refused to acknowledge the truth it highlighted. No, he could see that she had never really cared for the routines of his life. He was there only to serve her. And yet when, in the beginning, he had walked across the floor of the restaurant to-wards her smiling face and welcoming eyes he felt as though the decision was all his.

He picked up a cloth and rubbed hard at his reflection in the stainless steel but instead of coming clearer it remained there, blurred and indistinct.

Chapter 17

She had lied to him, of course.

When he met Sonya, they were both in their early thirties, both established and experienced and up until then, neither had seriously entertained the thought of having children. The subject originally came up on their first trip to Vienna together. Oliver was still delighted to be caught in the whirlwind of Sonya's energy as she led him around the ancient city. They ate at restaurants where she was known to the staff and it did just occur to him if she had done this with anyone else.

'Of course not, darling. There's a lot of money in Vienna and some of it, as you might have guessed, has found its way to 3MS. But you have to sing for your supper.'

She took him to the Spanish Riding School and she gave him a running commentary on the manoeuvres the riders were putting the horses through. Some seemed to him rather cruel and contrived, the tip toe steps, the crabbing movements, the standing on hind legs and Sonya mocked his ignorance of the riders' technical brilliance.

It was the children waiting to go on the Ferris Wheel that prompted Oliver's question. 'Can you imagine it?' He nodded towards a family whose three children were each clutching ice creams with varying degrees of success.

'Heaven forbid,' Sonya replied, rolling her large eyes to the skies. These were Oliver's sentiments and they laughed as the youngest of the children, in turning to point up at the giant wheel, tipped the melting ball of ice cream on to his face. Oliver was an only child and in the early days of freedom with Sonya, he could not imagine being encumbered with a similar small, disruptive life.

Later he was to think differently and now, as he walked towards Au Fil du Temps on a bright Sunday morning, he wondered if his change of heart had been an attempt, subliminally at least, to repair the fault lines that had begun to widen in their relationship.

He raised the subject of children with Sonya exactly three years after their first trip to Vienna. They marked the anniversary by going to an interminable performance of Schoenberg's *Moses and Aaron* at the State Opera House. He felt that the hours had been wasted and in an odd, slightly improbable leap of logic, asked Sonya if she thought that marriage without children was a waste of that marriage.

'No, not at all,' she said firmly. 'But I see what you mean. Why? Are you getting broody?' He remembered that particular phrase. So typical of Sonya to cut to the chase immediately. He had told her, tentatively, that he was warming to the idea and that, on balance, he would like to have children, not one, perhaps two. And she leaned towards him and kissed him gently on the lips. 'Let's do it,' she said.

She didn't mean it, but it took him another year to find out. It was a year in which their sexual life began to change. At first he had wondered, now that their sex had a purpose, if this had affected its frequency and quality. But, a few days before he caught the ill-fated train to Paris, he had found a half-empty packet of contraceptive pills which had spilled from Sonya's handbag. Once again, so many thoughts rushed into his head that they neutralised each other. The betrayal had ramifications, he knew, but he was unable to grasp what they were. The incident seemed to come on top of so many others, that he wasn't able to filter a logic or a pattern. Perhaps he would see things differently in France.

Today the lunch tables would be filled with families, the dining room alive with the voices of children.

For a brief second, between a multitude of tasks, Oliver looked through the hatch, *la passe*, which separated his kitchen from the dining room. It was Sunday lunchtime, the weekly ritual which revealed the true contradiction in French life, at one and the same time revolutionary and conservative. In the noisy, relaxed atmosphere of the restaurant were the same families that Oliver had grown to recognise in the months since he had taken over as chef. Each was a market researcher's delight, a generational mix brought together by ritual once a week, grandparents, parents, children and grandchildren around one table. The country which overthrew governments, built barricades against authority and took *action direct* whenever it felt like it, was corralled and calmed by this Sunday gathering. In England, Oliver mused, the power of the Sunday lunch had diminished in direct relation to the influence of the family. Gone were the strong patriarchs, the fearsome matriarchs, who would issue three line whips for family events. The extended family did its own thing, perhaps only at Christmas agreeing to be coalesced into an uneasy and uncomfortable group. This erosion was not evident at the tables Oliver observed. Respect and affection seemed to go hand in hand and there appeared genuine warmth across the spread of years. Oliver felt himself slipping into some rose-tinted view of the French family. 'Maybe they're just good at hiding their murderous feelings towards each other,' he thought as he returned to removing a serving of *os à la moelle* from the oven. If ever a dish represented the French lunch, this was it. Barely seen in England, it was a staple delight of many of his regular customers who relished scooping the glutinous bone marrow from a shin bone standing upright in its own *jus*.

In the beginning, Oliver had been glad of days like this, when a full restaurant had allowed him to disappear into hard work and where a fourteen-hour day gave him little or no time to reflect on what he was doing. But now, as he watched the animated faces and the excited gestures of children and grandchildren he once again felt as he had done in Amiens cathedral, an outsider removed from the realities of life. And the memory of his feelings in this kitchen the previous morning stayed with him like unfinished business, asking for resolution but in the physical pressure of the day, pushed quite literally to the back burner.

'Chef. Chef.' He was being called to oversee two dishes of rabbit and honey, one of his specialities. Bending over the plates in the way that all chefs do before they consign their creations to the scrutiny of the restaurant, he wiped a small splash of gravy from the corner of one of the plates and nodded his approval. It's curious, he thought, that in moments of emotional intensity one's other senses seem to diminish so he barely heard the calls of his sous chef. 'We're nearly there, chef. Just the *os à la moelle* for *grand-papa* Joseph. Maybe that's why he's lasted ninety-five years.' Oliver smiled and looked back to the dining room where old Joseph sat in his crumpled dark blue suit, his face ruddy from years of farm life and not a little sturdy red burgundy.

It was *grand-papa* Joseph who was last to leave, a little unsteady on his feet, led to the door by his granddaughter, seventy years between them, children of hugely different ages bound by family and, today, one table. Oliver offered them a cheery *au revoir* and returned to the kitchen to help finish the cleaning. A little while later, with a glass of wine in his hand, he sat in the chair that had been Joseph's. He imagined his position at the head of the table, the blur of faces all around him, the family resemblances, the memories triggered, connections made and lost across three different centuries.

Oliver, still wearing his whites, pulled out the chair nearest to him in order to rest his feet on it. As he did so, one of the Sunday papers the restaurant bought for the customers, slipped to the floor. Oliver bent down to pick it up but in a pose not dissimilar to the one he used at *la passe*, he remained stooped, as if looking at something far below him. Slowly, as if offering his hand to a dog who may or may not bite, he stretched forward and picked a magazine off the floor and raised it up to the table. Again he tilted forward to observe what was in front of him. By now his other senses had retreated almost completely. He could not hear the cars in the square, nor the rumble of the dishwashers in the kitchen, not even the distant drone of a chainsaw cutting wood for the winter. He was focused entirely on Karyn Baird as she offered a cup of cheer, it seemed, directly to him. Gently he placed his hand over her body, so just her head remained, her face looking at his. He was aware only of her presence which for him, at that moment, was overwhelming. Then his eyes began to see the words under his fingers and he slid his hand away to read 'The Lynx Lives in France. The extraordinary story of one woman's quest . . .' He skipped the headlines and quickly turned to the story inside. She had told him about the Pyrénées and the hotel that her father took her to, and here it was now. He was so intent on reading that he did not hear the departure of his team who all offered unreturned 'bonne soirée' to his stooped back. And now the photograph, spread over two pages, of the lynx caught in the sun surveying the early morning mist hovering in the valleys below. It was a magical picture and he wanted to tell her so now, this instant. He flipped back to the cover and looked again into her eyes. He needed to hear her speak, for her to finish the sentence that seemed to be on her lips. He lowered his head to the table so his forehead was resting on her feet and he remained there for some time as one thought percolated through his system. He was trapped in a cul-de-sac of his own making.

He stood up and looked around the room. Although the restaurant would be shut tonight and tomorrow, all the tables had been neatly laid, save for the place at which he had been reading. Methodically, he fetched cutlery and a napkin, putting them in position along with the others before finishing the setting with two wine glasses. Standing back, he adjusted the angle of a fork to match the symmetry of the others. He then went to the counter which held the cash register and where the *apéritifs* and *digestifs* were served, to find the jar of biros and pencils kept underneath. From an order pad he pulled a sheet of paper and wrote a short note and addressed it simply to 'Bernard' and left it on the counter along with his keys. Turning off the lights and shutting the door behind him he headed into the autumn evening. At the walls of the Abbey, just as he turned towards his apartment, he paused and looked back at the restaurant. The sign bearing the name Au Fil du Temps was rocking gently in the wind and dried leaves scuttled underneath. He turned away and walked into the shadows of the ancient wall.

Oliver felt curiously calm. He unzipped his kit bag and put it on the bed. He went carefully through his chest of drawers, discarding some items but folding others neatly into the soft bag. He spread a set of clean clothes on the bed and the items he didn't want he put into a black bin bag. He had accumulated very little in the months he had been in the town and the job was quickly done. Finally, he took off his whites and added them to the bin bag. His room was lit by a small bedside lamp with a yellow tassled shade which lit one side of his body now reflected in the window which gave on to the old walls. He paused to study it, half almost in darkness, the other half over-exposed in a parchment yellow. His long hair was barely visible in the darkened glass, but his thick stubble bordered the lower half of his face. This incomplete image was at odds with the way he felt. He went into the tiny bathroom with its stained claw-foot bath and looked at himself in the small oval mirror on the cabinet above the sink. He ran some hot water and began the painful process of shaving, something he hadn't done for weeks, pre-ferring instead to occasionally snip away at his beard with a small pair of nail scissors. Gradually, the face he recognised emerged from its disguise. He took a small glass from the cabinet, filled it with water, and raised it to the mirror in a similar gesture to the one that Karyn had used in her self-portrait.

Later, on the bus to Abbeville, he glanced back at the Abbey, its pale walls stark in the floodlights and watched until it disappeared. The effect was almost filmic, a dark green wipe sliding across his field of vision so that, when it was lost, he turned back into the bus, the sole passenger on this darkening November evening. He was picturing the tiny steps that Karyn used when marking out the shape of the bar at La Mission. She was wearing brown Campers with black tights and a very darkly patterned tartan skirt. It had been cold on the site and she had on a black parka, unzipped at the front with a narrow red and yellow scarf loose around her neck. Did he realise then that he was falling in love with her? He was so limited, he realised, for his only point of reference was Sonya and so what was happening with Karyn came without instructions. It was only when he saw the picture of her in *Le Figaro* magazine that he felt something crystallise inside him. The shape of her face, the half-formed words on her lips, the appeal in her eyes and the questioning gesture of her hand to the camera cut straight through to him. Somehow he knew that she was speaking directly to him, that she wanted him to share in that moment. The magazine had been the last item he had packed and as the bus rattled towards Abbeville he slowly and carefully unzipped the bag so that, as the teeth parted, Karyn's steadfast gaze was revealed. He glanced away, into the dark night and wondered if he was being fanciful and asking why he had allowed himself to fall into this strange limbo. At one and the same time, the accident had both clouded his vision and ultimately brought him face to face with himself. Slowly but surely in his old life he had been failing, slipping further and further from reality whilst remaining mired in the routines of leading it.

Sonya dominated that old life, a massive presence intellectually and physically. He had not begun to fully understand exactly why he had allowed her to loom so large and why he had abdicated responsibility for his own feelings with her. But he knew he would have to if the journey he was now on was to have any meaning at all. Part of him wanted to blame her but even now he was able to see that this would be futile for he had contributed as much as her to his own downfall.

The foundations of his life, so carefully and deliberately constructed by him, were faulty from the start. The accident had metaphorically destroyed them and only now could he see beyond the wreckage and register the opportunity that had been given to him from the moment he met Karyn. He did not think love could be like this, something precious that could grow without the initial stimulus of sex.

At Abbeville, he boarded the local train for Amiens and it was some minutes later, as it rattled along the banks of the Somme, now hidden in the darkness to his left, that he realised he had overcome another barrier. He felt no fear in the train, only a calm certainty. He eased back into his seat and closed his eyes and, for the first time in months, he thought about the future. By the time the train pulled into the ornate glory of Amiens station and he had crossed the platform for the TGV to Paris, a plan had formed in his mind.

Chapter 18

Karyn returned to Paris as a cold dusk began to grip the city. She was driving against the traffic, a steady congealed mass of headlights moving relentlessly towards her through the dreary *banlieus* to the north. St Denis, Drancy, Bobigny drifted by before she entered inner Paris at Porte de la Chapelle, passing under the stationary traffic on the Périphérique. During the journey, the realisation that Oliver was alive had triggered a series of responses, one after the other, like dominoes falling in sequence. This man, whom she had barely touched, let alone kissed, had been at the forefront of her thoughts in the months since the accident. Indeed, ever since she had met him, the focus of her life had changed, at first gradually and then with increasing urgency. She had known, well before she skipped happily towards the Gare du Nord that fateful morning, the balance of her life had shifted profoundly.

The car nosed down one of the narrow cobbled streets in the Marais as she made her way towards Pont Sully. She felt the tremor of the stones through the steering wheel and the thrum of the tyres filling the cabin of the car. To the west, the body of Notre Dame was floodlit and the shadows of the trees in the gardens flanking its boundary were gaunt against the huge stone walls. Her faith, not only a religious commodity, had enabled her to rationalise the fact that Oliver had not been in touch since the accident, but it had propelled her to think about the basis of her feelings. Love was not a word Karyn entertained lightly. Before Oliver, it had barely raised its complicated head for, despite one fairly important relationship, she had never felt deeply moved by her boyfriends. She acknowledged that she was an awkward proposition for most men who found her intelligence and strongly held opinions difficult to master, as master they must. Oliver had never given one hint that he wanted to change her or bring her round to his way of thinking. But, Karyn now wondered, if the first test of their relationship had been his response to the accident, should she not be disappointed? She dismissed this instantly by reminding herself that they had not even begun a proper relationship, merely a working friendship. So, what were the roots of this feeling which now gave her such certainty? Did she need to question them or should she continue to respond to them in the way that birds did about migration, without thought and by instinct?

'I love the process of falling in love,' a colleague had told her over a cappuccino in the cold bowels of La Mission. Karyn had been mildly shocked, although she had said nothing to her friend. Is it possible to keep falling in love? Just how many times can you say 'I love you'? Was it a game you played for the thrills of the process, like taking drugs? She heard a car horn and turned towards the sound. Karyn was stationary in a jam as was the man sitting in a car going the other way. He smiled at her and blew her a kiss. This incessant flirtation was part of her life, a part of any young woman's life and it made Karyn wish for a more formal and restricted code between men and women. She did not consider herself prim or old-fashioned, but in a world where the moral boundaries of sex and social interaction had been breached to the point of redundancy, her instincts were self-protecting. She had little doubt that she loved Oliver but she knew the moment for saying the three words was some distance in the future. She shrugged and smiled at the man as their cars moved off in opposite directions, a harmless exchange in the City of Love.

The stone hallway of Karyn's apartment was tiled in a series of geometric shapes which gave the impression that the floor was made up of three-dimensional rectangular steps. Karyn loved this *trompe-l'œil* in black and shades of grey but as she walked across it to put her coat into a pale blue armoire, she couldn't help see it as a metaphor for her feelings of frustration. It was an illusion to think that she could now find Oliver. What had, just a few hours ago, appeared solid and achievable was nothing more than a mirage. Towards the end of her journey in the car, she had begun to pick at every conversation she had had with Oliver in a vain attempt to find any clues to where he might have fled. She knew in her heart that if she could be surrounded by Oliver's possessions then by a process of forensic deduction and sheer instinct, she would find the clues that would lead her to him. As she sat on the old wooden chair in the hall and heard it creak under her weight, she realised that the elation she had felt in the café in Beaumarchais was rapidly fading.

She remained in the hallway for some time and between the slow blinks of her eyes the floor moved from two to three dimensions and back again so that at one point she felt compelled to stoop down and run her hands over the smooth, cold surface. She didn't doubt its flatness, as she didn't doubt her feelings for Oliver, and so she smiled at her gesture. She felt certain, if the roles were reversed and Oliver had to find her, he would remember all that she had told him about the Pyrénées. She had sensed him there the day she had seen the lynx, her powerful need to share that moment making him an almost physical presence by her side. What had he told her about himself, what clues had he given her? Perhaps, if she waited in this hallway and simply concentrated hard for his return, the door would eventually push open and his shadow would fall across the patterned floor. Jean-Paul thinks he saw him outside her apartment; the man at the hotel is fairly certain that he stayed there the night after the accident. She stood up and, putting the door on the latch, ran down the shallow stairs two at a time, across the courtyard, to the green door. She quickly pushed it open and stepped through, half expecting him to be standing there. But the line of street lamps, making yellow pompoms along the pavement, revealed nothing. She walked to the other side of the street hoping for a glimpse of a dark haired man in a three-quarter length leather coat walking surely towards her so that she could begin again what should have ignited under the giant roof of the Gare du Nord.

She returned to her apartment to collect her coat. Afterwards, she walked along to the rue du Cherche-Midi and the rue du Dragon without looking left or right at the shops that normally slowed her passage, until she came to the boulevard St Germain. The rush hour traffic paid no attention to the slight figure with her coat collar pulled up over her mouth. Crossing the road, she took a cobbled street which linked the boulevard with the Seine, but before she reached the river she turned left into a narrow passage not far from the Musée d'Orsay. The Bistro du Quai had once been a *cordonnerie* and the faint outline of the words proclaiming its previous use were just visible on the panel above the front door. Inside was a small bar and perhaps a dozen tables. Even if all the tables had been taken, Karyn knew the owner, Patricia, would have found space for her. As it was, the table she preferred, just the other side of the bar and slightly protected from the entrance, was free. This was where she came to eat alone, that is until she had met Oliver. After their last meeting at La Mission she had brought him here, not revealing the importance of her decision. By this time she had decided to include him in her world and wait for him to register the importance of what was developing between them. It didn't really matter what they ate that night, but she remembered, as she did everything they had done together, that they began with grilled oysters followed by confit of duck. Patricia had watched the man sitting opposite her friend and later declared to Karyn that he must be important. Karyn merely put her finger to her lips. Nothing passed between them that night; he did not hold her hand nor hint at changing the nature of their relationship. But he talked about her, asked her questions about her life and her wishes. He was a gentle inquisitor and a gentle listener. She hadn't been back to the restaurant since for fear of what the memories might do to her.

'It's good to see you again,' Patricia announced as she placed a glass of Beaujolais in front of her friend. 'I thought you might have found somewhere else.'

'No you didn't Patricia. You thought that I had split up with the boy I brought in here and I was licking my wounds.'

Patricia smiled and raised her eyebrows. 'Well, I knew he must be someone important for you to bring him here. Perhaps he is joining you here later?'

Karyn hesitated. 'If I told you he was, but he might not arrive tonight, would you understand?'

'Mmm . . . I would know that it wasn't something simple, like a row earlier today. But I can't begin to figure out what the answer might be.' Patricia wiped the top of the wooden table with a clean white cloth. The table didn't need it, but it was a gesture which would allow the conversation to come to a conclusion if Karyn wanted. She did.

Karyn sipped her red wine and ate a *salade landaise*. She had a plan. It was to do nothing. Work had slowed to a trickle at La Mission, but she was able to continue site visits and the routines of the rest of her life, the ones that Oliver knew about, for somewhere deep inside her she knew that he would find her.

Later that night, on the way home, she decided to drop in on the bar in the rue de Buci where Oliver and she would drink after their meetings. She ordered a cognac and, as she expected, before long a man had offered to buy her another. He was perfectly pleasant, in the style of Daniel Auteuil, mousy hair flopping over his forehead, a blue Oxford shirt under a herring-bone jacket, small featured and eager. She let him flatter her with compliments about her face and hair, safe in the comfort that she was impregnable, impervious to whatever he might say.

'What are you doing later this evening?' he asked her, inevitably.

'I am waiting for someone.' Her reply was equally inevitable.

He cocked his head.

'I am waiting for my boyfriend,' she responded, smiling at him.

'And when will he be arriving?'

'Ah,' said Karyn, 'that is the question.' Slipping off the bar stool, she kissed him on the cheek, shouldered open the swing door and left the warm, smoky atmosphere of the bar for the cold of a Paris night.

Chapter 19

Sonya Dreyfuss was angry. She kicked open the door of Oliver's study and waited for it to bounce back to her open palm. There was a crash as some object rolled off the shelving and smashed on to the floor. It was only as Sonya pushed open the door again did she realise how distant her relationship with her husband used to be, how little curiosity she used to have about his life. Although she had been in this room many times, the bric-à-brac and mementos meant nothing to her. But now she was forced to get involved with this very evidence of Oliver's life and it caused the fury to rise inside her once again. It was as if Oliver was controlling her, dictating her actions, and as she stepped into the room the crunch of broken china under her feet was a suitable accompaniment to her mood.

When they were together, Sonya used to present their separate lives as their respect for each other's independence, but now she knew it was simply because she didn't care that much. In some ways she had contempt for Oliver, as she did with all men. She knew she had power over him, could use her body to mesmerise him. He was no different to most of them except he didn't care about her money. That made him slightly rarer than the others. Oliver was blind and unsuspecting. When he began to achieve greater fame independently of her she had the guile and the intelligence to put a fatal flaw in his new found celebrity. La Mission was going to be a failure from the very start because she had made sure it could never succeed. But now, for the first time, the reins had been taken away from her. So, at the very moment when his life seemed beyond her control, she needed to discover Oliver in a way she never had before. She stood and scanned the room, her eyes moving along the bookshelves, over the computer and the jumble of papers on his desk, across the small sofa to the low coffee table piled with books. The walls were covered with pictures, many of them photographs, all in the same thin black frames. Whilst this room was full of what mattered to Oliver, she felt not the remotest sense of the man himself. This was a museum reconstruction of her husband's study, long after his death. This very absence merely increased her anger.

The postcard that Karyn had sent Oliver was still propped on the screen of his computer. She snatched it up, tearing it roughly in half and tossed it aside so that the two parts of the aircraft carrier dropped to the wooden floorboards. The long mirror along the wall behind, festooned with other postcards, clippings and Post-it notes, reflected her movements as she worked her way roughly through his possessions, pulling open the drawers of his desk, running her hands over his books as her eyes read the titles for clues and examined the scraps of paper that fell from between their pages.

She was interrupted by the ring of her mobile. She answered it as she continued to search through Oliver's belongings. It was Gordon and she abruptly ordered him to come over and join her. When he asked what she was doing, she said: 'I am looking for Oliver.' There was a pause.

'I'm sorry. Am I missing something? Oliver is surely dead.'

'Well, perhaps he's not,' Sonya barked. 'Come and help me find him.' She cut him off and pushed the handset along the desk towards its receiver.

The archaeology of Oliver's study slowly revealed a man she only partly recognised. There were cuttings from newspapers, photographs torn from magazines, pieces of broken pottery, restaurant reviews, letters of complaint from customers, a kaleidoscope of references that made up a collage of Oliver's life. She found a map of Paris with various positions circled in ink and realised that one of them marked the site of La Mission in St Sulpice. He couldn't hide there, she knew, so where had he gone? She slammed shut one drawer and pulled open another which was full of photographs. She rifled through them, discarding those of herself of which, she noted, there were precious few. Most of the images were familiar, people and places common to them both, but at the back of the drawer she found a manilla envelope and she spilled its contents onto the desk top. Some of the stills were black and white, others in washed out colour. There were faded sepia pictures of his parents which she had never seen before and she registered the pin prick of annoyance that he should have kept them from her. There was a photo of Oliver as a teenager, leaning against a racing bike, his trousers tucked into his socks and another of him beaming at the camera wearing a chef's toque.

In the background she heard Gordon arrive, his familiar call of her name coinciding with the turn of his key in the lock. She shouted his name and he followed the sound to find her at Oliver's desk. He kissed the top of her head and looked around at the chaos of papers and pictures.

'My, you are having fun,' he said, waiting for her to tell him more. Without turning around she told him of her conversation with Jean-Paul Patrese. 'He thinks he has seen him. Outside *her* apartment. He thinks, can you believe it, that Oliver might have survived the crash because he went through to the first six carriages before the tanker crashed over the bridge. The little bastard could still be out there.' She spat out the words as she swung round on the typist chair. 'Even though I have just received the official notification of his death from the insurance company, damn it.' She thrust the letter at Gordon.

It was almost impossible to make Gordon angry and he marvelled at the venom being expressed in front of him. 'And now you want to find him,' he said calmly picking up a torn section of the aircraft carrier and turning it over to see Karyn's signature.

'I didn't know I hated him so much,' she replied, taking the fragment from his hand and throwing it away. Once again she swung around in the chair, so that her back was to him. He stood up and put his hands on the top of her back, massaging her shoulders and he felt her head arch back towards him in an unmistakeable gesture. He leant down and kissed her ear, his hand undoing the buttons of her shirt. She was wearing a silk bra in diagonal mauve and black stripes which barely covered her nipples. Without turning, she manoeuvred the chair half around so that she could see herself in the mirror. She watched Gordon slip her breast out from its silk container and spread his fingers around her nipple. As she pushed the chair back, the wheels ran over the remains of the battleship and she felt the bulk of Gordon's erection at the back of her head. In the mirror she could see him release his penis and move it around to her mouth. It was like taking it in duplicate and as she drew it into her open mouth, she watched herself. Gordon's head was cut off above the mirror, so all she could see was his midrift and her head moving forwards and backwards, pausing now so she could see the tip of his shaft around her lips. She was wearing tight black slacks which she now unzipped and pulled down to her knees. She pushed him away and sat on the edge of the desk, lifting her legs so that she could see that part of herself reflected in the glass. Gordon now blocked her view as, pushing her knees against his chest, he entered her. Photos and cuttings were trapped under her body, or floated to the floor. The plate that Oliver had won as Restaurateur of the Year was pushed off the edge by Sonya's outstretched hand and if Gordon didn't hear it break into pieces, Sonya took a certain erotic thrill in its destruction. She was traducing all that was Oliver's, marking his territory as a cat would squirt her scent amongst the bushes. She looked down in pleasure as Gordon moved in and out of her, seeing the photos rucked up underneath them, soiled and crushed by their passion.

Afterwards she sat, her legs brazenly apart, as Gordon brought in glasses of wine to the dishevelled study. She was looking at a photograph which she exchanged for the wine which Gordon now offered her.

'What do you think of that?' she asked.

'I think it's wonderful,' he replied, looking at her sprawled in the chair. She smiled and brought her legs together.

'It's an early picture of our hero,' Gordon continued, examining the photo. 'It seems to be a little damp. I wonder why?' He smiled at her and added, 'I didn't know he was a chef so early.'

'He wasn't,' she said. 'I think this picture was taken on one of the *stages* he did in the early days in France. I wish I could remember where it was.'

'Well, it shouldn't be difficult,' said Gordon, 'with a magnifying glass, at least. Do you have one?' She got up and left the room and he watched the smooth white rounds of her bottom moving away from him. He leant over to switch on the computer. She returned and gave him a magnifying glass with a malachite handle. 'In the window behind the group there is a brass menu holder. It looks like it might have a name on it.' He slid the glass over the top of the picture, moving it until the focus was correct. 'Mmm . . . almost,' he said. 'I can see Restaurant de L'A and then it's lost. Underneath I can just make out St Ri, but no more.'

'Wait,' said Sonya, stretching over the desk, her back to him, so that Gordon could just see the tufts of pubic hair at the apex of her legs. 'Got it.' She handed him a postcard. He looked at a picture of an ancient white building outlined against trees which rose on a hill behind. He turned it over. The card was blank but for the title: L'Abbaye de St-Riquier. Gothic. Picardie.

'Who knows?' said Sonya, pulling on her knickers. 'But let's try.' As she left the study, she picked up the torn halves of Karyn's postcard to Oliver. After she dressed, she put them in her wallet, permanent fuel for her anger.

*　　*　　*

Sonya flinched as the trains crossed at high speed. Seconds later, her view was restored towards the low unenclosed fields criss-crossed with tracks which disappeared and reappeared with the rise and fall of the land. Her face was passive and contained since she now had a purpose and was doing what she liked best, employing her logic in the pursuit of a goal. Oliver was no longer a husband, he was an object, a prey, in the process of becoming the sort of document she prepared on the companies she traded, devoid of emotion, stripped of conjecture, cold and precise.

Sonya was a pragmatist. It did not concern her that four hundred people had been killed on a similar train only a few weeks ago. This would not be her fate and her imagination was closed tight against the images that might have assailed another traveller. In her mind, the fact that the crash had happened so recently made the chances of a similar accident that much more remote. That Oliver had escaped was all that pre-occupied her and she now tried to put herself in Oliver's place in the days that followed the disaster. She knew her husband was a creature of habit, finding comfort in familiar routines and places. She knew also that he had removed no money from his account, although she had no idea if he had any money on him at the time of the accident. He could not have planned to disappear, this much she knew, so she doubted he would have had funds to survive for long. So, unless he took to crime, he would need to work. Unless, of course, he was being funded by Karyn, the very thought of which made her tap the table in front of her with impatience. No, she could not allow this thought to impede her. For now she was satisfied that the only way Oliver was surviving in France was by working.

And the thing that Oliver did best was cook.

They took the local train to Amiens where they hired a car and Gordon followed the N1 before turning towards St-Riquier at Ailly-le-Haut-Clocher, its church tower dominating the land-scape. Apart from the Abbey, there seemed nothing remarkable about the small town of St-Riquier, south of the Forest of Crécy. Gordon had a Michelin Guide open on his knee and he told her that it was, nevertheless, famous for its restaurants boasting at one time, perhaps the time Oliver was here, Gordon added, no less than two Michelin-starred restaurants. Sonya knew that he had been here. It was the sort of place he would have liked. She shuddered at the thought of having to live here, wrapping her camel coat more firmly around her body.

She thought this part of the expedition would be simple, but before she entered the first restaurant she hesitated. She held in her hand the photograph of Oliver wearing the toque but another instinct in her told her to be cautious. If Oliver had worked here he would have done so illegally, as a dead man. In a town where everyone knew everyone else, tracing him might be simple but exposing him and thereby herself, she might regret.

'I am a freelance journalist writing about the extraordinary history of food in this town', she asked in the first restaurant. 'Can you help me locate where this photograph was taken, please?' An elderly waiter, who had read any number of articles on the local restaurants, directed her further up the main road with a wave of his thumb. She arrived at Au Fil du Temps still uncertain how her questioning would unfold. Lunch was over and, but for a plume of smoke rising from behind the bar, Sonya might have assumed the place was empty. The cause of the smoke looked up as she entered. Sonya saw a once handsome man with a face run ragged by life under a jumble of grey hair, looking at her over a pair of reading spectacles. She introduced herself as she had done in the other restaurant, but kept the photograph in her pocket. The opportunity to talk about food and his days of glory brought Bernard Chichilian out from behind the counter with half a bottle of wine and two glasses.

He spoke eloquently about the heyday of the town when, once upon a time, it had two restaurants holding two Michelin stars each and in desperate competition with one another to be the first to win the nigh impossible third. 'Of course,' he said, with a shrug of modesty, 'in my first restaurant I only ever achieved one star but I have to say my cooking was *pas mal, pas mal.*' He looked over to her now with a tired smile and added, almost as an afterthought, 'and we have just won our first star here. But that is another story.'

Sonya decided now was the time to show him the photograph. 'We found this picture in the archives,' she told him, 'and we believe it was taken outside what was probably the Restaurant de l'Abbaye some years ago.' He took the picture and regarded it through a haze of blue smoke.

'Yes,' he confirmed. 'This must have been taken fifteen or twenty years ago. It had two stars right up to the death of the chef, *le patron*, Guy Samartin. Sad, really. It went downhill after that and then changed its name to Au Fil du Temps shortly before I bought it. Perhaps,' he said, glancing behind him towards the kitchen, 'this place is bad luck for chefs.'

He turned back and looked down at the picture. 'And who is this man wearing the toque, I wonder,' he said, holding the photograph closer to him and pushing his glasses back up his nose. 'A good chef is hard to find. Believe me, I know.' He took another mouthful of wine and swilled it around his mouth before swallowing it with a grimace.

Sonya let him wander on, not clear where the conversation was heading.

'It's like a law,' he continued. 'All chefs have problems. Take me. It was drink. OK, I have wine, yes, but before it was wine and brandy. And that was before lunch. If it's not drink, it's women, or drugs, or all three. The chef who's just walked out on me was brilliant but he had so many problems he couldn't even begin to tell me about them, or even who he was. Oliver Cobden he said. Ha! He wanted cash and no questions and a life on the black. That wasn't difficult for me. And then he was gone. I was hurt, I tell you. But maybe this is just another chapter for your history of St-Riquier.'

At first, Sonya did not realise the significance of what Bernard Chichilian had just told her and when she did she had to control the way she asked the next question. 'What, he just upped and left?' she inquired casually.

'Yes,' the old chef said, ignorant of the fact that the woman opposite was now leaning forward anticipating his answer. 'He left me a note saying he would never forget what I had done for him and that one day he would explain everything. But I doubt I will ever see him again. Here, I'll show you.' He returned to the bar and found the letter and handed it to her.

Sonya looked down at the handwriting she knew so well. 'How long ago was this?' She asked her question as lightly as she could. Bernard Chichilian glanced down at his watch.

'About this time yesterday,' he said simply. 'But where he went is anyone's guess.'

Sonya had the familiar feeling rising in her chest again, a barely contained frustration at being thwarted. 'But he must have lived near here. Perhaps he's there?'

'No, it was just around the corner, but it was bare. He'd just packed up and gone. Like he never existed, really.' Sonya stood up suddenly and held out her hand to thank him. Bernard Chichilian was surprised that she wanted to leave so quickly. He was on the point of opening another bottle. He watched her move towards the door, admiring the shape of her body under the cashmere coat and saw her come to a sudden halt.

'Jesus Christ,' she said. Staring at her from a rack of newspapers to one side of the front door was the face of Karyn Baird. 'That bloody woman.' She snatched the magazine and held it in front of her before turning to the article inside, not really reading but flicking furiously though the pages. She looked back at Bernard who was watching her from the table.

'Can I borrow this, please?' She was already rolling it up and stuffing it into her pocket so Bernard's response was not really necessary.

'Certainly,' he said, puzzled at her behaviour, but she was already half-way through the door.

'Goodbye,' he said to her back as he lit another cigarette.

Gordon was waiting for her in the car. He had tuned the car radio to a French classical station and was conducting with his finger the slow movement of Bach's D minor Double Violin Concerto when Sonya opened the door. Her mood was in direct opposition to his.

'He was here,' she told him furiously. 'The bugger was here all that time, working as a chef, can you believe?' He could and he waited for her to continue, watching the by now familiar route of her anger. 'And I think I know where he has gone.' She tossed the magazine at Gordon. He looked at the front cover and then glanced back at Sonya as she climbed into the car. They spoke together.

'Karyn Baird.'

PART THREE

Dessert

Chapter 20

She was black, with large eyes and a pig-tail, and she carried across her arms a sub-machine gun which she cradled like a baby. Welcome to Paris. Oliver's arrival at the Gare du Nord brought him yet again face to face with his anonymity, the end of a journey on a ghost train that was three months late. He was once again under scrutiny and the black face of the policewoman followed him closely as he slowly made his way up the platform, his resolve of three hours earlier now draining from him just as the damp Paris night seeped into his clothing. The station was claustrophobic; the indiscriminate cameras all around, the press of people against him and the metallic ring of the public address system above the trapped rumble of half a dozen powerful diesel engines. It was the chance failure to arrive at this terminus which had catapulted him into retreat and now, having finally arrived, he felt half-way between shedding his old identity and emerging with his new. At one point the journey had felt like a metamorphosis, the speed of the train frightening him as it hurtled through the night. He had gripped tightly to the retractable arm of his seat and when the express plunged into a tunnel, the sound in the carriage suddenly closer and more intimate, he put his hands to his ears in expectation of the worst. He had looked along the walkway between the seats towards the entrance to the next car imagining only too easily it tearing open to reveal a night sky full of red and orange flame. The train emerged from the tunnel and he breathed more easily, sucking the air in through his nose and feeling his heartbeat return to normal.

By the time the train reached the Gare du Nord he had regained his composure.

But, for all his resolve he still hesitated, wanting to be in charge of this next phase of his reincarnation and sensing that, at midnight, it would not be wise to confront the catalyst of this change with his resurrection. So, still not having sloughed off his temporary identity, he signed into to a small hotel near the rue La Fayette, still as Oliver Cobden and, in front of the porter, added the number of his passport in the required box, making just two small errors. He paid in advance, saying that he had to depart early in the morning, too early for breakfast. He was left with just forty euros in his pocket with which to finish one life and start another.

The following morning, a bright blue day at the beginning of December, he walked down through the Marais, a marsh of boutiques and cafés, towards the river. The balconies of the upper floors were lit golden by the low sun and for a city at the endless mercy of the motor car, the air was unusually sharp and clear. Oliver, carrying his bag over his shoulder, could not compose the script for his opening exchange with Karyn. He stopped in front of Notre Dame and watched a man on the end of a bright yellow scissor-arm scrub the pigeon droppings off the head of Charlemagne, frozen massively on horseback and flanked by his foot soldiers. All around, as if in some new Nazi salute, irregular groups of tourists held their cameras out in front of them to record yet further images of the two gothic towers. Oliver had read that it was impossible to see Paris for the first time since no city offers so many images of itself in advance. We go, thought Oliver, to reaffirm what we already know. The carved saints, high above the twin entrances to the cathedral, lined up like footballers in a defensive wall, paid no attention to the rash of tiny flash lights.

It occurred to him that he had never been to Paris with Sonya, a fact he wrapped around him like a security blanket. When they had first met she had taken him several times to Vienna. She would make decisions unilaterally and he was more than content to exist in the slip stream of his decisive wife. He did not inquire how she knew the city so well and she did not volunteer the information. It lay between them, like so much else, unspoken. Vienna, darker and more introspective than Paris, he learned to admire rather than love. It didn't share itself like Paris, a part of it buttoned up like a reserved and discreet bank manager. Nevertheless, he had gone along with her, been happy to be escorted here and there. He grimaced at the memory and now, with the bulk of Notre Dame looming behind him as if demanding an explanation, he was compelled to examine why he had been drawn into a relationship with Sonya in the first place. To say there was a strong physical attraction would be to offer a smoke screen to the truth, he realised. Sonya provided a series of answers to questions which Oliver had yet to ask. By the time he realised that these weren't the answers he was looking for, not because they were untrue but because he had neglected to offer his own questions in the first place, the gradual erosion of his own life was well under way.

A *bateau mouche* grumbled under the bridge in the narrow passage to the south side of the cathedral, the close proximity of the embankment walls reflecting upwards the noise of the big diesel engines. His discomfort had been like this, a low level unease not dramatic enough to acknowledge, nor strong enough to address. He unwittingly accepted the status quo. But Sonya had changed in direct proportion to his success. It was as if, when they first met, she had discovered his local celebrity and been part of its promotion but as soon as it had its own momentum, carried forward by the recognition of other people, she drew back from it. And, at the same time, she withdrew her sexuality and used it sparingly with him, as a negotiating device. He never could see the whole Sonya and in many ways he had never wanted to. Steadily she became even more autonomous, their twin lives even more defined than ever.

Across the Pont Neuf the land began to rise and Oliver climbed up towards the Luxembourg Gardens, keeping to the east, away from Karyn's apartment and La Mission. For all he knew, Karyn could be walking a hundred paces ahead of him, or along a parallel street. The very idea increased his anxiety and he quickened his step as he crossed the rue des Écoles, the strangely anonymous dome of the Pantheon high in the sky to his left and entered the Gardens. The heavily pollarded sycamores were at their worst, barely hanging onto the last of their long brown limp leaves. Oliver sat down between the Queens of France, the black and ugly stump of the Montparnasse Tower looming to the south and the tip of the tapering Eiffel Tower beyond the trees ahead of him, across the round pond. Joggers and children, dogs and tourists, police patrolling the back of the Senate, came and went as Oliver began his announcement to Karyn that he was still alive. She was on his knees, looking up at him and he placed the paper gently over her face, before taking a pen from his pocket. For the passers-by he was just another visitor to the Gardens, transported back to the eighteenth century by its curves and statues. Oliver was surprised how quickly he finished, but what he had put down had been distilled over the previous twenty-four hours, if not three months. He slipped the paper into an envelope, stood, nodded upwards at Queen Beatrice, and walked towards Karyn's apartment. He knew it was a risk but he assumed that she would be at work. Even so, he waited opposite the green door with the message clutched in his right hand, the bustle of Paris dead to his ears.

*   *   *

Sonya was made for driving in Paris, forceful, unyielding, unafraid and able to swap the rudest gestures with the most committed French taxi driver, which she now did as she swung into place de la Concorde, the wide open spaces of cobble alive with the criss-cross of cars. Gordon, as impassive as ever, trusted her judgement, in matters of driving at least. He understood perfectly her need to establish whether her husband was alive, but the fierceness of her resolve had quite surprised him, as much as anything ever did surprise him. In St-Riquier they had debated driving to the Pyrénées but Sonya quickly dismissed the idea. Oliver would go to find Karyn in Paris and the very idea that he might be with her already was reflected in the unforgiving way she was driving.

'And you think he will be there?' Gordon's question came at the end of a long silence following an impassioned outburst from Sonya accusing Oliver of deception and selfishness at which Gordon could merely raise his pale ginger eyebrows. 'He will go to her, I know it,' she said firmly as she handed him the address which her PA had found weeks ago before Karyn's visit to her. 'It's somewhere in the 6th.' That had been half an hour earlier and with a map open on his knee, he had led them to the Pont de la Concorde and the boulevard St Germain, which would lead them up to St Sulpice.

'Even if he got there before us,' she said, not really replying to Gordon's question, 'they will come back.'

'And then what?'

She glanced at him as they waited at the pedestrian lights in front of the National Assembly.

'I don't know. I don't know.'

This was not the Sonya he had met over drinks almost a year ago, although her startling physicality remained unchanged. She was wearing a skirt and he looked at her legs as she lifted her foot off the clutch, her calf and thigh muscles clearly defined as the car pulled away from the lights. Her face was similarly spare, a fine, narrow nose and small mouth and shortish hair pushed back behind her ears so that, even after a three hour drive, she looked as though she had just stepped out of the shower. He had been drawn to her instantly and it amused him to think that he had been invited to the party as a 'high worth individual' but afterwards his value to her was marked in something other than money. There had been a certainty about her, a directness which afforded him a perfect harbour for his practised indifference to life. There were no great declarations of love. Their importance to each other was secretly acknowledged, like a gentleman's agreement. Both had an amoral approach to life, a sliding scale of right and wrong depending on how it suited them. It was just the merest of concerns for Gordon that the absence of Oliver had disturbed the apparently simple equation and that Sonya was still seeking the answer to the puzzle.

'Where'm I going?' she demanded, as if in echo to his thoughts. He directed her up the boulevard to the ancient church where they turned right into the rue des Rennes. Gordon gave her two more instructions and they nosed into the narrow street where Karyn lived. He was watching her face again and he realised it reflected no concern, merely an intense concentration. Suddenly he was thrown forward towards the windscreen, the snap of his seat belt restraining him from colliding with the dashboard.

'Christ. There he is.' Sonya's statement was cold and clear and was spoken over the short, resistant squeal of the tyres.

Gordon would not immediately have recognised the figure hunched up under the trees on the pavement perhaps fifty metres away, but as it looked towards the noise the car made, he could see it was Oliver. Gordon had to admit that he felt just the tiniest hint of pleasure that this man, the husband of his lover, was indeed alive and that, by some miracle, he had survived the awful accident. The moment was fleeting, for Sonya cut into his thoughts with a commentary on what Oliver was now doing.

'He's crossing the road. Someone is coming out of the door. He's gone in.' There was no sense in her tone of voice that she felt relieved to see Oliver alive, quite the opposite. They both stared in silence at the green door. Moments later, Oliver reappeared and walked off quickly in the opposite direction. Sonya pushed open the car door and was half-way out when Gordon put a restraining hand on her arm.

'Wait,' he said quietly, his calmness causing her to hesitate. 'Let him go.'

Sonya looked back, puzzled.

'I think he has just left Karyn a letter,' Gordon said simply. 'He was carrying an envelope in his hand which was gone when he came back. I think he hasn't seen her since the accident.'

Sonya banged her palms against the steering wheel and shouted.

'Well, why the hell should I sit here and allow him to do that? I want to stop him.'

Gordon supposed he understood, but nevertheless could not stop himself asking:

'Why?'

Sonya got out of the car and slammed the door, hard, before resting against the bonnet with her arms folded. He waited inside and listened to the gentle tick of the clock on the dashboard.

Sonya was remembering the time that her younger sister was given a pony. It was a Christmas that she would never forget and even now, a quarter of a century later, she could feel her stomach shift with the memory. Why should her sister have the pony when she herself had been denied one at the same age? The injustice created a poison which remained with her now and the sight of Oliver crossing the road to that woman's apartment had produced the same bile as her parent's betrayal of her all those years ago.

'No, Oliver,' she said to herself, 'you won't have what you want.'

She opened the door and said 'Wait'.

She walked slowly up the pavement, crossing to the side where she had first seen Oliver. And then she watched, just as Oliver had done. An elderly woman leading two smooth haired dachshunds, each wearing a rainproof coat trimmed in tartan, came towards her in stages, stopping at each tree for her dogs to explore. The two women nodded at each other as they crossed, the dogs pausing to sniff Sonya's feet. Sonya waited another fifteen minutes before a man carrying a thin leather briefcase stepped out of the door and even before he had time to shut it behind him, Sonya was calling to him from the middle of the road.

'Excuse me, *monsieur*, Karyn Baird asked me to leave something for her.' On hearing his neighbour's name, the man offered her a dignified '*bonjour*' and continued on his way. Inside, the stone hallway led through an open arch to a courtyard within at the centre of which a stone fountain quietly filled the space with sound. Sonya found the light switch and looked around the lobby to discover, just to the left of the door, a series of open pigeon holes marked with apartment numbers. Sonya took a masochistic pleasure in this next stage, pulling the white envelope from its wooden slot and holding it in her hands. She was quite calm as she reflected on what its contents might be. It wasn't sealed and she carefully opened the flap and gently removed the single sheet of paper that lay within. Her eyes, prepared to see words, were confused at the series of lines in front of her, so she turned the paper upside down to be sure. But it had been the right way up and as she turned it back again she could see the strange cartoon. It showed some sort of outsized cat sitting on the deck of a crudely drawn aircraft carrier. Underneath were the words:

'Sorry. The silence means nothing and everything. Let me take *you* to dinner now? Tonight or any night. I want to tell you something. And, yes, "look if you like but you will have to leap". X. Oliver.'

Sonya kicked the base of the pigeon holes, so that some of the letters shot out and scattered on to the tiled floor. She looked at them around her feet and stooped down to pick them up, laying them neatly on top of the compartments before gently putting Oliver's sheet back into the envelope and carefully returning it to its slot. She let herself out and walked back to the car.

'You're right. We'll wait. But she won't be back until later.

She'll be at work. Take me to the hotel.' All this was said to the windscreen.

*   *   *

Karyn stood in the middle of La Mission and breathed in the familiar mix of brick dust and dried cement. In the weak band of sunlight which filtered through the oriel window above her she could just make out the swirls of dust dancing in the late after-noon light. The building was eerily silent. Earlier that morning, she and her colleagues had been informed that all work on the restaurant was to cease and the project mothballed for the foreseeable future. There was a moment when she wanted to interrupt the announcement and shout, 'No don't! Oliver's still alive, he'll find a way out of this', but she couldn't and the sense of frustration and futility remained with her now. She had been asked to stay behind and make an audit of the assets and her hand now rested on the zinc bar, shrouded in milky plastic. 'Hurry up, Oliver, hurry,' she said quietly to the empty interior.

Karyn knew that Oliver would not come to La Mission to find her so now, as she walked along the rue du Cherche-Midi in order to buy a baguette, she looked at all the faces coming towards her wishing, expecting to see his smiling face. It was busy and the pavements along the narrow street were crowded with people, hurrying home, criss-crossing in front of her. So many people, she thought. What strange randomness makes any one of them more important than the other? What was the mixture that defined Oliver differently for her, made him unique from all the other men shouldering their way towards her?

She retraced her steps, baguette under her arm, passing in front of the church of St Sulpice where one of its twin towers was completely shrouded in scaffolding, masking its outline and upsetting its natural symmetry. She glanced up at its cockeyed appearance, feeling similarly lopsided and incomplete. The unlit church was sombre but opposite the windows of the shops, decked in red and gold and silver were alive with Christmas lights. '*Joyeux Noel*', they proclaimed but Karyn was not quite yet ready to join in.

It was dark by the time she turned into her street and wandered in and out of the pools of light to her front door where she hesitated, looking around, wanting Oliver to emerge from the shadows. She let herself in with one final glance up and down the street. At first she did not realise the importance of the envelope, marked simply with her name in capitals, but the moment she saw the drawing she could feel her body fill with warmth, as though her blood was suddenly alive, and for a second she leant back against the stone wall. She stared at the paper as she climbed the stairs to her apartment, smiling as she crossed her geometric hallway to sit at her kitchen table where she began to cry. Her tears fell onto the cartoon lynx and blurred the outline of the battleship but amidst the tears she began to laugh as she realised that in her hand was the first real proof that Oliver Dreyfuss was still alive.

She placed the tear-stained note on her mirror, sliding it into the frame and pressing it in place. She showered and washed her hair, coming back into the living room wrapped in a towel in order to look at it again. As she dressed, she repeated the small journey, each time adding another item of clothing until she stood, finally, looking at herself. She was a mixture of colours and patterns which, taken together, worked perfectly and complemented her simple good looks. 'I'm looking, Oliver. And I'm leaping,' she said to herself in the mirror.

Chapter 21

The men's room on the second floor of Bon Marché seemed a strange place for Oliver to spend the afternoon of one of the most important days of his life. At first he was absorbed into the anonymity of the large store, just another pre-Christmas shopper swept from department to department under a canopy of fir tree branches, tiny white lights and gentle music. Although the store was close to both La Mission and Karyn's home, he felt safe here as he wasted the afternoon hours wandering aimlessly around the carefully inoffensive interior. The store had recently been refurbished and the men's room was a subtle mix of pale stone and mirror, with diffused down lighters which did much to improve the pallor of his face and the grey lines under his eyes. He washed his face and looked more closely at himself in the mirror, aware of the tensions of the previous months and considered what he was about to present to Karyn. He was the part owner of a failing business, undoubtedly bankrupt, *sans domicile* and, if and when he was declared alive, an illegal immigrant. But these negatives were all on the outside. Oliver could measure them and decide on a course of action. It was the dormant part of him that now faced a challenge and his natural defences were down. The careful armour that Oliver had built around himself since an early age had suited the previous three months. He was adapted for this kind of life, neither giving much nor asking for help or guidance. He was well practised at self-sufficiency but what was about to happen next he could neither predict nor rehearse for. He wet his hand and drew the open fingers through his hair.

And he knew, even as he had these thoughts, that they were

the route of his downfall with Sonya, for she had never tried to penetrate that armour. She was a master of the art of deception, skillful at disguising her motives and, as he saw it now, able to justify all her own actions because she had her own rule book of morality. Sonya was only interested in herself. He was destined to learn nothing from her and, at first, he was happy to accept this. It was an abdication of responsibility. But what Oliver couldn't grasp intellectually, his body did naturally and when given the chance, it offered Oliver an escape route, one which he took blindly. Only now could he see the logic of it all.

He left the store on to the rue du Bac, heading towards the river, glad to be away from the press of people. Oliver's certainty that Karyn would come to the little restaurant where she had once taken him was an enormous assumption, he realised. In his mind's eye he could see the small bistro tucked down a cobbled passage barely visible from the main street but he took several false turns before he located it. Having done so and as the last light was drained from the sky, Oliver walked along the Seine, crossing the Pont Neuf to the Île de la Cité. He made for the westerly tip and sat on a bench looking down river, a chill wind blowing into his face. Karyn told him that she used to come here to think and he looked at the empty space by his side and imagined her there.

The Seine ran quickly left and right of him so that he had the impression of moving forward, a sensation emphasised by the headlights of the cars coming towards him on the Quai du Louvre. He sank his chin into the collar of his jacket, the captain of a ship with no rudder or power, adrift in the current. Behind him the great bells of Notre Dame cut through the wind and filled the evening darkness. A *bateau mouche* throbbed up river, brightly lit and full of Christmas tourists staring up and beyond him towards the cathedral. If Karyn was to come to the bistro tonight, he wanted to be there before her, so, stiff and cold, he retraced his steps back to the Left Bank, walking against the wind towards the Musée d'Orsay, crossing the wide plaza in front of the museum, doubt and hope fighting for position in his chest.

He hesitated at the entrance to the passage, the light from the bistro spilling on to the damp cobbles. The conflicting emotions of the previous months seemed to collide and congeal inside him. His desire to see Karyn was countered by his inability to form the words with which he would try and explain to her what he had been doing. And then, at the pit of his stomach, was the drag anchor of his guilt weighing him down. The walls of the passage loomed around him, pressed against him, compressing his thoughts so that the thinking part of his brain became paralysed and refused to make any logic from the contradictory messages it was receiving. Each step he took towards the oasis of light seemed slower and more difficult than the one before so that when he arrived at the window he was barely moving at all. He knew, without looking, that she was sitting alone in the restaurant and the feeling that rose in him caused him to reach out and hold on to the frame of the window. It was probably this movement that made Karyn look up from the book she was reading. He was incapable of turning towards her, his resources now totally diminished. He had reached the end of his powers of improvisation and denial. It was not only his feet that had stopped moving, but his whole being.

He was conscious of her standing, turning over her book to mark that page she had been reading and moving towards the door. He felt her take his hand and lead him back into the bistro and sit him in the chair opposite her. She still held his hand and he looked down at it now, aware of its warmth and stillness. His own hand was shaking slightly, reflecting the tumult that was rising inside him. He was frightened that movement or speech would cause him to act in a way he could not anticipate. He felt the tears behind his eyes and an enormous and ever expanding balloon in his chest.

'Oliver,' she said quietly, and he sensed the balloon move

further up his body and his breathing becoming shallower.

'Oliver,' she repeated. 'Hello.'

He looked up at her now and saw her dark eyes under her black hair and the small smile on her face. He could not speak and he dipped his head as his chest began to shake and the first tears fought their way through his defences. And now he could not stop as the balloon released itself through his mouth, causing him to make a strange and ugly sound. This is not what he wanted but he could do nothing about it as wave after wave of emotion rose through and out of him, his body jerking as he attempted in vain to stop the invasion. Through the blur of his tears he could see her watching him, the smile now wider, her hand not simply resting on his, but holding it. The night-light on the table under a dome of pebbled glass, increased the distortion of his tears so that Karyn appeared to him as an impressionist painting, a mix of colours and shapes, an illusion almost more real than reality. How long he sobbed he couldn't say, but as time went by he experienced a growing calm, as if his body had been emptied, the balloon expelled. He still did not dare to speak, though, not for fear of what he might say as much as what he might sound like.

'I knew you would come, Oliver. I knew you never went. Even in the beginning, I knew you were still here.'

His chest rose again, but his breathing was deeper now and he was able to nod his head and then look into her eyes and see her clearly.

'I cannot imagine what it has been like for you,' she continued, now placing her other hand on his. 'But I do know that you never died for me. Even high up in the Pyrénées you were still real to me, you were with me.'

'That's what did it,' Oliver said, surprised that he sounded so normal. 'I somehow knew that you were speaking to me in that photograph. How is that possible, do you think?'

'That's easy Oliver. It's possible because it was true. There was no point in the moment unless I could share it with you. And I did. And now you are here.'

He watched her as she spoke, his body suffused with a relaxation that he could barely recall experiencing before. It was as if he had shed more than just the burdens of the previous three months and had touched somewhere far inside himself that had remained lost for years. She had allowed him to cry in front of her without seeing it as a sign of weakness because she knew that this had been a necessary journey for him. How could he have taken so long to acknowledge what an extraordinary woman she was?

'I was running away, I suppose,' he said. 'The crash just accelerated the process. I barely thought about what I was doing in the immediate aftermath, I just fled.'

'No, Oliver. You weren't running away, you were running towards yourself, but you didn't realise it. I thank God that you escaped the accident not just because you are alive but because, strangely, it has brought you to this point with me, here.'

Oliver was astonished at her certainty, as if she had an infallible emotional route map in front of her. Other people had now begun to drift into the bistro and he wondered if she had stage-managed the whole evening, allowing him time alone with her to cry before the others arrived. As if to make the point, Patricia come over to their table and without saying anything placed two drinks in front of them.

'So, welcome back,' said Karyn, raising her glass. He lifted his glass and held it against hers. He wanted to embrace this moment for as long as he could.

'I'm sorry,' he said, 'that I could not, or did not, or was unable to tell you what had happened. I cannot explain it . . . .' She was about to reply when he held up his hand and continued. 'It has taken me over a year to recognise something that happened the first time I met you. I fell in love but did not know what it meant.'

Karyn's tears were quite different from his. At first they lit up her eyes and then one or two tears, no more, ran down her left cheek and around the large crease made by her smile, to disappear in the corner of her mouth. Only then did they clink glasses and for the first time in as long as he could remember, he felt safe.

Later they walked back up the rue du Bac, across the boulevard St Germain towards St Sulpice, a route they had taken several times before, but never like this. He walked slowly with Karyn's arm tucked in his and his bag slung over his other shoulder. Oliver felt exhausted and elated by turns, wanting nothing more than to be contained in this moment. Somewhere he registered that they were going back to Karyn's apartment but he did not allow his imagination to run any further than the comfort he felt now. He knew there were a thousand questions to be asked and answered but unlike the denial he felt when he worked in the restaurant, or even, as he now acknowledged, in his previous life, he felt equipped to deal with them. Nevertheless, Oliver felt strange to be walking towards the green door to Karyn's apartment. He was about to tell her this when he was suddenly blinded by a fierce white light which made them both shield their eyes and move apart. It took Oliver several seconds to realise that they were in the main beam of a car's headlights. There was a similar delay in comprehension when he heard his name called out. The familiar tones came from another life. But, beyond the lights, he was staring into blackness.

*   *   *

Sonya opened the car door and moved towards the front of the bonnet. The two figures in front of her were revealed in a harsh white light and behind them their shadows were cast high across the fronts of several buildings like giant graffiti.

'So there you are Oliver. Not quite as dead as you have lead us to believe.' Sonya felt calm again now, in charge of the situation.

'I see you have been enjoying the evening in the company of *Mademoiselle* Baird. How very nice of you for letting me know that you are alive and well and taking in the joys of Paris. It was most considerate.'

'Mrs Dreyfuss, would you please turn off those lights. This is not necessary.'

'Don't you tell me what is or is not necessary, Karyn Baird. Remember, you are arm in arm with my husband.' Sonya spat out these words, her eyes fixed on Karyn who now moved against Oliver.

A thin drizzle had begun and it drifted and whirled in the headlights. 'I think we should talk about this in my apartment,' she heard Karyn say and the very reasonableness of her voice grated on Sonya and caused a vicious and immediate response.

'No. I'm not here on your terms. You are here on mine. So listen. I want this little affair of yours to end. Now.'

She saw them turn to one another and a feeling of impotence flooded through her. She stepped two paces back to the car, flicked off the headlights and then moments later put them on again. She knew they would have been overwhelmed by darkness and then blinded again with the light.

'The situation is simple. Are you listening? Oliver, you have been committing deliberate fraud. You are a bankrupt and you wanted to escape your debts. And you have been having an affair with one of your colleagues. And you wanted to avoid the consequences. You were conveniently offered the opportunity to do both. And you took it. You have been working illegally in France and you have deliberately deceived your family and friends. It won't look good, Oliver, believe me. You can't afford lawyers and I can.' She turned off the headlights as she finished. In the darkness she heard Oliver's voice for the first time in months.

'Would you answer me a question, Sonya?' His voice was small and he did not wait for a reply. 'Were you, are you, glad that I am alive? I need to know. Out of curiosity.'

Sonya's eyes had now adjusted to the darkness and she could see the shapes of Oliver and Karyn standing by the entrance to the apartment block. Her voice was slow and deliberate.

'No, Oliver, I'm not. From the moment you took that train without telling me until now when I find you in the arms of your lover, your life, or lack of it, has been nothing but an irritant to me. Why should I be glad that you are alive to carry on deceiving me? Just consider your position, Oliver.' Sonya slammed the car door and thrust the gear lever into Drive and accelerated quickly away. Later, in bed with Gordon, she recounted the story but deliberately left out the thought that had occurred to her as she sped away into the Paris night.

*   *   *

Karyn listened with astonishment and dismay to Sonya's outburst which seemed both ridiculous and unnecessary and which had brought to an abrupt end an evening of extraordinary tenderness. To watch Oliver emerging from the tangle of the previous months enough to trust her with his emotions had profoundly touched her. She had not predicted how he might be, but now, afterwards, she knew that this was the only way and that his tears were as powerful as any words of love he might have spoken to her. How had Oliver managed to live with a woman so clearly unable to give any emotional nourishment? This was an easy question to answer, she realised instantly, for Oliver had never demanded this from Sonya in the first place.

It was in the darkness, listening to the threats from Sonya, that Karyn, on the point of condemning her for being hypocritical, realised that she was in possession of information that might hurt Oliver. He was unaware, as far as she knew, of the existence of Sonya's lover. As they climbed the stairs to her apartment she knew that this was not the right time to pass on the information. She unlocked the door and they stood together looking at each other. Without taking her eyes from his, she pushed open the door and watched him move in ahead of her. She heard the door click shut behind her and she sat on the wooden chair in the hall as he continued into the living room. She saw him look around, taking in his new surroundings before walking towards the mirror where he removed his own letter which she had tucked into the frame. She was peering around the corner as he came back towards her and offered his hand. She stood up and he leant forward and embraced her. She sank into his chest and felt his warmth. Minutes passed before she eventually led him to the sofa where she watched him sit, heavy with tiredness. She went into the kitchen to prepare him peppermint tea but when she returned she found him slumped and asleep. She took off his shoes and lifted his legs onto the sofa and later brought a duvet to cover him. She sat and watched him, his dark hair tumbling over his brow, his breathing deep and regular, his face still and realised that she had never kissed the lips of the man she loved. She knelt down by the sofa and softly, as if she was kissing a sleeping baby, put her lips on his.

Chapter 22

Somewhere in a vast house of many rooms a telephone was ringing, faintly at first and then louder and louder. Karyn felt the panic rising in her as she ran from room to room in a desperate attempt to find the phone before it stopped, for she was certain it was Oliver. And then the dream became a reality and she woke up, still half-believing that the ringing phone was in some distant room. Finally she picked up the handset by her bed which was pulsing with a dull green light.

'I wasn't sure whether *you* would answer or my husband.' Karyn hesitated, moving her digital clock from behind the pile of books on her bedside table. It was 3.40 a.m. She waited for Sonya to continue, as she knew she would.

'And I hope I didn't *wake* you. I thought perhaps I would. Now, where was I? Ah, yes. Oliver, *my* husband.' Sonya was speaking slowly, enunciating each word as though she was talking to a ten-year-old child with learning difficulties. 'Have you, Karyn, had time to think about what I had to say?'

From the moment that Karyn had first met Sonya she had detected a disturbing coldness which was masked by her disarming smile and undoubted elegance. There was about her a predatory quality which women detect in their own sex much more quickly than men.

'Do you want to see him destroyed, Karyn? For destroy him I will. If you walk away from him now, I will rescue his company and he can give himself up to the authorities. Post-traumatic stress disorder, I think they call it these days. You wouldn't want to spoil the chances of him getting back on his feet, would you? Think of what a celebrity he will be.'

There were so many things that Karyn wanted to say but she continued to keep her counsel, sensing that her words would make no impression on this woman.

'Cat got your tongue?'

Karyn pressed the red symbol on the handset and unplugged the receiver from the wall. She pushed the pillows up behind her head and lay there until the first grey light was visible through the crack in the shutters. She then carefully opened her door and saw that Oliver was still sleeping, on his back now, with his feet neatly together so that he looked like a marble effigy on top of a tomb, his face pale in the weak light of early morning. She showered, all the time wondering what to tell Oliver when he woke.

She was tiptoeing to the kitchen when she heard him begin to stir. She put the *cafetière* on the stove and when the smell of the coffee percolated through to the living room, she heard him call her name. She was wearing a silk dressing gown with a brightly coloured chintz pattern made of large, bursting thistles. Although she was naked underneath she knew this was not the time to make love to Oliver. That time would come.

'Karyn.' He called her name again and she pushed open the door with her foot, carrying two cups of coffee over to the sofa. 'Karyn,' he said again, 'you look beautiful.' She nodded and with small, Japanese steps and still holding the coffee cups, turned around in front of him. He was smiling now, remembering her little steps in La Mission in the days when he was falling under her spell and didn't know anything about it.

'How come it has taken me so long to realise that I loved you from the moment we met?'

' . . . and had to pretend to be dead for three months just to be certain,' she added as she gave him the cup. At this moment she knew that Oliver felt just as she did, that to make love, to even kiss, would be taking the stages of their courtship in the wrong order. As if to mirror her thoughts, Oliver reached for her hand and she sat on the edge of the sofa.

'I want to know what to do now,' he said. 'I want to know what *we* should do now, for I seem to have lost my bearings for the time being.'

'You didn't hear the phone last night?' Oliver shook his head. 'It was Sonya at about 4 o'clock in the morning wondering if she was waking me up. She told me that if I left you she would save your business and would tell the authorities that you had suffered from traumatic stress after the accident. You would be free to finish La Mission. And you could sell your story for lots of money. Simple.'

He pulled her towards him so that their faces were almost touching. 'I could no more go back to Sonya than fly to the moon. I think you will have to do better than that. I have been with you less than twenty-four hours and I've been asleep for twelve of those.'

'She won't let go, Oliver. There is something in your wife beyond reason. She's clever and she's cold. And she'll do what she can to destroy us not because she wants you back . . . ' Here she paused, 'but because she senses that you have something she doesn't. She's not sure what it is but she doesn't want you to have it.'

'So?'

'So,' Karyn stood up and walked towards the mirror and spoke to his reflection, 'my head tells me that we should go to the British Embassy now and explain what has happened.' Now she turned to face him. 'But my heart wants some time alone with you. We need to be away from here, from her.' She made a gesture with her head towards the window. 'For now we should think of us. We need to be a couple.'

It was a bright, clear morning and a thick frost covered the cars in the street. They walked across the Luxembourg Gardens under the stern gaze of the Queens of France, around the Pantheon, towards the market in the rue Mouffetard. 'Let us have coffee and be normal,' she shouted to him earlier, as he showered. 'We'll go to a café I know and watch the world go by.'

And so they now sat under a domed heater and observed an old woman in a voluminous overcoat shuffling between the stalls. Just visible were a pair of ancient trainers and around her neck was a grey, woollen scarf which covered her mouth and nose. Every so often she would stoop down and scoop up a discarded parsnip or mis-shapen carrot and almost in the same movement deposit these finds in the pockets of the coat.

'I imagine she might have been beautiful once,' Karyn told Oliver, 'the *belle* of the thirties with an apartment overlooking the park. Now she will go back to her tiny room over in Ivry and make a vegetable soup to last the week.'

Oliver picked up the story. 'She was married only once, to a race horse owner who gambled away his fortune and all of her jewellery and died young. She never replaced him and despite a string of suitors remained steadfastly single and loyal to him. She worked as a buyer for Bon Marché and now she barely gets by on the state pension and people ignore her. What a lot they miss.'

The old woman had disappeared into the crowd. There were crumbs of bread on Oliver's mouth, which Karyn brushed away gently. 'Well, make sure that doesn't happen to me,' she said and she could see Oliver coming back to life, his face taking on the softer shapes that she remembered.

'You know that photograph. The one of me toasting you up the mountains. I want to take you there, to a place away from here which is mine. I want to share it with you. In a way, it's where I want to start. I want some time with you before you become public property. Will you come?'

'I would deem it a great honour,' said Oliver leaning towards her and for the first time kissing her gently, his hand placed lightly against her face.

'For a dead man, Mr Dreyfuss, you have surprisingly warm lips.'

*   *   *

Sonya had booked a small L shaped suite at the Montalembert with a bedroom and a small sitting room off at right angles. It was from here that she phoned Karyn, holding the handset in one hand and swirling a glass of brandy in the other. When she returned to the bedroom Gordon was propped up and wide awake. She was wearing one of his shirts, done up with one button and on her feet were a pair of tapestry slippers she had bought that afternoon in a boutique in the rue St Honoré.

'I like it when you have that look on your face,' he told her. They had made love violently and noisily and she had left him asleep some time before dawn to walk over to Karyn's apartment. With a carton of coffee and a brioche she had waited until Karyn and Oliver emerged, hand-in-hand. She had followed them to a café in the Arab quarter where, just another shopper in the busy market, Sonya had watched them sit and talk. When he leaned over to kiss Karyn, she experienced the familiar anger fill her body. Sonya had a small digital camera and as his hand came to rest against Karyn's face, she recorded the image with an electronic click. She took other photographs of them as they retraced their steps, stopping at a bench in the Gardens where it appeared that Oliver was telling an amusing story standing next to a tall statue of a woman. Instead of returning to the apartment, she watched them make a diversion to a Europcar office in the rue de Rennes. She waited and after a while they emerged and crossed the road to a multi-storey car park where, shortly afterwards, they reappeared with Karyn driving a pale grey Renault Modus.

For a moment, Sonya panicked fearing she would lose touch with them but she saw the car indicate and turn down a street in the direction of Karyn's apartment. When she arrived there the car was parked not far from the green entrance and she called Gordon on her mobile and asked him to pick her up as soon as possible. She was going to make life as difficult as she could for the man she could now barely acknowledge was her husband.

* * *

The telephone rang and for a moment Karyn thought that it might be Sonya again and considered not answering it. Oliver was watching her and she decided she could always cut her off, so she picked up the receiver. It was Jean-Paul who, in typical fashion, launched into a series of questions. As he did so, she looked over to Oliver and put a finger to her lips.

'Have you had a visit from Sonya Dreyfuss? She promised to see me but she hasn't shown up. I just wondered if she had talked to you.' Karyn doubted that Sonya had ever promised a visit to Jean-Paul, but she could imagine Sonya using the television producer for her own ends.

'Jean-Paul, I'm just about to go out. Could I talk to you later?'

'Look, Karyn,' ignoring, as was his habit, what Karyn had just said, 'I told Sonya that I thought Oliver might still be alive and she was coming over here to find out more. I was sure she might have spoken to you.'

Karyn found it very difficult to lie so she told Jean-Paul that Sonya was in Paris and had called the night before. She felt strange talking to him with Oliver sitting opposite her and her apprehension was well founded.

'We're going to run with the story that there is a possibility that Oliver Dreyfuss is still alive,' he said excitedly. 'We may be wrong but at the moment we can't be proved right or wrong.' She was looking intently at Oliver now and at the frown which had creased his brow. 'Sonya was going to talk about her reaction to this. Would you be interested in contributing?'

'Let me think about it,' she said, hoping that this would make him stop.

'Well, we could talk about it over supper tonight. Are you free?'

She told him she wasn't and really had to rush and eventually she was able to put down the phone.

'Who was that?' Oliver asked immediately.

'That was a man who thinks you are still alive,' she replied. 'A man, a television producer I know, whose next documentary is going to show how you might have survived.'

'Was this man a boyfriend of yours?' She could see the anxiety in his face.

'He was not, Oliver. He would like to be but there was never a chance. How funny it is that this worries you and not the film he's making.'

'The crazy thing is, Karyn, I came to Paris to see you about a month ago and as I approached your door a nice-looking chap rang your bell and spoke to you in a very familiar way. I think he said his name to you. Jean-Paul. It knocked the wind out of me and made me realise how little I knew about you and how I could not take you for granted. I couldn't believe it. I fled. For a day I didn't know what I was doing. I can't believe it now, but then . . . .'

'Well, you're a fool Oliver. Which is why we need some time without people like Jean-Paul and your dear Sonya. But first I'm going to find out how much time we have got.'

Karyn called Jean-Paul back and asked him when the documentary was due to be finished. She assumed, correctly, that he would think that this indicated she wanted to take part and he told her that it depended on the interviews he got but it would be at least a month.

'We have two weeks,' she told Oliver afterwards. 'Two weeks in which to bring you back to life.'

Chapter 23

Before long it was quite clear that she was much fitter, climbing steadily ahead of him up a stony path under lugubrious conifers. Every so often he would slip on the scree underfoot whilst she seemed light and surefooted. Somewhere, beyond the dense canopy, he glimpsed the faint shape of the outstretched wings of a large bird slowly wheeling in the wind far above the valley. Every so often she would wait for him to catch up, watching expectantly as he drew level. She was smaller than him so just before he arrived their eyes were on the same level and he could kiss her without bending down. This was another stage in what he saw as the dance of their courtship, almost medieval in its formality.

He had been entirely in her hands as they left Paris and he had watched in admiration as she wove her way through the suburbs to the south of the city quite clearly following a route she had taken many times before. They had avoided the great auto-routes and stuck to the minor roads through the countryside, a succession of nearly empty roads which allowed them to fill in the stages of their lives to one another. Although he was aware that he had swapped one capsule for another, this one offered him a future. In St-Riquier, he was only interested in the present and to project his thoughts further than the actions in front of him produced instant anxiety which he combatted with yet further activity. With Karyn he was slowly beginning to glimpse the future, to look forward to tomorrow. As they drove on he would occasionally rest a hand on her shoulder, or she would take a hand from the wheel and place it over his. In one way their intimacy was complete. In another it had yet to begin.

They were completely engrossed in themselves and Sonya was banished and left behind, a relic of another life.

Ahead of him he could see the trees begin to thin and the ground slowly level out and soon they had emerged onto a small plateau. All around the mountains loomed and this small patch of open ground showed them how far they had come and what lay above them. Her face was more beautiful than ever, her cheeks touched with the cold of the morning, her eyes bright with the chill air and her short dark hair unruly as the wind came up from the valley and pushed it off her forehead on its way to suspending the buzzards above them. They kissed again and then, as they drank water and ate fruit, she told how she had first come to the Pyrénées and what the mountains meant to her.

'Sure, my father gave me the connection and I will always be grateful to him. But I now think I have claimed them for myself. And do you know why, Oliver?'

He shook his head and waited, for by now he knew that she said nothing by accident, or carelessly. There was a certainty and wisdom about her that took his breath away.

'Because,' she continued, looking out over the valley as the sunlight lit up the slopes in the distance, 'I know I can now give this to you to share. It is as if I have reached a point where I can release something of my father by sharing this with you. Do you understand?'

He knew precisely what she meant and he marvelled that this verbal commitment to him had come before the physical equivalent. 'You mean,' he said, looking out across the valley as well, 'that it is a way of leaving your father behind but not betraying him.' He felt her turn towards him and another part of their dance was complete.

Yesterday, as the night fell on the seemingly endless French countryside, Karyn had pulled into a small hotel just beyond Cognac. It was tall and somewhat weary and the room they were shown was the largest in the house with a high and slightly bowed ceiling, two enormous windows and, in keeping, a mahogany bed large enough for a family. They had eaten, alone, in the equally large dining room, lost in one corner surrounded by tapestries and imitation flowers. He had told her about Au Fil du Temps and how he had filled his days since the accident. He described the aftermath of the crash, speaking softly even though there was no one to hear, knowing that he should not hold back the shocking images. It was not easy for him and when he came to tell her of the women who had been in his carriage and the chance that had spared him but not them, he could not prevent himself from crying, not in the way he had in Paris but quietly and as he spoke. 'And, now, it is worse.' Karyn spoke softly and in a way that caused him to look up into her face. 'Not only were you spared when the others died, now you have this, me, us. You feel you don't deserve it and if I tell you that you do, it may not make any difference. It is difficult to escape this, Oliver. It will take time. We have time.' And now, again, Oliver wondered at her ability to understand what he was thinking almost before he did, as though she had seen a rehearsal of this scene earlier.

Their food came and went; there was no menu and the only decision they had to make was to choose between a *pichet* of red or white wine.

'I never thought once about contacting Sonya,' he had told Karyn. 'Sitting here now, I can see that the crash acted as a violent case of shock therapy, although, of course, I didn't see it that way at the time.'

'But now can I tell you something?' And he looked at her knowing absolutely that this exchange could not have taken place with Sonya and glad that, no matter what he had been through, he was certain of this. 'The moment I met Sonya I became a part of her life. Unquestioningly. I remember going to Vienna with her because she knew it well. I now find myself going to the Pyrénées with you because that is part of your life. I don't want to repeat my mistakes, Karyn.'

She returned his gaze. 'And did you cry in front of Sonya?' she asked simply. 'And did Sonya ask you about the places that mattered to you? Don't worry, Oliver, for whatever lay undiscovered in you by Sonya, we will find together.'

He knew that there was no question of them making love that night. This was in her hands and this added to his calmness. There was nothing to engineer, no cartwheels to turn, no strategies to devise. They were beyond all that.

They continued climbing and the trees became smaller and the open spaces more frequent and the wind colder. There was snow in patches all around them which he could see lay thicker above them. The path was now following a contour, with the mountain rising sharply to their right and dropping away steeply on the other side. He could see the line of the path ahead of them cutting across the contours up to a col and Karyn walked on to this distant point with the confidence of someone who had done it many times before.

Last night he had seen her body completely. He was bone weary when they climbed the creaking wooden staircase to their room and when she went to the bathroom he undressed and got into the bed. When she reappeared he watched her take off her clothes. She was not shy nor did she undress to tease him. Her body was that of a dancer except for her breasts which were surprisingly large for her frame. She was not the least self-conscious and although the room was cold, got into bed beside him naked. 'Well, Mr Dreyfuss, here we are. I am excited and I want to make love to you, but I want us to wait.' He was neither surprised nor disappointed. They slept facing each other and woke in the same position.

Although her body was shrouded in protective clothing she could not disguise the sway of her body and as he followed her he could see her naked as he had the night before. He recalled the mass of dark pubic hair which disguised the space between her legs and which she made no attempt to control. It was wild

and exciting and seemed to represent her, natural and uncon-
ditional. She was walking more quickly now, for although it was
only early afternoon the winter sun was beginning to touch the
tops of the higher peaks and would soon dip behind them completely. He knew that soon they would pass the point of no
return, if they had not done so already, but he trusted her knowledge of the mountains. And then gradually the scenery became
somehow familiar and he could see her slowing down. The path
came to a right angle because in front of them was a great chasm
with the steep hills opposite plunging into the dark valley far
below them. And then the images came together, her photograph in his mind and the reality in front of him. When she
stopped and turned and raised her right hand to him, both were
complete.

'Here's to you, Oliver. I wanted to have you here so much
then. And now you are. In the fairytales the lynx would now
appear behind me but this is not a fairy tale, this is reality.' He
kissed her then, with the wind tugging at their anoraks, rushing
in their ears so that in the end they had to pull apart, laughing, in
case it pushed them over the edge.

When they had arrived at the hotel in the mountains late the
previous afternoon he stood back as Karyn was greeted as warmly
as any daughter. He felt shy, an outsider to this world he was just
beginning to glimpse but he, too, was embraced with a bear-like
hug by the patron and his wife. Even before they were shown
into their separate rooms, they had sat down to a table of *foie
gras* and sweet Jurançon and their hosts toasted Karyn and the
success of her article on the lynx. 'Even during these winter
months,' the old man said, raising a glass of the yellow wine to
Karyn, 'we are full almost all of the time, thanks to you. But they
will never find the lynx. Only you have that eye.' The *foie gras*
had been followed by *sanglier* in a rich wine sauce and then
cheese and salad. It was late before they went to their rooms,
kissing on the landing. Early the next morning, Karyn arrived in

his room with two back packs each holding a sleeping bag and a thin, bright yellow roll tied up on the back. 'That's a therma vest,' she told him. 'You have to blow it up before you sleep on it.' He was lying in bed smiling at her as she pulled out a red anorak and modelled it for him, her figure lost in its bulk. 'This is for you,' she told him. 'So hurry.' They had left for the mountains half an hour later, following the red and white flashes of a *sentier de grande randonnée*, climbing out of the village and into the trees.

They left the point where she had taken the picture and she led him along the path for a further two kilometres or so with the light falling all the time and the clouds above shades of orange, pink and in the distance to the east, a more uniform grey. They were in the lee of the wind although it was still very cold and the patches of snow underfoot were frozen and crunched as they walked over them. The refuge St Antoine was a plain stone hut with two small shuttered windows flanking a studded wooden door which she pushed open. She flicked on the light and they were in a simple room with wood-boarded walls and a stove against the right-hand wall. Opposite was a simple work surface, a sink and a hob. But the most obvious feature, an enormous bunk bed, was directly ahead of them running the width of the room. 'These are the shelves for human beings,' she informed him. 'Welcome to our home for the night.'

He knew about refuges but he had never been to one. 'It's so immaculately tidy,' he said, walking around the room. Karyn explained that for half the year the refuge was looked after by a guardian but in the winter it was empty and used only for emergencies. She came over and put her arms around him. 'And this is an emergency,' she said. 'It is a matter of great honour amongst walkers,' she continued, 'to leave this place exactly as one finds it so the next visitors have as little to do as us.' She kissed him quickly and opened the door of the stove to find it laid with kindling. She took a box of matches out of her rucksack and lit the bed of paper. A large stack of wood was piled neatly by the side of the stove.

'Now,' she said, delving again into her pack, 'we have *soupe à l'oignon*' and she tossed him a packet, 'and cold *magret de canard*. And to go with it, some red wine.' She raised the bottle to him like a trophy. 'And some subtle lighting.' She placed a stubby red candle on the work surface. 'Tell me, do you want the top bunk or the bottom?' And then she laughed and they kissed again.

By the time the stove began to warm the room, the first snow was flickering down outside. It was dark and the light from the windows lit the irregular pattern of the flakes. 'I think now we will be alone,' she told him, looking out into the night and she went over to a cupboard built into the wall and took out several blankets which she spread in the centre of the lower bunk-bed. She took the lit candle and placed it to one side and then turned to look at Oliver. He watched as she undid her salopettes and stepped carefully out of them. Underneath she was wearing walking tights which she peeled off and he saw again the muscled legs. She unzipped the thin polo neck, crossing her arms to pull it over her head. She immediately unhooked her bra and released her breasts. All she was wearing now were small white panties which, while not taking her eyes from his, she flicked off and at arms length dropped to the floor. She walked to him and the warmth of her body astounded him.

When he entered her, he heard her inhale and then sigh and he looked at her face. She had an impish smile which widened as he pushed against her. He returned the smile, gradually feeling the boundaries of his body and her's disappear. He knew then that this part of the dance was not an end but another beginning and when they both came he experienced a peace so overwhelming that, even as he laughed he was crying and his tears joined hers and once again ran around her wide and smiling mouth. They lay there in silence, his hand on her warm, wet pubic hairs, his face against her cheek.

'Did you know it would be like this from the start?'

'Oh, yes, Oliver, I think I did.'

They ate and drank and watched the snow flakes, thicker now, tumble outside the window. Later they made love again and despite the formality of their courtship she gave her body openly without coyness. They slept arm in arm on the giant bunk bed as the candle burnt down and out. In the morning they opened the door and an intense whiteness stretched in every direction.

'How very appropriate,' Oliver said to Karyn.

Chapter 24

The screen was filled with a white flash.

'Too long. Needs to be a fraction shorter.' Jean-Paul sat in the edit suite, lying back in a swivel chair with his feet on the desk. In front of him were several monitors, some showing the same images. To his left was a young woman, his editor, whose fingers were running up and down a keyboard as though she were playing an organ.

'Why do you do that with your thumb along the keys, Chantal?'

'Why,' she replied, 'does it annoy you?'

'No. It just amuses me, that's all.' Her fingers continued to flick over the keyboard. 'Yes, that's much better,' he said, as she played the sequence to him again.

The white flash, now almost subliminal, exploded between two almost identical images.

'Now do that three times,' ordered Jean-Paul, 'so that in the end we're left with his full body.' Chantal tapped the keyboard and swept it several times with her thumb before he could review what she had done. She played the images to him. It was the CCTV footage of the six carriages which had survived the crash and the succession of white flashes separated a series of steadily less clear close-ups of the scene until the final image was of a heavily pixilated figure walking across the tracks. It was impossible to identify who it was, so distorted was the picture.

'That's great,' he said. 'Now show me the other stuff.' Chantal went into a different electronic bin and a still shot of Oliver Dreyfuss appeared on two of the screens. He was wearing a dinner jacket and his hair was long and shiny. Chantal animated the image and they watched as Oliver walked between tables of applauding people, up some steps and then across a stage to be greeted by a pretty blonde woman holding a large plate. Jean-Paul was not interested in the sound and he watched the sequence mute. He saw Oliver accept the plate, make a short speech and then turn to retrace his steps back to his table.

'I think that last piece should do it, but we'll leave it to the expert. Let's light this place now and I'll go and have a word with him.'

An hour and a half later he returned to see the scene transformed. A wash of sharp blue light spilled across the back of the edit suite. In the chair where Jean-Paul had been lounging, the cameraman was now sitting looking alternately between a camera on a tripod in the corner and at the small monitor on his lap. On the table was a laptop computer which was flickering.

'I'll have to adjust the shutter,' the cameraman told him, handing him the monitor and he got up to adjust his camera. Jean-Paul watched the monitor and saw the image of the laptop flicker at different speeds and then stop. He nodded approval and then sat in the seat. His head was back-lit with two monitors at eye level close behind him, one showing the still frame of Oliver on the tracks after the accident and the other an image of Oliver walking off stage at the awards. The laptop screen was placed down to the right side of frame.

'That's great,' Jean-Paul concluded. 'Let's get him in.'

Jean-Paul could only describe Dr Michael King as a geek, a large bulky American with a loud voice and pasty skin. He had invented MRS, movement recognition software, which had been used by the police in many countries. Jean-Paul regarded him as a geek because he had no real interest in the story that the documentary was attempting to tell, merely the cleverness of his own invention.

'If we play the close-up sequence of the figure on the train into the computer,' Dr King told Jean-Paul, who was prompting him from beside the camera, 'the software will detect specific movements and turn them into three dimensional grids. We've fed in the material from the railway line. Now watch.'

On the laptop a transparent figure made of green chicken wire appeared and was tracked across the screen. A little while later, after Jean-Paul had completed various close-ups, the American repeated the exercise with pictures of the awards ceremony. 'Although the camera is at a different plane once the movement is in the computer, it will adjust and compensate.'

Dr King's fingers pattered over the keys and moments later another green wire figure appeared. 'Now, this is the interesting bit,' he said, looking up for approval. 'We place the images one above the other for comparison. The software will match the pace of the two walks.'

Jean-Paul watched as the two artificial images mirrored each other across the screen. He asked the cameraman to give him a big close-up of the green men reflected in the Doctor's spectacles.

'But that's not all,' the expert continued once the camera had re-set. 'We can superimpose the two images.' And there, in front of him, the two outlines walked, almost as one.

'I'm as certain as I can be,' the American said with a self-satisfied smile, 'that the man in the CCTV footage and the one at the awards are one and the same person. But, of course, there is always an element of doubt.'

The following day, Jean-Paul took a crew to the vast marshalling yards in St Denis where he had permission to film in a train in one of the many sidings. Of the eighteen coaches, he concentrated on number eleven into which he put actors representing the passengers known to have been in that fateful carriage. At one table sat a group of women and diagonally opposite the actor he had chosen to play Oliver. He wanted to show how easy it would have been for Oliver to exit the carriage moments before the accident, leaving his mobile phone and possessions on the table. He would edit this sequence by distancing the voices and adding a single tone of music and inter-cut it with the

CCTV footage of the accident he had used in the first pro-gramme. And then, when the six carriages emerged unscathed from the carnage, he would use the montage of ever increasing close-ups of the figure leaving the train before introducing Dr King.

As the day wore on, the more confident he was that Oliver was still alive. At any point in the journey, he showed, the buffet car would have had at least two customers and usually many more. Some of these would have walked the length of the train to be there. The case for Oliver Dreyfuss having survived the crash was powerful, but it lacked one crucial element. Sonya Dreyfuss. Well, two, in fact. It would have been nice to track down Oliver Dreyfuss, as well.

He had been too involved with the filming to try calling her but now he brought up her mobile number. He was surprised when she answered. It sounded as though she was in a car, but he couldn't be sure.

'Hello, Mrs Dreyfuss. It is Jean-Paul.' There was no response and he listened to the atmosphere which could have been the interior of a car or the exterior of a quiet country lane. 'I wonder,' he continued, 'if you have given any more thought to appearing in my documentary?' Eventually she spoke.

'And why should I help make your career?' Jean-Paul was used to the suspicions of the public about television, but he thought that since he was attempting to prove her husband was still alive she might be more co-operative. He said something along these lines but she remained impregnable.

'I doubt that you do have my best interests at heart, *Monsieur* Patrese. I imagine yours coming somewhat higher up the pecking order. Nevertheless, tell me, do you have any more information?'

'I do but I want to interview you on camera about it. I don't want to tell you over the phone.'

'Ah, you make my point for me. If you tell me now, you will lose the moment of surprise or shock on my face and your film will be the weaker for it. Don't lecture me on self-interest, *Monsieur* Patrese.'

He tried to ignore this. 'Yes, we do have some powerful new evidence. The film is virtually finished and it is due for transmission in a couple of weeks. Your contribution, though, would make it complete.'

'Would be the cherry on the cake, you mean.'

He waited for her to continue but all he heard was the dull whine of a terminated call. He stood up and began walking along the carriage. Alongside the yard, all the walls had been covered in a rash of graffiti. Hardly a flat surface remained unsprayed. He went through into the next carriage, the buffet car and leaned against the bar and began to think about Sonya Dreyfuss along rather different lines. Maybe she wasn't just the victim of a dreadful accident. What if she was conspiring with her husband to pretend he was dead? When he had last spoken to her she had told him that their insurance company was satisfied that Oliver was dead and he presumed, therefore, that they had paid out on his life. He knew also that work had been suspended on La Mission. Was Sonya now on her way to see him carrying the cheque and to celebrate the success of their improvised deception? Jean-Paul wondered if he had been so interested in merely proving that Oliver was still alive that he had not considered what his motives might have been for not getting in touch with anyone after the accident. Perhaps his film was less complete than he thought. Instinctively he called Karyn.

'Karyn, it's me. Listen, I've just spoken to Sonya Dreyfuss and she doesn't seem the least concerned that I might have proved that Oliver is still alive. Don't you find that extraordinary?'

For the second time in a matter of minutes, Jean-Paul was surprised at a woman's response on the phone. He heard Karyn laugh. 'Oh, Jean-Paul, you don't waste any time, do you? Yes, thank you, I am fine and well. And how are you? Good. As to your question, no, it does not surprise me.'

Jean-Paul heard a lightness in her tone, as if she was smiling into the phone.

'Where are you?'

'I have gone away for a few days, Jean-Paul.'

He was disappointed. 'Listen, Karyn, we have further proof that Oliver almost certainly walked away from the crash. This is good news for you and the project at La Mission, isn't it? Won't you talk to me about that?'

'Oh, Jean-Paul, you're obsessed. Let me enjoy the mountains and I'll speak to you when I get back.'

And, again, he heard the line terminated. He went over to the window and watched a TGV slide slowly through a giant train-wash. A stubby diesel engine bustled by and the waste paper on the track rose and whirled in its wake. His instincts were alerted but like the tumbling rubbish on the lines, he was unable to make a pattern out of them. He knew, though, that his programme, even without the contribution of Sonya, would almost certainly produce a visit from the police. But, as a producer, he was fiercely protective of his material. He couldn't bear the thought that the police might then go on and find the missing pieces to this puzzle. His instincts as a journalist told him that somewhere in the swirl of information blowing around his mind was the clue that would take him further along the road to finding Oliver Dreyfuss.

He turned and stood by the door that would lead him back to carriage eleven. He imagined the scene that Oliver and the other occupants on the buffet car would have seen on that day four months ago, the smoke and flames and chaos from the stricken train at the bridge in the distance. He tried to put himself in Oliver's position as he walked along the tracks towards the inferno. What would the scenes have done to him? How would he have reacted? He had escaped death by chance, a few metres and a handful of minutes separating him from life and death. Whatever Oliver did next was not premeditated. It was improvised.

Or, perhaps, all this was part of his imagination and Oliver was burned to oblivion under a non-descript railway bridge to the north of Paris on a bright autumn day.

Chapter 25

Gordon had brought their hire car to pick Sonya up by Karyn's apartment and together they had followed the grey car through France. Sonya did not bother to try and examine or understand her emotions. Feelings of exclusion were alien to her and she refused to acknowledge them, preferring to interpret them as indignation and righteous fury.

'Why are you doing this?' Gordon asked her again as they maintained a safe distance behind Karyn and Oliver. She hadn't been able to give him an answer but she had no doubts about the pursuit. It was as if she was being driven along by some inner motor, a primitive animal instinct and the urge intensified whenever she saw Oliver and Karyn together. It was easy to follow them. Karyn's article in *Le Figaro* magazine had told her all she needed to know. Too much, in fact. The village high in the Pyrénées where as a child she used to go with her father and the little hotel, still run by the old couple whom she had grown to love. The image set Sonya's teeth on edge.

But she didn't want to lose them, she wanted to stalk them, watch them together. She knew where they were going and, once they had left Paris, she could second guess the route they were following. But it was more than that. Sonya could see, even from a distance, how involved Oliver and Karyn were, the way they were speaking, his arm occasionally on the back of her head as they drove. Not once did they look around. They were separate, in a capsule of their own. She hated them for it.

When they stopped in Cognac she saw him open her car door and when Karyn climbed out they kissed and she watched as he buried his head into her hair. Her hands had tightened on the steering wheel to the point of pain. This was not jealousy she told herself, far from it. Negative emotions would only slow her down. All she wanted was to regain the control that had once allowed her to guide Oliver one way or the other.

Next day, further south in the Pyrénées, up through the twists and turns of the mountain roads, she could feel the pressure increasing in her. Gordon had asked her on a couple of occasions what she intended to do, but she had been curt in her responses.

'He has used the accident as a way of continuing his relationship with Karyn and I don't see why I should allow this to go on,' she had told him crisply.

'But he couldn't have planned the accident,' Gordon replied calmly. 'And, anyway, I don't really see that you can prevent their affair, just as you wouldn't accept anyone trying to prevent our relationship.'

She couldn't tell him that her thoughts had run much further than his. She could not entertain that she was a woman scorned for Oliver had never given her any indication that he was dissatisfied. But then, she thought, yanking the steering wheel sharply to the right to negotiate a hairpin, neither had he expressed undying love. It was this neutrality she enjoyed, a safe middle ground which allowed her the freedom to do what she wanted. And now he had spoiled it all.

'Darling, I think you want to slow down. However much I like this countryside I would rather not be violently introduced to it.'

It had been easy to track the grey Renault up into the hills where there were so few auxiliary roads. The problem occurred when they came to the small village just beyond Vicdessos, after which a succession of *pics* rose to almost three thousand metres. The hotel was perched on the edge of a ravine so that its southern walls were merely an extension of the rock face. Sonya rounded yet another corner to see the Renault parked in front of the hotel. She pulled into a passing place and walked across the road where the edge was marked by black and white concrete blocks warning of the steep drop into the valley. She sat on one of the blocks, far enough away not to draw attention but near enough to see what was happening. She saw them climb stiffly out of the car and at the same moment she heard the cries of 'Karyn' as a portly man and woman came down the wooden steps of the hotel with their arms open. She saw Oliver stand back as they embraced Karyn, the old man waltzing her around the tarmac. And then Karyn introduced Oliver and even at this distance she could see the pleasure in her face, the proud way she looked at him. And when she took his arm as they carried the baggage into the hotel, Sonya kicked a stone and watched it plummet and bounce down the cliffside, the sound of its clattering descent gradually weakening as the wind took over.

It was as she drove back down to Vicdessos that her mobile phone rang. She could see from the display that it was Jean-Paul Patrese and she hesitated before answering it. She said very little but what she learned gave her a time-scale in which to work. It didn't matter to her what new evidence there was to show Oliver was alive for in two week's time the producer's film would be shown and Oliver would be on the front page of every European newspaper. And when he was found, he would have Karyn by his side. So this bubble of isolation they all found themselves in was about to burst. She drove on in silence aware of Gordon looking questioningly at her as she negotiated the sinuous turns back to the village.

They checked into a hotel with a wooden 'A'-shaped frame which, just beneath its peak, made the space for their bedroom. The views across the valley were stupendous but as Sonya stood looking out she did not see the high peaks on the horizon nor the patchwork green of the high plateau beneath her. She did watch the slow, drifting flight of a dark bird with a majestic wingspan crabbing high above the valley almost in line with her balcony. She admired the relaxed freedom of the bird, its haughty disdain of all around it, its singular grandeur. She imagined its eyes, round, cold, golden, as it patrolled its territory. And in that moment a realisation came to her which made her glance around at Gordon in case, somehow, he knew what she was thinking. She looked back and her eyes once again found the bird sailing on in the distance, unaware. A seed of an idea had planted itself in her mind and, as she would do in business, she was going to turn it this way and that to see if it was worth pursuing.

Gordon was lying on the bed, having kicked off his shoes and was reading a magazine about the high Pyrénées. She was less distracted now having once again given herself a purpose and a timescale. She took her small case into the bathroom and ran a bath, lying in the hot, foamy water as the idea marinated inside her. She washed, the warm water lapping over her breasts and allowing the soap to dip slightly into her vagina. By the time she was dried she was very aroused and she put on a pair of silk pyjama shorts and vest before returning to the bedroom. She could see Gordon watching from the bed and she deliberately bent down to put down her bag by the door so that he could watch her from behind. She enjoyed this overt sexuality, the voyeuristic glimpses of forbidden parts, the game of sex, predator and prey. She sat in a chair opposite the bed and picked up a book and pretended to read it. As she did, she raised her legs so that her heels were on the edge of the chair. Her blue silk shorts barely covered the tops of her thighs and she could feel that part of her vagina was exposed. She moved her legs and felt the focus of pleasure between her legs. She could hear Gordon unzip his fly and when she looked up from her book she said, in mock surprise.

'Oh, I didn't mean to disturb you.'

She looked back down at the book and heard him get off the bed. Without taking her eyes from the book, she felt him move aside the silk of her pants. Then the touch of his penis, probing her exposed vagina, just as it had done in Oliver's study. They both grunted together as he pushed it in further. She put her legs over his shoulders as he moved in and out of her and she sensed her wetness facilitating its passage. Making love to Oliver had been perfunctory, more prosaic and much less exciting. She wanted sex to be an adventure and she enjoyed the cameos she played with Gordon and his willing participation. He pulled out of her and she enjoyed him looking down at her, open and wet, anticipating his tongue and running the palm of her hand over her nipples. She felt his tongue around her clitoris, an intense pleasure filling every part of her body and she pushed against his face. And then she came again, her face reflecting both extreme pain and sheer ecstasy, her head bumping back against the chair. He now pulled her to the floor and she felt the weight of him on her and his mounting excitement. The shortening of his breath and the jerk of his body against hers brought another orgasm and she raised herself off the ground to extend the moment of pleasure for as long as possible.

He got off her and lay back on the bed. She remained on the floor, feeling his semen run down the inside of her legs. Her arms were outstretched and her legs open and she felt she had been pierced to the ground. The white light from the window was above and behind her, the intense sky bleached out and almost painful. She shut her eyes and told herself that sex between Oliver and Karyn could not be anything like this and with that very thought she shivered and realised the floor was cold and that the wind was beating against the balcony doors sending a draft through the room. She got into bed and drifted into sleep and dreamed of Oliver bounding up a steep slope like a mountain goat towards a distant figure on a hill-top. She never found out who it was, for she woke to find Gordon gently snoring besides her and a profound darkness outside her window.

Standing there at the window, looking out into the night and still wearing her silk pyjamas, Sonya realised that she was not dressed for the mountains. They had little appeal for her and the occasional skiing holidays she had taken with Oliver had merely confirmed her antipathy. She dressed and went downstairs and enquired of the concierge where she might buy suitable clothes for walking in the mountains. *Madame* gave her details about shops in Tarascon-sur-Ariège where she might shop tomorrow and as she did so she nodded towards a framed article on the wall.

'You may want to try and find one of those', she said with a strange accent tinged with Spanish. 'Lots of people come here since that was published in the paper.'

As she got closer, Sonya felt another wave of coldness sweep over her for she was confronted with the photograph of Karyn waving at a camera. The reactions she experienced were so strong that it was difficult for her to read the small type within the frame. It was the article she had taken from the restaurant at St-Riquier, with another one from a local paper. She skipped down the columns and soon got the gist: Karyn Baird was some sort of local hero for having photographed a Eurasian lynx which everyone had thought extinct in these parts. Her feelings of resentment towards them both became blacker. She wanted to smash the picture off the wall and might well have done if the woman hadn't been behind the counter beaming at her.

She gave a brief '*merci Madame*', before stepping out into the night. The cold wind almost took her breath away but it was the sudden blast that she needed to calm her down. She walked up to a bar in the small square where she ordered a cognac. On the wall a smouldering Johnny Halliday leered at her from astride a huge motorbike and on the juke box an incomprehensible French pop record churned away. She tossed back the drink in one gulp and ordered another. While waiting she looked above the bar where a series of animal heads stared at the opposite wall. There was a gnarled old boar, a couple of deer and a silvery fox.

'Do you like hunting?' The bar man handed her the drink as he asked the question. She looked up again at the trophies.

'Yes, I do. Very much. Thank you.' And in another single movement, drank down the cognac and, with a nod of the head, left the bar. She bent her body against the wind and walked back to the hotel, the clip-clop of her heels in the dark clear testimony to her anger.

The following morning she woke early, leaving Gordon asleep and drove out of Vicdessos towards the hotel where Karyn and Oliver were staying. An hour later, she had seen them leave and set off into the mountains. It was getting colder and she pulled up the collar of her camel coat as the clouds raced across the sky. She watched with growing distaste as the figures disappeared into the trees and she assumed they would be gone for the day. She turned and drove back down the tortuous road to Tarascon-sur-Ariège, a non-descript town hardly worth the hard work of getting there. But, being close to the tallest mountains in the Pyrénées, as she was told in the shop, she was able to pick from a vast array of the best protective clothing and boots. A rather charming man with closed cropped wiry hair and an equally spare face, helped her and was patient with her succession of questions. Perversely she started with the smallest item she needed and pulled over her head a soft balaclava which covered all but her nose and eyes. During the next half-hour she added all the other equipment which would enable her to walk at high altitude, close to the Spanish border. She was in search of the elusive lynx, she told him. 'You must be careful at this time of year,' the assistant had counselled. 'We have many who have come to see the animal and do not know how unfriendly the mountains can be.' She thanked him for his concern. Finally, she tried on a pair of walking boots before looking at herself in a full length mirror. She had zipped up the anorak and pulled down the hood so that only the whites of her eyes could be seen. The shape of her body was reduced by the over-trousers and several layers of lightweight clothing.

She was unrecognisable.

Chapter 26

For Karyn, her first step into the perfect bed of white snow marked the beginning of their re-entry to the world. The sky above her was sharp blue and the snow had covered and smoothed every surface so that she had to shield her eyes from the glare. She could not help but think that this moment was perfection but the very act of moving forward would spoil the scene, their footprints scarring the pristine landscape. The night on the mountain had been the closing of one chapter and the opening of another. She looked back into the simple room, as clean and tidy as when they first arrived and registered all the details, for it would be stored deep in her soul to draw on in the future. With small gestures of her hand she made the sign of the cross and said a quiet thank you to St Antoine. She felt Oliver come up behind her and with his embrace push her forward into the snow. He shut the door and took her hand and they walked into the whiteness. A hundred metres or so later, as the path turned behind a tall outcrop of rock, Karyn paused and looked back at the refuge. The scuffed snow marked their passage, two irregular lines side by side. A tremble of apprehension ran through her, at first an imprecise sensation, like a cloud blocking the sun, then a more nagging anxiety.

The snow had smothered nearly every trace of the path ahead of them and it was only the small pyramids of stone and the occasional red and white flashes painted on the rocks and her knowledge of the footpath which allowed them to begin the long descent. The going was difficult and she was thankful that she was familiar with the land. When, after a couple of hours, they stopped she could see that the colour had returned to

Oliver's cheeks and although he was breathing quite heavily, the steam rising from his mouth, she could see him beginning to regain himself.

'I think I could do this forever.' He laughed and launched his apple core over the side of the cliff. Then he looked at her and held out his gloved hands which she took between her own.

'But, I know, we have to come down from this mountain and resume normal service. It's just that the last few days have been such a blessed relief and joy I hardly want it to end.' He embraced her and she rested her head on his shoulder, looking over the valley to the soaring cliffs beyond which the snow had barely touched. The lynx, the nocturnal roamer of this windswept and isolated place, had managed to escape detection for years. And Oliver, too, had remained elusive for several months. But just as the world would surely catch up with the lynx so too would it press down on them. The conventional part of Karyn was eager to admit that Oliver was still alive and to go through the rigmarole of resuming life. But, now, another increasingly powerful side of her wanted to maintain this separateness, this splendid isolation which Oliver had created for himself and which she was now extending. Karyn could not shake off the shroud of uncertainty which had begun to grip her, an animalistic sense that danger was near.

'You're shaking.' Oliver looked at her and she could not hide the concern on her face.

'I was thinking, maybe I should keep you up here like the lynx,' she said. 'Keep you as far away from the world as possible. And then again I think, no, I want normality with you. But up here, alone, I just sense that the next stage is going to be more difficult than we imagine.'

'You even told the couple at the hotel to pretend I didn't exist and that you were up here to get away from things for a bit. But what's the worst that is going to happen? Sonya will accuse me of deception. We will divorce. La Mission will go to the wall.

But I'll have some money from the house and I still have the other restaurant. And then we have the future. I've begun to be able to glimpse it again, thanks to you.'

She saw the eagerness in his face, the very spirit that had drawn her to him in the first place. She smiled and pushed her doubts away, kissing his gloved hand before pulling him along the path.

*   *   *

'My dear, how frightfully unlike you.'

Gordon had watched her dress and she registered the frisson of sexual excitement she felt putting on even these clothes in front of him. She zipped up the soft polo neck aware that her nipples showed against the pale green material.

'Let me guess the reason for this sudden keenness for Alpine activity.' She noted a certain sternness in his voice. 'What are you going to do now?'

It had snowed during the night and she looked down on a snow plough pushing its way up the road. 'I'm not really sure,' she lied, lacing up her boots.

'And you don't want me to come with you now?'

'No,' she answered. 'I need some time to think. I'll see you later.'

She liked the sensation of being encased in the clothes, detached from the world around her. She scraped the snow from her car and drove slowly up towards the other hotel, turning over in her mind what her next moves were going to be. Despite the fact she was more visible against the white snow, she was less concerned about being seen. With her hood up and balaclava on she was just another walker. It was the weekend and the snow had brought people into the mountains and in front of the hotel groups of walkers and skiers stood in their brightly coloured anoraks. She walked up and past them and around the side of the hotel where the cars were parked. The Renault was there under a layer of snow. She had no idea of knowing if they were in the hotel or still walking in the mountains, but for the moment it didn't really matter. She cleared two neat portholes on the windscreen, so the car looked as though it had spectacles. She then took off one of her mittens and put her hand in the inside pocket of her anorak. She pulled out two pieces of torn card and freeing the windscreen wipers, used them to hold the two halves in the centre of the circles. Then she adjusted the cards so that closer to it was possible to see that they were two halves of the same picture. An aircraft carrier. And then, just as deliberately, she took a photograph out of her wallet. It was the snap she had taken of Oliver and Karyn in Paris. She carefully tore it down the middle, so that the two pieces came apart at the point where Oliver's lips met Karyn's. She tucked the separated couple opposite each other under the wipers along with the broken warship.

She returned to her car and waited. The low sun moved slowly across the sky and the walkers came and went. She unscrewed a flask of coffee and sipped at the hot liquid. The sky to the west was tinged with a cold grey pink before she saw them coming down the slope behind the hotel. She watched them stop and turn towards the sunset. She looked away when they kissed. The couple would have to pass through the car park on their way to the main entrance. It was Karyn who pointed at the car first and Sonya could see her laugh. Just wait, she thought. She watched as they walked towards the car, thinking it was some practical joke. And then they stopped. Their movements were identical. First they glanced at each other and then they both turned and looked up and around. The smile was gone from Karyn's face and she saw Oliver walk around the bonnet and take her hand.

'This is just the beginning, my precious little love birds. Just the beginning,' Sonya said to herself. She waited until they had gone into the hotel before swinging the car around and driving back down the hill.

*   *   *

'It means that she is here.' Karyn was by the window as the last of the daylight began to fade. The doubts she felt earlier in the day still fluttered around inside her, but now she could give them more definition.

'Oliver,' she said. 'Despite Sonya's behaviour, I don't think it is right for me to criticise her. And, anyway, it would be a waste of time. But there is something I should tell you, which may hurt you, I don't know.' Oliver, who had been standing by the bed, now sat on a wooden chair against the wall.

'And I only tell you this because I am worried about Sonya and about what Sonya might do next.' Karyn came over and sat on the edge of the bed and faced Oliver. 'Sonya has been seeing another man for some time. She has been having an affair.' She watched Oliver frown slightly and then nod his head. Before he could speak, she carried on.

'She came to Paris to accuse me of having an affair with you – and we had never even kissed – whilst having another man herself. Your wife does not comprehend reason, or right and wrong, as everyone else does. She can only see herself. She doesn't care that you're alive. She's furious that you spoilt her perfect world. And she is angry Oliver, very angry.'

Karyn watched Oliver's face change. The frown evaporated and was replaced with a grin. 'You know,' he said, kneeling in front of her, 'we were having an affair from the very start, but I couldn't see it. No wonder I couldn't or wouldn't speak to Sonya after the accident. I didn't want to go back. I don't want to go back and I couldn't care what Sonya was doing with some other man. It doesn't matter. That is the past. Let us sidestep Sonya now.'

He stood up and paced over to the window, which he opened. 'Can you hear me Sonya?,' he shouted at the top of his voice. 'You can't touch us. You can't touch us.'

She laughed, not so much at the sight of Oliver bellowing out of the window but at the new energy that was running through him. She remembered the candle she had lit in the gloom of Notre Dame all those weeks ago and now dipped her head in acknowledgement.

And then he shut the window with a finite clunk.

'Why don't I tell my story to that television friend of yours?' Karyn was taken aback and let the question sink in before she replied. She was surprised but the more she thought about it, the more she could see that it might be a very neat solution.

'But wouldn't he want to speak to Sonya, as well?'

'So? I've done nothing wrong. She would just be shown up for what she is.'

Karyn looked over to the window, half expecting to see Sonya reflected in the black glass. The business of the postcard was not the act of a jealous woman, but of someone who enjoyed inflicting pain and anxiety. She could have informed the police of Oliver's whereabouts, but she was after a different conclusion. No, Sonya would not go away that easily. Karyn stared out into the blackness knowing that she could not be far away.

'Oliver, how did you live with her so long?'

He answered as though this had been a question he had been expecting for some time. 'I'm not sure I did "live" with her. We co-existed. We didn't really engage. She wasn't really interested in me and I didn't have the mechanism or desire to find out more about her. We got by in our own worlds. But it's a question that I came to ask myself the further away I got from the crash and the closer I came to you. When you told me she was having an affair rather than offend or make me angry, I felt things drop into place. There was a separateness about Sonya which at first I thought was attractive but in the end I came to regard as something quite sinister. Not that I could put it in so many words, but I do remember certain looks on her face, her reactions to what we were doing, which caused a strange reaction in me. You could never conquer Sonya, nor could you induce remorse in her. But I married her and I married her because I knew she would never ask about me. Now, with you, I want to tell you everything and know everything about you. So will you take me to dinner, please? Now.'

And, for the evening at least, Karyn banished Sonya from her mind and listened to Oliver Dreyfuss come to life in front of her.

*　　*　　*

He rewound the sequence and read the script out loud again, removing a couple of words and marking a pause. It was late and the building was quiet. It was the time that Jean-Paul liked best when he could work undisturbed.

'So the question is, did Oliver Dreyfuss leave his seat in the fateful coach eleven and walk through to the buffet car, a journey of no more than thirty metres but one which may have saved his life?' On the screen the pictures he had shot on the train in St Denis, deliberately treated to look like CCTV footage, showed the actor playing Oliver put down his mobile phone and make his way to the door through to the next carriage.

'If so,' Jean-Paul continued, reading to a montage of different still images of Oliver, 'what has happened to him since? Why has he not come forward to the authorities, or spoken to his wife?'

At this point, Jean-Paul picked up his pencil and threw it at the screen. 'And why have *I* not spoken to his wife and why is this a film without a bloody ending?' He stood up and paced around the edit suite. Earlier in the day he had telephoned Sonya's office in London and been told that she was away indefinitely on business. Was she in France? Was she with Oliver? He couldn't rest until he had answered these questions. He didn't want to make a fool of himself but if his documentary went out as it was now only for him to discover a few days later that Oliver had committed deliberate fraud with his wife, he would look foolish. He was pleased with his basic premise, that Oliver was still alive and the sequence that he had cut together about movement recognition was strong evidence. But was there a much bigger story lurking here?

When the phone rang he picked it up with an irritated 'yes'.

Then, half way to sitting down, he paused as he realised who it was. The programme controller was as direct as ever. 'I assume you have finished the assembly by now?' It wasn't really a question.

'I'm just stripping in the commentary. I'll be through in about half an hour.'

'Good. That's when I should be arriving. With Thomas.'

He put the phone down with a groan. Thomas was the channel lawyer. By the time they arrived he had finished recording the guide voice-over and he played the documentary to them. At the end, he watched his two visitors look at each other before they responded. The lawyer spoke first.

'Nothing directly problematical here, but we may come unstuck on good taste and decency. Do we have permission from Mrs Dreyfuss to run this?'

Jean-Paul shook his head.

Thomas looked across at the programme controller whose ultimate decision to broadcast the film it would be.

'It's good, Jean-Paul,' she said brightly and he knew immediately that she was going to pull it. 'But I'm afraid we can't. The new evidence is good but we will be accused of playing with people's emotions. And this is all still too fresh for us to risk our reputation. And the advertisers won't like that. I'm sorry.'

They got up and left. Jean-Paul picked up the pages of his script and flung them at the screen and pushed the typists' chair against the radiator.

'Fuck you Oliver Dreyfuss. Wherever you are.'

Chapter 27

You cannot kill a man who is already dead.

She liked the phrase, rolled it around in her mind and spoke it gently aloud. 'You cannot kill a man who is already dead.' With a steady hand she applied her eye liner and pursed her lips into the mirror. The face that looked back at her was calm and she moved her head to the right and then to the left as she continued staring at her image. The interior lights in the car emphasised the cut of her jaw and the slight hollowness of her cheeks which, with her short cropped hair and tight black roll-neck sweater, she thought made her look like an athlete. She snapped shut her make-up bag and turned off the cabin light. Ahead of her she could see that the grey Renault was still under its blanket of snow in the car park of the hotel. It was just after dawn and the thin white light around the half moon emphasised the coldness of the morning. She drove back down the valley, glancing up at her own hotel where she assumed that Gordon was still sleeping. He demanded so little of her that it was easy to leave him behind now as she followed her obsession along a path which she needed to travel alone.

'You cannot kill a man who is already dead.'

She parked the car by the old bridge in Tarascon-sur-Ariège and put on her anorak before walking across a small square, smelling the coffee from a café outside which two tall, pollarded trees stood bare and bleak. She had been told of the shop by the good-looking boy when she bought her outdoor clothes. In the centre of the window was a large and ugly stuffed boar with pale glassy eyes. Standing on either side of it were two male dummies dressed in camouflage outfits, each sporting a rifle slung casually across their arms. The rest of the window was alive with knives, nets, rods, pistols and green and brown waterproof clothing, the paraphernalia of hunting. She wondered how many women set foot in such a place.

She was greeted by a middle-aged man whose dark hair was scraped across the dome of his head to hide his baldness. 'I would like to buy a rifle for my husband's birthday.'

With the sweep of his hand the man gestured to his shop. 'We have everything here. It depends on what he wants to shoot.'

'He's a boar man,' she said, imagining what it would take to penetrate the tough bony hide of the specimen in the window.

The man pulled a rifle from the rack behind him and laid it on the table. 'This is effective at seventy-five metres,' he said, picking up the rifle and holding it to his shoulder. 'I take it that he has used something like this before.'

She nodded and then again when the shopkeeper inquired whether he was English.

'I assume, then, that you have his licence to hunt in France? It would have been given to him in England.'

'I'm sure he has it somewhere,' she said, 'but I wanted this to be a surprise so I could not ask him.'

'Alas, madam, since the shootings in Montpellier it is more than my job is worth to sell you a rifle without a permit.'

'Does this apply to all rifles?' He shrugged his shoulders and she watched him as he walked along behind the counter to bring back what appeared to her to be a slightly less sophisticated version of the first gun he had shown her. 'He could kill pigeons with this, although some of the bigger ones might laugh at him.' He broke the air rifle and showed her the lead pellets it used. 'Not quite in the same league, I'm afraid.'

Sonya bought it. 'I suppose I can at least practise *my* shooting with it,' she said. She only had a half-formed idea of how she would use it, but it was enough to maintain her focus and take her forward. Just outside the town, on the way back up the valley, she parked the car in a small clearing in the woods just off the road. She lowered the window and loaded the gun and looked around. On a conifer about twenty metres away she could see the grey-pink breast of a wood pigeon. She raised the rifle and looking along the barrel pulled the trigger. She saw the bird flinch and then miss its footing on the branch before tumbling clumsily from the tree. On the soft bed of fir needles beneath the tree it raised a wing in a vain attempt to stand. She shot again and the bird stopped moving. And then down to her right she saw the yellow flash of another, much smaller bird. She put another pellet into the gun and raised it towards her target. This time the bird was knocked back and fell instantly to the ground. She got out of the car and went over to look at it. The lead shot had entered the yellow breast of the tiny bird and its red and black head lay crooked and still. She scooped it up and tossed it into the undergrowth.

She knew the rifle would barely mark the skin of a human but somehow it made her feel better.

*   *   *

Oliver woke with the sun streaming in through the balcony window. In the distance he could see the Pic d'Estats which Karyn had pointed out to him on the walk up to the refuge. 'It is the tallest in the Pyrénées,' she had told him, 'and I once climbed it with my father. In summer, of course.'

Karyn now stood by the bed, holding a tray which she handed to him before climbing into bed beside him. He watched her take a large croissant and dunk it in a cup of black coffee. As she ate it the crumbs spilled on to her chest and he picked them off as she continued to eat.

'So, is this my last day as a dead man? And, if so, can we do something special, please?' Karyn's mouth was full of jam and croissant so she widened her eyes and nodded agreement. 'Have you ever been to Mirepoix?' she managed to say. He shook his head. 'It's market day and if we get a move on we can be there well before midday.' And he nodded again and he watched her lick her fingers just as her mobile rang. She looked at him with alarm. 'It's Jean-Paul', she told Oliver glancing down at the screen. 'Shall I answer it?'

'Yes, but tell him you are about to go out and that you promise to phone back later.'

'Hello, Jean-Paul. How are you?' He watched as she listened, her beautiful face full of concern. Her dressing gown had fallen open exposing one of her breasts. She had folded one of her legs underneath her and this complete image, the tilt of her head, the shape of her body, the stillness of her face, he knew he would hold onto forever.

He heard her promise to call him later that afternoon and she lobbed the phone into her bag. 'They won't let him show the film,' she told him, 'unless he has an interview with or permission from Sonya. I imagine, though, you might solve his problems.' She crawled forward and kissed him. 'We could arrive a little later, couldn't we?'

It was only as they approached the car, hand in hand, that he remembered Sonya and he automatically looked around him half expecting her to be standing in the car park. Even as he cleaned the windscreen his eyes scanned the surrounding slopes and as the engine warmed up he watched the faces of the passing hikers. He had not wanted to lose the mood he had experienced in the bedroom, but now the outside world was tugging at his sleeves.

They headed off towards Tarascon-sur-Ariège and every kilometre he covered was distance between himself and his wife.

*   *   *

She was driving quickly, increasingly familiar with the road and she was enjoying clipping the apexes of the tight corners. The surface had been salted and gritted and the road was a snaking black line between banks of snow. She rose higher, the piled snow almost obliterating the safety barriers between her and the gorge below. She entered an S bend, her body automatically leaning into the first curve, enjoying the momentum of the drive. She almost didn't see the Renault coming the other way and the two cars swerved past each other. Sonya had just time to register that Oliver was driving before the car disappeared from view. She turned around as quickly as she could, bumping against the heaped snow on both sides of the road. She quickly caught them and followed at a safe distance through Tarascon-sur-Ariège and on towards Foix, the road becoming easier and wider the further they went. She had no idea if they had left the hotel for good but when they slowed down in Foix and she could see Karyn pointing to the castle up on the hill she assumed that this might be a daytrip. They continued on down the valley where the land began to open out, the rounder hills making a gentler landscape. They forked off towards Mirepoix and Sonya felt curiously relaxed as though she was part of their excursion as well. As they entered Mirepoix the small roads were milling with cars and people and she saw the Renault back into a small parking place. Sonya looked desperately for another space, aware that Oliver and Karyn were now walking away from her. She bumped up on to a curve in the driveway of a small house allowing just enough space for the owner to get in and out. Then she joined the current of people moving towards the church and the first market stalls. If she had worried about losing sight of the couple, she need not have worried for the heart of Mirepoix, she discovered, was an old, arcaded square not much bigger than a rugby pitch. She was aware of the noise of the market, the throng of people talking, the different music in the air, the whirring stone of the knife grinder and the calls from the various stalls. '*Profitez, profitez*', an old woman shouted from behind two upturned boxes from which she was selling bundles of muddy vegetables.

She observed them from a parallel aisle as they meandered from stall to stall. Even in the centre of the protected square it was cold and her face was well hidden by the neck of her anorak and the scarf she wore round her mouth. Through a string of hanging garlic she saw them pause by a woman selling jewellery. Oliver, placing his hands on Karyn's shoulders, turned her towards him, picking up a round purple furry brooch from the table, which he then carefully pinned to the beret she was wearing. The stall holder offered a small mirror to Karyn who beamed with pleasure at the addition, leaning her body forward and kissing Oliver gently on his mouth.

Sonya had become very still, her breathing shallow. She sensed an intimacy that had never been hers. Not that she wanted it, she told herself but why should he have it? Oliver and Karyn sat down for coffee and she watched as Karyn placed her hand on his when she wanted to make a point. Sonya despised this confident, pretty woman and this fusion with her husband. When they went into a restaurant she waited in a nearby café, not wanting to watch their sentimental pawings. It was not anger she felt now but an emotion much colder, much more rational and in charge of itself. For she, Sonya, was not dependent on anyone for her completeness.

*   *   *

By the time they left the restaurant, the market had begun to disperse, the stalls broken down and the long mobile shops shuttered up and ready for departure. Oliver saw that the cafés were still full as people watched the dismantling like some kind of opera. He took Karyn's hand and thought about the words before he said them, conscious of their power but also of their ability to embarrass. He realised that he had never said them before.

'Do you know something?' She stopped and looked up at him. 'I love you.'

'I do know that Oliver. And I love you. I cannot tell when exactly it began, but it was a long time ago.'

He embraced her, aware of the flow of people leaving the market parting to either side of them, one or two regarding them and smiling.

They knew, as they drove back into the hills, that this was their last chance of peace before they spoke to Jean-Paul. In the cocoon of the car, the grey clouds accumulating ahead of them, Oliver spoke of what he would say and they imagined together what the consequences might be. They were resolved now and began to discuss where they would live once all the fuss was over. It was safe to do this for the factors that would be brought into play when it was known he was alive, were still dormant and unknown. This was the last day in what Oliver could see was the demi-world he had stumbled into in the aftermath of the crash. He was in the penumbra now, neither free of its peculiar gravitational pull, nor in the freer orbit of what would come next. He pushed back in his seat and watched Karyn drive, still wearing her beret and brooch, hardly able to believe what had happened to him.

The snow began to fall just after Foix, thin and powdery at first swirling lightly in the traffic. Towards Tarascon-sur-Ariège it thickened, although the visibility was still reasonable. The grey skies had brought a premature darkness to the afternoon sky but it was countered by the white of the snow reflected in their headlights. The weather intensified the pleasure of being in the car alone with her, enjoying the sensation of being at the heart of one of those glass domes he had been given as a child, the dots of whiteness racing all around them.

The long series of bends which would eventually take them to their hotel and the top of the valley now began. Karyn was driving steadily and he noticed her glancing in the rear view mirror as the glare from the headlights of the car behind them reflected in her face. He turned and looked behind him. The car was quite close and at first he judged this as normal, the other car allowing Karyn to do all the work. And then a doubt began to creep in and he stared harder at the following vehicle, but it was impossible to see the driver against the sharp headlights. Karyn looked across at him and he knew that she was thinking the same as him. As she speeded up, so did the car behind, creeping even closer now. A sign for an S bend flashed by and Karyn swung to the right, the other vehicle matching her movement. It was as she positioned the car for the upcoming sweep to the left that Oliver was aware of a darkness in the cabin. The other car had momentarily disappeared but suddenly it was by their side, running parallel with them and he was able to see the driver. At that instant Sonya looked across at him and in that brief second he registered her cold and motionless face. Karyn had also seen her and gripping hard the wheel began to turn into the next bend.

Sonya's car slipped half-a-car's length behind them and, as Karyn reached the middle of the corner, Oliver was about to speak to her when he saw Sonya's car coming at them from an angle. It hit the driver's door and the appalling noise of the crash coincided with a grunt from Karyn as her window smashed and scattered glass over them. Their car was sliding now and as it hit the snow piled at the side of the road it was launched into the air, landing on its undercarriage before coming to a stop. Karyn was slumped over the wheel. He could see her clearly in the single headlight of Sonya's car, which was backing away. He put his hand to his forehead and felt the warmth of his own blood. He unclipped his seat belt and leant over to Karyn, who was still motionless. And then his mind slipped and he was watching the blazing train, staring at the ripped and broken bodies, hearing the cries of the dying and the roar and crackle of the burning carriages. He pushed open his door and almost stepped out into a black void. Letting out an involuntary cry, he scrambled over to the back seat and opened the rear door on the other side. As he did so, he heard the other car revving and looked up to see it driving hard towards him, its engine roaring. His scream was lost in the noise and as he dived out of the way into the snow he registered the thump of Sonya's car hitting the drift. Then, after a fraction of a second, there was another terrible crash as it hit the other vehicle followed by another brief silence before further, more distant and muffled sounds of breaking glass.

The cold of the snow seeped through his jacket and in his mouth he could taste blood. He could not will himself to move. He did not want to accept the consequences of what had just happened. Some part of him hoped that it was the train and not the car. Was it seconds or minutes before he staggered to his feet to find the cars were gone? The impact of the second car had taken them both over the edge. He stood on the hardened snow drift and looked over the side where, below, he could just make out a dim light. He struggled down the steep slope, slithering in the deep snow, an awful dread invading every part of him.

He came to Sonya's car first and her body lay half out of the open door, held in place by her seat belt. He scrambled on beyond her to the car trapped underneath it, lodged against a tree. In the bent shell of the cabin he saw Karyn, the interior light spilling a dull white light over her twisted body. Her neck was broken. Although he knew she was dead, he still took her hand and felt her wrist. There was no pulse. He let out a roar of pain into the black sky.

He climbed back up to Sonya. He grabbed her and in his anger, yanked her head around to face his. He did not know what he was going to say or do and it was only as he looked into her open eyes that he realised that she, too, was dead. It was his massive anger against Sonya that, just for an instant, blotted out his misery. He let her head drop and it banged against the bent, metal pillar of the roof and her mouth sagged open. Oliver searched around the interior of the car until he found her purse.

He removed what money there was and slithered back down to Karyn. He was beyond tears now, beyond conscious reason and he crawled into the cabin and kissed her lips. 'Goodbye Karyn. I, too, am dead.'

And he disappeared into the night.

Chapter 28

Jean-Paul waited for Karyn's call but it never came so in the end he telephoned her and an automatic voice told him her mobile had been switched off. He felt disappointed and let down, for Karyn always kept her word. He poured another glass of wine and later stumbled to bed wondering why it was fortune had so turned against him. When the phone did ring in the small hours of the morning he snatched it up.

'Karyn,' he said immediately. There was a pause.

'No, I'm afraid not, Jean-Paul.' It was one of his colleagues in the news room at the channel and the tone of his voice made Jean-Paul sit up in bed.

'Karyn Baird and Sonya Dreyfuss were killed in a car accident in the Pyrénées last night. We think you should go down there as soon as possible.' The call was more professional than personal, although the news editor was aware of his connection with both women.

'In the same car?' He asked, incredulously.

'No, apparently they collided in a bizarre accident, but you'll find out for yourself.'

There were so many questions that rushed into his mind that they rendered him speechless. 'What happened? How was it possible? Surely the coincidence was too great? Was no one else in the cars?' He tried hard to resolve the two emotions that were rising up inside him, the excitement that the incident would allow him to continue with his film and the sadness at the death of Karyn. He could barely acknowledge that the former was stronger than the latter.

By midday he had reached the site of the accident. The cars had been removed and the snow had filled in all traces of the accident and the footmarks of those whose job it had been to recover the dead and winch away the twisted vehicles. A policeman stood on top of the snow drift at the point where the crash had occurred. It was a freak accident, he told Jean-Paul. The way the snow had been pushed against the side of the road and the subsequent drifting had created a launch pad so after the cars collided they were catapulted over the barrier. The local police inspector confirmed this story and told him where Karyn had been staying.

The old couple at the hotel looked tired, but he watched their red-rimmed eyes become suspicious when he introduced himself as a friend of Karyn's and a journalist. 'Was Karyn staying here alone?' He had been in many of these situations before and he asked the question gently and sincerely. The old man regarded him coolly and spoke calmly.

'*Monsieur*, at the best of times your question would be impertinent. At this moment it is insolent and discourteous. But I will tell you. She was here alone. These mountains were her partner. But I don't expect you to understand that. Goodbye.'

Jean-Paul sat down in the foyer and watched the snow falling outside, a dense whiteness that hid the magnificent view that he could see displayed in the photographs on the walls. His own view on what had happened was just as obscured. Sonya must have spoken to Karyn and come down here to see her. But why? Could it be that Oliver was down here as well?

Two hours later, following further advice from the police, he was in Vicdessos asking similar questions in a different hotel. 'No,' the concierge told him, 'Madame Dreyfuss had been with a gentleman. Such a tragedy for him.' 'A tragedy,' Jean-Paul agreed, his mind racing ahead. He produced a picture of Oliver which he had brought with him for this very purpose. 'Was this the man she was with?' He could barely wait for her to study the photograph and reply.

'Oh, no, *monsieur*. This is not the man at all. This one is dark with long hair whereas the man with Madame Dreyfuss, God rest her soul, had gingery hair slightly grey at the sides and looked quite different.'

She handed the photograph back to Jean-Paul and it was all he could do to smile and thank her.

*   *   *

By mid-afternoon Gordon was in the departure lounge at Toulouse airport. He was calling a friend about Cheltenham.

'George. It's Gordon. Yes, I've been away rather a lot recently doing this and that. More of that than this, let me tell you. I wonder if there's a chance you could squeeze me in for the meeting tomorrow? My dear chap, how kind. I should be with you by midday tomorrow.' He flicked the phone shut and watched his plane touch down, taxi towards the small terminal and disgorge its passengers. Soon he would be aboard and away from here, he reassured himself.

He had been woken by a visit from the police shortly after dawn and told the news. He had received it calmly. Even having to identify Sonya's body at the hospital morgue had not unduly disturbed him. She still looked perfect, her sculptured face white against the unflinching lamps but still undoubtedly beautiful. The crash appeared not to have marked her at all. He leant forward and kissed her forehead and the coldness of the skin surprised him.

Afterwards he received a bigger surprise. The other victim of the accident, he was told, was a woman called Karyn Baird. He accepted the news with barely a nod of his head, his unblinking eyes meeting those of the policeman in front of him.

'A tragic accident, *monsieur*. I am sorry for your loss.'

And that was the way Gordon wanted to leave it. In recent weeks Sonya had become more and more obsessed with Karyn and Oliver so that he was no more than a mere observer of her life. He did not want to know what had happened the night

231

before. It was history now and the less he knew, the better.

Back at the hotel he had ordered a taxi to take him to Toulouse and on the way he booked on the afternoon flight to London. And now, in the terminal, Sonya was already a half-forgotten dream, another passage in his life which he had taken for the enjoyment it gave him.

*   *   *

When Oliver stumbled into the refuge St Antoine he had been walking for almost five hours, since just after first light. He had hidden in the trees and watched the police arrive and the ambulances take away the two women. The cold had barely penetrated his misery and afterwards he was driven upwards with a furious anger. Bursting into the refuge, he had pulled out the blankets and collapsed on the lower bunk bed where he cried, not the tears of joy and relief he had released in this room with Karyn, but ugly tears, his body wracked with a pain he had never before experienced. The best day in his life was separated from the worst by just twenty-four hours. He raged, shouting her name, until finally he had fallen into a dull sleep, too tired even to dream.

When he awoke the following morning the dread was still with him. There was not even a second of peace between sleep and remembering. He had looked around the room where they had so recently been together and the pain of the memory drained all the energy from him. He had spent a second night on the mountain, the howl of the wind matching the bleakness of his thoughts.

And now, pushing open the door of the refuge he once again stepped out into the whiteness. He was about to shut the door when Karyn's voice came to him so clearly that he turned round expecting to find her. 'Everyone leaves the hut as they find it.' He went back in and folded the blankets and wiped down the surfaces where he had opened and warmed the packaged soups. No matter how hard he tried, he could not imagine a time that he would return to replace them.

He shut the door and walked away, not looking back, until after a while he came to the point on the path where she had taken the photograph. He stood there and felt the wind against his face. The sky all around was uniformly grey, but the snow had stopped. He wanted to believe that out there in the distance, the lynx would suddenly appear and look in his direction, its feathered ears alert but its eyes calm and clear. He sat on a rock and waited, he could not say for how long. His eyes hurt with the staring, the trees blurring under the intensity of his gaze. He wanted it to be her, the lynx, alone in the landscape, elusive and beautiful. The cold was beginning to encircle him and he rose stiffly, wrapping his arms around himself as much for warmth as regret. He was just shuffling away when a tiny movement in the distance flickered in the corner of his vision. The animal, silver grey against the snow, came out from the trees onto the open ground. It looked out over the valley and remained there, without movement. Oliver, too, was motionless and as he stood there he felt a warmth flow through his body. And, then, in the gesture that Karyn had used to him, he raised his arm in salute.

'I wish you were here, Karyn. But I think perhaps you are'.

And at this point it all became clear to him, like the peak of a mountain emerging from driven cloud. He was not here by accident and Karyn was not dead. She would not allow him just to stumble off into oblivion. He could feel her presence in him like a tangible force. This is where, barely a day ago, she had affirmed her belief in his life and he, in his way, had a similar duty to her's now. Oliver had never felt so certain in his life. He would not allow her death to be in vain. With the wind rushing up from the valley, the misery lifted from him and he let himself imagine that she was that lynx, free to roam the land that was spiritually hers.

He turned and walked down between the rocks, the wind behind him and the snow soft under his feet.

PART FOUR

Left Overs

Chapter 29

With infinite care he lifted the *foie gras* from the bowl of tepid water in which it had been softening. He lay it on the marble surface and began to remove the veins and nerves and the green pieces which marred its appearance. He then spread out a piece of damp linen cloth and lifted the goose liver on to it. He threw on a sprinkle of salt and a few turns of the pepper mill before shaping it into a longish sausage, twisting the ends tightly and tying them up with string. On the stove a large pan of stock was simmering and into the bubbling brown liquid he gently placed the sausage. He added a bottle of St Croix du Mont to sweeten the meat. He left it to cook and turned to preparing the legs of lamb. Tomorrow was Bastille Day and it was also Sunday, so the town would be *en fête*. He would begin cooking the *gigots* at about nine-thirty so that, four hours later, they would be ready for the busy lunch time service. He returned to the *ballotine* of *foie gras* which, with two flat spoons pierced with holes, he lifted from the cooking liquid and into another saucepan containing iced water. He took this pan to the large fridge and put it inside. Tomorrow the *ballotine* would be firm and he would serve *tranches* of it alongside the slow-cooked lamb. He wiped his hands carefully and removed his apron.

It was high summer and although it was not yet nine, both he and the sun had been up for hours. The route was familiar by now, along the chalk and flint path through the beech copse and out onto the open, undulating farm land. On either side of the path the yellow corn stood guard, rustling in the dry, warm wind. In a few days it would be harvested but now it defined the narrow passage ahead. He rose up through the fields until he reached the gently rounded summit and the point where the four paths met and the old elm tree offered its ancient gnarled branches for shade. The shadows of the clouds were still being chased across the waving corn and the skylarks somewhere high above were still creating a canopy of song. The sun was warm on his face and he lay back under the tree feeling the comfort flow through his body. He could smell the corn ripening. He had stopped asking questions these days and had learnt that life was about a series of linked moments like this, each to be taken on its own terms. When he thought of Karyn, which he did often, it was without pain or regret. She had shown him how to do what he was doing now and he had absorbed her spirit by a process of human osmosis. Sometimes, when he had decisions to make or was troubled, he would speak out loud to her. Gradually he became calmer, less anxious. Nothing worse could happen to him and as the months went by he slowly began to take control of his life again. When he thought of Sonya, which he occasionally did, it was without anger. To blame her would be pointless for he had learnt, thanks to Karyn, to see Sonya as a painful stage on a long road. If he had been unable to see Sonya for what she truly was, he had been equally unable to see himself.

He walked along the ridge above the town, making a large semi-circle with the Abbey at its centre. It was over a year since Karyn had died although she was still so real to him that she might have been by his side now. At first the images haunted him; her body in the car, the terrible night on the mountain, the shape of her sitting on the bed on the day she died. But slowly, almost imperceptibly, the happier memories began to take precedent. What he had become now was both thanks to Karyn and for Karyn. It was as if he could not betray the trust she had placed in him and the more he thought like this the stronger he became. This was not the man, he came to realise, who stumbled around in the aftermath of the rail crash. Karyn had equipped him to do more than merely survive. The whole of Picardie was around and about him, a vast pattern of fields merging under a sky of suspended clouds. He raised his arm towards the panorama as he always did at this point and saluted Karyn with the familiar gesture she had given him in the mountains.

He continued along the ridge path before turning off and slowly descending to the white walls of the Abbey. The butcher called to him from his shop and he paused to talk about his orders for the following week. At the restaurant, Bernard Chichillian was drinking coffee and he went over and embraced the tousled haired owner before continuing on to the kitchen. Preparations for the lunchtime service were under way and his two assistants greeted him from behind their stations. It was curious, Oliver thought, that when he worked here before he had never really registered his surroundings. In those days this kitchen was a protection from a life he was keeping at bay, a place he scurried to for safety. Now the opposite was true. Bernard Chichillian had welcomed him back with unreserved pleasure and relief. As before, he had asked no questions and Oliver slipped back into the same routines.

'You look well,' he heard Bernard call from the restaurant. Oliver wiped his hands and went back to join his patron, making an espresso on the way.

'And here's to you, too,' he said, raising his small cup and clinking it against Bernard's. 'It looks like we have a full house again tomorrow. I thought we might squeeze an extra table outside. What do you think?'

Bernard smiled back. 'It is already done,' he replied. 'And thank you for making it possible.'

'It's a great pleasure, Bernard. I have much ground to make up with you, as you know. You have done so much for me it is the least I can do to fill your restaurant as often as I can.'

'You owe me nothing, young man,' Bernard told him but Oliver knew that soon he would tell the whole story to this gentle bear of a man. What Bernard did with the information he could not predict but whatever it was he felt it would be for the good.

The following morning dawned hot and still. The hills around St-Riquier shimmered in the heat and at nine o'clock Oliver felt he could hear the wheat crackling as it dried under the relentless sun. The red, white and blue bunting hung limply above the main street. Oliver stood outside the restaurant where the smell of a hot summer day was laced with garlic and roast lamb. The first groups began to arrive just after midday and an hour later the restaurant was full, the tables of white linen spilling on to the pavement. Once upon a time, providing food for a hundred and twenty people, each demanding service at a different time, would have provided Oliver the perfect opportunity to lose himself in his work, to become anonymous. Now, although the routines were the same, his motives were different. Whereas before he would fear the moment when the intensity of work would end, now he enjoyed the penumbra between extreme effort and gradual relaxation, the slow passage between the tables, the mingling with the customers, most of whom he knew and liked.

He cut another *tranche* of *foie gras* and laid it alongside the lamb, adding a dribble of garlicky *jus* and watched the waitress take the plate into the noisy restaurant. He scanned the tables of tanned faces made even browner by light summer clothes and ample wine. Oliver's eyes stopped on a young man in the corner who was, unusually for a day like this, eating alone. It was one of the few faces he didn't recognise in a room full of regular diners, families who came together here several times a year and came regularly as individuals or with their partners the rest of the time.

It was four o'clock before the restaurant began to empty. Oliver had worked his way to most of the tables, accepting wine, discussing the food and a jumble of local gossip. He could, by now, write a fairly detailed account of the lives of the people in

this room, the progress of their sons and daughters, the problems of their marriages, the complaints of the local farmers and
their united love of food and wine. He was aware that the man in
the corner had been watching him move between the tables. As
Oliver approached him, he stood up and offered his hand.

'Hello. I am Jean-Paul Patrese. Pleased to meet you. Thank
you for an excellent meal. Will you join me for a digestif?'

Oliver nodded and sat down. The man ordered coffee and
cognac and Oliver regarded him. He seemed on edge as though
he was expecting something to happen and even as he noticed
this, Oliver felt a small wave of apprehension sweep over him.

'I don't think I have seen you in these parts before,' Oliver
ventured, raising his brandy glass in thanks.

'No, this is the first time I have been to St-Riquier.'

'And what brings you here, apart from my splendid cooking?'
Oliver asked.

'You do, actually. But it's not just for your cooking, which is
excellent, *monsieur.*' Oliver watched as the man produced a
brown folder from a bag beneath the table. He opened the flap
and slid out several photographs. Oliver could see that they were
all of him. Two years ago he had hidden his face with a beard
and his hair had grown to his shoulders. These pictures, several
of which he recognised, showed him looking similar to the way
he did now. Now Oliver knew who this man was but he noted
that he felt neither surprise nor concern.

'You are, I believe, Oliver Dreyfuss. Am I not right?'

Oliver looked at him for a moment before turning towards the
counter behind which Bernard was preparing the final bills, the
plume of blue smoke indicating that lunch was officially over.

'Bernard, can you join us please.' Bernard looked up, perhaps
detecting a certain strangeness in Oliver's voice, and shuffled
over to join them. Oliver introduced the two men.

'Bernard Chichillian, I would like you to meet Jean-Paul
Patrese. Jean-Paul is a television producer. We have, we had, a

mutual friend called Karyn Baird.' As he spoke, Oliver kept his gaze on Jean-Paul and saw his eyes widen in surprise. He then turned to Bernard.

'Jean-Paul has been working on a documentary about the train crash of a couple of years ago. He is here to tell me that I am not dead.'

He saw Bernard's head look first towards Jean-Paul and return to him.

'Whatever is said next, I want you to hear it as well, Bernard, for it is no less than you deserve.' Bernard silently acknowledged Oliver's statement and they both turned to Jean-Paul. Oliver could see that he was confused and uncertain how to proceed.

'Let me help you, Jean-Paul. Just over a year ago, on a cold winter's day high in the Pyrénées, I watched Karyn call your mobile. Karyn', he explained to Bernard, 'was the woman I loved and is the reason I am here.' He resumed his story to Jean-Paul. 'She told you that she would call you later. She never did, as you know. Later that night she died in what we shall call an accident. But had she not, she would have made that call and you would then have spoken to me and I would have proved your instincts right. I did not die in the rail crash. By a fluke, I survived. Not long after the accident I found myself here and had the good fortune of meeting you, Bernard. You had the grace not to ask too many questions and for a while I became a working recluse here.' Bernard was leaning forward as if to capture all he was saying. Jean-Paul had barely moved since he began talking.

'And then, sitting one Sunday in this very room, just as we are now, I saw Karyn on the front cover of a magazine. She was the woman, you may remember, who found the lynx in the Pyrénées. It was then that I realised I had to go to her and I did. She had never given up believing I was alive. Strangely,' he continued, looking directly at Jean-Paul, 'we were not having an affair although my wife, Sonya, came to believe otherwise. When you told her, Jean-Paul, that you believed I might still be alive, she began to pursue me and eventually threaten me. Finally, Bernard, she was killed with Karyn. They called it an accident but it wasn't really. Sonya's madness killed Karyn. Afterwards, I came back here. And, once again, Bernard took me in without question.'

There was a silence. And then Jean-Paul picked out a photograph from his folder and handed it to the old restaurateur. 'I have seen this before,' Bernard said, looking at the sepia picture of the old café. He passed it on to Oliver, who shook his head remembering this memento from his study in Wimbledon. He waited for Jean-Paul to continue.

'This was how Sonya began to track you down. This old postcard was one of a number of unclaimed items in the hotel room she was staying in when she died. I had a contact in the police there and he thought I might be interested. I did what she did and worked out that it was the picture of a restaurant in St-Riquier. I came here on the off-chance. I am glad to find you at last.'

Oliver ignored Jean-Paul and put his hand on Bernard's forearm. 'When I worked with you before, I wanted to be anonymous, to disappear. Now I don't. But this is my world now. This is where I have arrived.'

He could see Jean-Paul turning the information around in his mind, working out an appropriate response, weighing self-interest against the possible repercussions of his actions.

'What do you want, Jean-Paul?'

'May I interrupt?' Bernard spoke for the first time. It was a genuine question and he looked at the two men for permission before he continued.

'It is impossible for me to absorb all the information I have just learnt. But, in some ways, I don't have to. It was clear that Oliver was running from something or someone when he first arrived at my door. I needed a chef and I didn't ask any questions. And the more I realised how good he was, he is, the less I wanted to ask questions. When he suddenly disappeared, it was a blow. It was not the action of a man I had come to know. And then you came back, Oliver. You had changed. Can you be sadder and happier at the same time? This is what it seemed to me. And I knew then that at some stage you would tell me, as you had once promised to, the details of your life. And here we are now.'

Oliver waited for him to continue, sensing though the direction he was going.

'This man,' Bernard gestured to Jean-Paul, 'is a journalist. To ask him not to tell your story would like asking a lion not to eat meat. But this is only one side of the equation. You have a life to lead, Oliver, which you can only half live like this. You need your identity back.'

'I don't want that identity back.' Oliver spoke slowly. 'Little or nothing of that life remains. I am a different person. But, Bernard, I know what you are saying. I used to share a poem with Karyn. "The way is certainly both short and steep. However gradual it looks from here; Look if you like, but you will have to leap." '

He got up and left the restaurant. The heat of the day lay soaked in the pavements. He breathed in deeply. He had spent almost two years denying the existence of Oliver Dreyfuss. Even in those few precious days with Karyn he had extended his isolation. Should he step out of it now? He looked up into the sky, waiting to hear Karyn's voice. The swifts skimmed and swerved all around him, scything by and banking sharply under the eves of the houses. Their screaming seemed to block out all other sound, a fierce wild, abandoned noise. Their cart-wheeling acrobatics, slender black bodies outlined against the grey and white walls, were an expression of pure freedom.

Oliver returned to the restaurant and the gaze of the two men.

'I know that Karyn would not have wanted me to carry on like this. And I realise, also, that it would be unfair to Bernard. There is too much unfinished business in my life.' Bernard was watching him now and Jean-Paul once again looked confused. 'I want to continue here but I must close the other chapter first. I will speak to you, Jean-Paul, and I will tell you the story.'

There was a silence before Bernard spoke. 'Do you know, Oliver, I once said that this restaurant seemed to bring only bad luck to those who worked in it. When you left, I felt the curse continue. But now I feel differently.' And he stood and took Oliver's hand. 'It's a good decision.'

* * *

A week later, Oliver sat under the lights in the centre of the restaurant. In front of him was Jean-Paul sitting as close to the camera as he could. In the background, just to one side of his eye line was Bernard trying to be as inconspicuous as possible.

'Jean-Paul.' The producer looked up from the monitor on the next table. 'Would it be possible, please, for Bernard to come and sit beside you for I feel I would like to tell the story to him?' It wasn't really a question and Jean-Paul moved aside for the big man.

Jean-Paul called for silence and with the quietness that followed, Oliver felt a stillness descend on him. He heard the producer say 'turn over' and indicate that he should start. Oliver looked at Bernard's face and began.

'I think I knew something was changing when I left home that morning and the big trees opposite began to rustle in a breeze I could not feel. I remember looking up and from that point on nothing in my life was ever the same again. Later that day, after the accident, they announced that I was dead and there were 'no identifiable remains' of my body. Oliver Dreyfuss didn't exist. They were right . . . '

Acknowledgements

I owe a debt of thanks to several people for helping this book see the light of day. Richard Barber and Lynne Woolfson for their constant encouragement and canny suggestions; Julia Hobsbawm, Rachel Pollard, Sarah Coombs, David and Nigel Evans Quiney, John and Maureen Fairclough, Susan Keverne, Kristel Kristjánsdóttir, Chiara Messineo, Mark Tagholm and Roger Tagholm for their sustaining enthusiasm. I would also like to thank Peter Denton for putting me right about the lynx. Most of all to my wife, Sally Tagholm, without whom it would never have started nor left the house.